Ms. Hui Jiang, a Chinese immigrant and a successful financial consultant, has written a fascinating novel about the lives of immigrants in the United States. Through this book, Ms. Jiang conveys a message that it is through life's most difficult moments that one can find truth and hope. The main character was a proud, self-reliant young lady; after struggling through unbelievable hardship and obstacles, she became a mature woman who depended on God for her life and her family. As a fellow Chinese immigrant, I have come to know the author through collaborative work for Asian Americans. I highly recommend her book to not only Asians and immigrants, but also all of us who are searching for strength and inspiration when we face challenges in our lives. This book will elevate your spirit and broaden your scope of vision for life and develop a renewed appreciation for God.

—Ming Wang, MD, PhD
CEO of Aier-USA
Director of Wang Vision Institute, Nashville, TN
Author of *From Darkness to Sight*

A beautifully written immigrant fairytale love story that turns unexpectedly dark. Discovering the hardships of coming to America to work to seek the American dream! Many Americans have no idea of what it takes to learn and to speak English, to work hard, to find your voice and to be recognized for successful work outcomes. The challenges of immigration when needing family to assist in difficult times make daily life unbearable. As this love story unfolds and the American dream comes true, the devil's grasp becomes a nightmare full of evil, fear, self-doubt and pain. Thankful for God to start a journey of believing, healing and appreciation of many blessings. In abundance, Ms. Hui Jiang is blessing and helping others by sharing this story.

—Donna F. Cole
President/CEO
Cole Chemical & Distributing, Inc.
Roy M. Huffington Award winner, Asia Society Texas
Order of the Rising Sun recipient, Japan

The COLOR RED

An Immigration Story to Eternity

HUI JIANG

Paperback ISBN 978-1-960007-65-0
eBook ISBN 978-1-960007-66-7

Published by

Orison Publishers, Inc.
PO Box 188
Grantham, PA 17027
www.OrisonPublishers.com

Contents

CHAPTER 1

New Millennium

On this beautiful early autumn evening before the new millennium, the sky was pure Texas blue. A few light clouds danced in the sky like ballerinas' skirts. The breeze was light and pleasant. Esther and her husband, Kevin, enjoyed their walk in their high-end gated community with custom-built houses in the city of Houston, Texas.

Their house was a symbol of their realized American dream. Its style was a fusion of Southern plantation and French cottage. The house featured huge arched windows on both sides of the front door. It had a yellow-stucco front and brown bricks all the way around. Two young oak trees were planted recently in the front yard. Shrubs were placed neatly in a row near the house with one pink myrtle tree on each end. Round, well-trimmed shrubs decorated the front walkway while two huge sago palm trees stood where the walkway met the sidewalk like welcoming hosts. To Esther, the house looked like a palace.

The property included a detached three-car garage. Kevin owned a shiny red race car and Esther drove a brand-new black Camry. The red race car made a big impression on Esther the first time she met Kevin. Esther always liked the color red; to her, red meant life and passion. However, she did not like to draw too much attention to herself; a conservative image and a practical vehicle were more important to her.

Directly across the street from their house was a beautiful large lake with a fountain in the center that continuously gushed out water and formed a huge flower in the air. Several ducks floated seemingly effortlessly in the water.

Esther was on an after-dinner neighborhood stroll with Kevin and her mother, Hua. The walks were recommended by her doctor because she was a gestational diabetic. Esther would give birth to their first child, David, with a scheduled inducing in two days. Hua had just arrived in the United States a week ago to help Esther and the young growing family.

Both Esther and Kevin came from China as international graduate students less than a decade ago. Kevin came right after the Tiananmen Square event. For a while, the Chinese government changed its policies for students wanting to study overseas almost every day. Young intellectuals had to change their life plans very quickly because their lives could be dramatically altered by one single policy. Kevin rushed out of China before a new national mandate of five-year service for all college graduates became effective. Esther managed to leave a few years later with the help of a very rare exception to the policy. All that either of them had when they arrived in this new country were two suitcases and hundreds of dollars in their pockets. Such was the story of many students leaving China to study elsewhere. Kevin and Esther met in Houston a few years after Esther came.

Esther felt very fortunate to have Kevin as her husband. Secretly, she thought she was a little too lucky. He was young and tall—at almost six feet, he was taller than most Chinese men—and good-looking. Esther was petite, but she had always liked tall men. Her boyfriend in college back in China had been tall and handsome. Were those her real desires? Or were they rather vanity?

Esther tried to justify her preference. In her mind, a man's being tall was nature's favor. Esther wanted her children to be tall. She believed her chance of having a tall child was higher with a tall husband. Besides, she was very smart and attractive. Surely, she could set her bar a little high for a husband.

More importantly, Kevin was ambitious and capable. He was so talented at software development that he had already acquired a few patents. During the high-tech boom of the 1990s, almost every high-achieving immigrant switched to this field. Kevin stood out from the crowd. He worked on high-paying contracts throughout the country and his hourly rate was jaw-dropping. He had settled down in Houston working for a trading company. Kevin had a passion for making money. He tried everything from importing and exporting silk flowers to starting his own high-tech company. What more could she ask for in a provider?

Still, the most important thing was that Kevin loved her and adored her. He often smiled at her with such contentment, as if he were the luckiest man in the world. Their mutual love and admiration for each other was strong. He was never stingy about showing his affection for her in front of others. He was even a little pushy about it in the beginning of their relationship. She was sure it was only because he wanted to be with her. They fell in love shortly after they met and rushed into marriage.

They were alone in the United States since all their families were still in China. Having each other provided them with much needed support like two little boats finally anchored in choppy water. They did not even go back and visit their families before getting married. In Esther's opinion, marriage was about two people who loved each other; it was not about their families, especially when those families were on the other side of the planet.

The American concept of marriage counseling made no sense to her. If a marriage required so much work, then what was the point of staying married? Esther was sure that Kevin was exactly what she was looking for—and even more. They would never need a marriage counselor.

Esther was not naïve, though. She knew quite a bit about relationships, and she knew that a similar family background was critical for a good marriage. She learned this lesson from watching her sister, Ling, and some other friends; a similar family background usually implied similarity in values and lifestyles, which were necessary for harmony in an intimate relationship. Kevin was from a big city in northern China, and both of his parents were college-educated engineers. Esther grew up in HangZhou, a beautiful city in China famous for its stunning natural scenery and rich history. Her dad, Qing, was a college professor, and her mom, Hua, a factory administrator. Thus, with similar family backgrounds, Esther was certain that she and Kevin would have more in common than not.

Esther was determined that she would have a better marriage than her parents had. Her parents, although both good people, argued all the time. She was very sure that her marriage, started very well, would only get better.

Esther planned her pregnancy meticulously. Her hope was to have a baby in the zodiac year of the tiger. To her, the sign of the tiger represented strength and leadership, and Esther hoped her child (preferably a son) would have these qualities. Throughout her life, Esther almost always achieved everything she planned—and even more.

However, this time she ran into mother nature, and her plan did not quite work out. Months went by, but she could not get pregnant. By the time the window for having a baby in the year of the tiger closed, she wondered whether she could get pregnant at all.

"If I can't give you a child, I will leave you so you can marry another woman and have children," Esther said to Kevin.

Kevin bore the responsibility of having an offspring since he was the only son of his family. In Chinese tradition, filial piety was one of the most important virtues. Having an offspring was the number one expression of filial piety.

"What are you talking about?" Kevin embraced Esther with a big hug. He blinked his eyes and gave her a gentle smile. "You will for sure get pregnant!"

His smile was so sweet and innocent. Esther was so grateful to him.

She did become pregnant when she stopped obsessing about it. It was such exciting news! The baby would be a rabbit, the sign right after the tiger. But this did not matter anymore. She would have taken any sign by then, even the rat. Her dad, Qing, was born in the year of the rat. Esther loved her dad, and he was always her favorite parent.

It was such a joyous journey for her to carry this ever-growing life inside her. She felt more alive and in touch with her body. It was such a miracle! She knew the baby was a little boy. She saw him a few times through ultrasound, and one time he was sucking his toe. He became very playful when he grew closer to full-term. Many times, when she sat down and remained still, a big bump would suddenly appear on her abdomen. Not sure whether it was a little fist or a little foot, she would tap on the bump, and it would shrink back down. Then, suddenly, with another "pong," another bump would show up in a different spot. Esther was sure the little boy was grinning.

Kevin was thrilled about their upcoming new child. He could not contain his excitement. He accompanied Esther to every new parent prep class and helped in preparing for the nursery. He even painted a brand-new cradle a lovely light blue.

Esther, Kevin and Hua kept walking with big smiles on their faces. Esther was in the middle with Kevin and Hua on either side. Hua was an energetic and hard-working individual, and she had a strong mind and hot temper. Hua was never Esther's favorite parent, and the relationship between mother and daughter was always strained.

From the time she started elementary school, Esther argued with Hua constantly. She was the youngest kid in the family, with an older brother, Jian, and an older sister, Ling. While her siblings were obedient, Esther was free-spirited and liked to challenge the status quo. She always insisted on finding the reasons and motives behind Hua's commands. This attitude annoyed Hua a great deal. With her limited formal education, many times Hua could not explain her thoughts clearly even when she tried.

Esther quickly became more educated than her mother, and she often felt that her mom was not good enough in many ways. She was even ashamed of her mother on a few occasions. This attitude probably irritated Hua even more and fueled further arguments between them.

"Why do I need to do this?" Esther would ask in a typical conversation.

"Why do you ask so many questions? Just do what I tell you!" Hua would angrily shout.

As a parent in Chinese culture, Hua had absolute power over her children. And to be fair, Esther thought now, a full day of work and long commutes on a bicycle had to be exhausting.

Hua favored Jian, who was her only son. Between her two daughters, Hua preferred Ling, who was not only much prettier but also much more obedient. In her youth, Esther often felt like she was a scapegoat for whatever happened in Hua's life. Nevertheless, Esther knew Hua loved her. Whenever she had a doubt about this love, she always remembered a midnight emergency when Hua woke her up. It was in the late 1970s of China, and she was about nine years old.

They were living in a college dorm, and her dad was on a business trip. Hua checked on the kids and found Esther hot to the touch. She took Esther's temperature and mistakenly read 42 degrees Celsius (108 degrees Fahrenheit). The thermometer in 1970s China was an ancient style; there was no digital display. Hua panicked, so she dressed the groggy Esther while half in tears.

"We need to go to the clinic. Your fever is way too high," Hua said and took her out of the dorm, but Esther was so sleepy that she could barely walk.

"Come up on my back and I will carry you," Hua directed and squatted down.

The dim streetlight fell on them, and everything was surrounded by warm, yellow fog.

"I can walk," Esther insisted. At that moment, she had pity for her mom and did not want to burden her.

Hua grabbed Esther's hand and took her to the overnight clinic. Esther was seen by a doctor and prescribed some medicine. Her temperature was 40.2 degrees Celsius (104 degrees Fahrenheit) instead of 42 degrees Celsius, but it was still serious. The doctor later became a family friend, and every time she met Hua, they would laugh at how panicked Hua was that night because of the wrong temperature reading.

When Esther told her mother that she was pregnant, Hua insisted that she needed to come to the United States and take care of Esther and her newborn. Hua knew from her own experiences that the Chinese tradition of "sitting a month" was great wisdom. Hua probably also felt guilty for what happened to Ling.

"Sitting a month" meant a new mother would refrain from all physical work and rest in her bed, eating and nursing her baby, for a whole month. In Chinese tradition, the first month after childbirth was considered so critical for the mother that it was like an opportunity for rebirth. If the mother was well taken care of, she would be much stronger physically and even get rid of some old illnesses. However, if she did not get enough rest and care, her health would deteriorate significantly. The impact might not be obvious at first, but the lack would show up later in chronic pains and illnesses.

Hua had retired from her job at age 50, but staying idle at home was difficult for her. She soon directed all her energy into a neighborhood association. She quickly advanced to manager level, even though she was barely qualified for the position due to her lack of education. After she stumbled through this position for ten years, dragging her husband and children with her, the manager position and all her achievements in it became the highlights of her life. Recently, though, Hua had to step down from the position.

The opportunity to take care of Esther and her upcoming baby came just in time; doing so became Hua's priority and focus. Once she arrived, she took charge of the household as if she were a drill sergeant. For the very first time ever since she came to the United States, Esther felt relaxed with her mom on her side.

What a perfect life!

Esther felt a little niggle of unease deep down, though. She had had a moment like this before, but it was so brief—then an accident struck that changed her life.

CHAPTER 2

Hometown

The trio walked along the backside of the large lake and passed the clubhouse and tennis courts. The clubhouse was magnificent; its roof was made of red shingles. It had a huge circular driveway with beautiful flower gardens on both sides filled with roses, cornflowers, asters and bluebells. Small lampposts built with bricks lined up like dutiful soldiers along the walkway.

The man-made circular lake was surrounded by white and pink myrtle trees. In the middle of the lake was a huge water fountain shaped like a beautiful lily flower in full bloom. The water reflected the blue Texas sky with white clouds. It rippled in lovely lines under the gentle breeze, turning the reflection into a wrinkled painting. At the other end of the lake was the entrance to the subdivision where security guards stopped and checked every visitor.

The lake reminded her of West Lake in her hometown of Hang-Zhou, China. West Lake was the heart and soul of HangZhou. She remembered her favorite view of West Lake from the top of Baoshi Mountain. She would climb the hill every morning during her summer breaks. On top of the hill were boulders so huge that she had to climb on her hands and feet to get to the very top. In a girls' outing during Esther's middle-school years, her best friend, May, tried everything she could but was unable to climb up the boulders. Esther still remembered how May's face filled with embarrassment.

Once Esther made it up to the top of a boulder, the whole West Lake would open up right in front of her eyes. The view just melted her heart. The beautiful and peaceful lake was surrounded by a series of blue mountains that towered in the distance, like a tender baby embraced in the strong arms of her loving mother. The city was on the east side of the lake, its skyline continuously changing throughout the years. The lake had thousands of years of history and thus was associated with many stories and fairy tales. A natural lake, its water came from the East Ocean. A few islets dotted the lake, and around it were many parks—all of them with their own unique sceneries and stories.

The water of West Lake shimmered like a silk dress; under the sunlight of early morning, it rippled with many sparkling gold streaks when the breeze passed through like gentle fingers. The Bai Causeway and the Su Causeway—named after two famous ancient Chinese poets—were like two heavily embroidered sashes for this shining silk dress. Boats and kayaks decorated the lake like many embroidered embellishments.

Willow trees and peach trees were planted alternately along the Bai Causeway on both sides. In the spring, the smoky green of willow trees and the warm pink of peach flowers decorated the causeway like a dream. The causeway divided the lake into two parts: an inner lake close to the hill and a much bigger lake that connected to the mountains far away. Inside the inner lake was a huge field of water lilies; in the summer red lily flowers in full bloom stand out from the rich, green leaves like many young and beautiful ballerinas.

The Bai Causeway was almost parallel to the hill. The entrance to the causeway was the Broken Bridge, which looked so close that Esther often felt she could almost take a step and stand on it. The Broken Bridge was named for its famous view on sunny winter mornings after a heavy snow. With white snow still covering the bridge except at the very top where the snow was already melted, the golden sunshine reflected by the snow made the bridge look broken on the very top when viewed from a distance. The bridge also was forever linked to a fairy tale of an ancient love story between a white snake incarnated as a beautiful young woman and a human man.

The Su Causeway connected with the Bai Causeway through an islet called GuShan and flowed out to the south end of the lake. Designed to be a tranquil place, the Su Causeway was connected by six bridges with willow trees on both sides. Esther always loved the thrill of riding a bicycle on the causeway, going up and down the bridges.

Many years had passed since Esther had left China. The longer she stayed away from West Lake, the more she loved it. She missed West Lake and her hometown.

Now the three of them walked into another small section of the neighborhood after crossing a bridge where they came upon another small lake surrounded by huge stones. Three water fountains shot water straight up like fireworks. A few white swans floated on the surface. A group of little ducklings watched over by their mother rested on top of the stones. Next to the lake was a little playground with swings and slides. Kevin and Esther sat on swings, and Hua walked around checking out the playground. This was going to be a great place for their child to play.

At times Esther was in awe of how far she had come. She was in the United States for less than ten years and thriving in both private life and professional life. She was the only female engineer for Pride Oil, a medium-sized oil company. Her job offered very good pay and many great benefits. She and Kevin could afford a wonderful custom house and two nice cars. More importantly, though, she had found a great husband in Kevin. Best of all, their first son was going to be born.

Esther was the only child in her family who successfully immigrated to the United States. Immigration to developed countries became increasingly popular in China in the 1980s, especially after the Tiananmen Square event in 1989. As a symbol of freedom and opportunity, the United States of America was considered a top choice for immigration.

Her older brother, Jian, was a kindhearted and handsome young man with few words. He was a great athlete in track and field but did not do well academically. After every track and field competition, he would receive many love letters from his admirers in addition to many trophies and awards. He always gave all the awards to his sisters to keep.

After graduating from college, Jian wanted to go to France and study culinary arts. The last time he applied for a visa was during the Tiananmen Square upheaval. For the twenty days he was there in Beijing, he did not send one single word back home, which made their parents very worried. After that rejection, he totally abandoned his dream and settled down in their hometown of HangZhou.

Her older sister, Ling, went much further on this journey but also fell short. She was successfully admitted to a doctorate program of biology with a full scholarship at a well-known American university. However, she gave up the program and returned to China six months after she started the program.

In addition to Ling's difficulties in adjusting to a brand-new environment and a challenging doctorate program, her husband was a major reason for this failed adventure. He went to visit her in the States but was eager to go back to his prized job in China. Yet, he did not want to leave his beautiful wife alone in America where so many single men, especially lonely Chinese graduate students, would find her attractive. Ling gave in to the pressure from her husband and the doctorate program.

Ling's return to China was quite a disappointment and considered a huge failure by the family and all the people around her. Esther was so embarrassed that she hid the fact of her return from her closest friends. As a result, Ling carried around tons of guilt and regrets.

Being the youngest in the family and probably the boldest, Esther carried the family torch and came to the United States and successfully settled down. She was one small drop of water in the enormous emigration tide of Chinese intellectuals after the Tiananmen Square event in 1989.

She would never forget her initial journey to the United States from mainland China. She traveled with Lan, who was her longtime friend since elementary school. Lan was the first friend Esther made. Lan was a very quiet and seemingly obedient girl, although, in fact, she was free-spirited and even wild in her thoughts. She was quite artistic but did not dare to pursue a career in art because of the uncertainty of an art career; instead, she studied engineering in college.

Esther came to America to study engineering in graduate school while Lan came to reunite with her husband. It was the very first flight ever for both, and it was an international flight! They were flying to a totally different country. At the Shanghai airport, they were running late and had to rush to the gate. They were in such a hurry that Lan tripped and fell.

"Ouch!" Lan was quite upset and wanted to take a break.

"Get up! We do not have time to waste!" Esther urged Lan and pulled her up.

Esther often felt the same way in this totally strange new country— you just had to get up quickly every time you fell, or you would be run over. Everybody was in a rush. Nobody waited for you.

After Lan was picked up by her husband in San Francisco, Esther began her lone journey to Houston, Texas. Esther did not know anybody in Houston and could not find anyone to pick her up. A search for an acquaintance in Houston by her family and friends turned out to be fruitless as well. Communications between China and the United States were limited to physical mail in the early 1990s. Very few households in China had a phone; phones with international access were almost unheard of. Besides, phone calls to the States cost a few dollars a minute and could quickly drain a typical Chinese monthly income. There was no internet at that time; looking back, it almost seemed like the Stone Age.

Esther went to the home of her friend, May, in Dallas instead. May was living with her sister and her brother-in-law. May came to the United States one year earlier, before she even finished college in China. May had to leave China swiftly because she did not want to be subject to the five-year service mandate. She joined her sister in the United States and continued her college education. This hurried decision cost May many years of struggle in getting her bachelor's degree in the United States.

Esther did not have to follow this five-year service requirement because of one exception that applied to college graduates whose direct relatives were overseas Chinese nationals. Esther's grandfather emigrated to Japan in the 1920s and returned to China on the eve of the Japanese invasion of China. Although this part of the family history had once seemed distant and irrelevant, suddenly it became a stroke of great family luck and saved Esther and her sister Ling five precious years of their youth to realize their American dreams.

Her father, Qing, took many trips to his hometown of WenZhou to get the required documents. It took great effort and smart tactics to work with local government agencies to verify this family history of five decades prior. Fifty years was a very long period! After almost one year of travel back and forth, Qing finally had his family history documented with red seals so that his two daughters could apply for passports.

It took the efforts of multiple generations and even a bit luck for a successful immigration!

Among Esther's friends, May was always the prettiest, best dressed, and most popular girl in the school. She was a kindhearted girl, but many times her kindness was overlooked because of her beauty and stylish clothing. Her parents were a model couple in Esther's eyes. May's dad was an accomplished professor and engineer and made good money on the side by working on building design contracts when the Chinese economy had been booming in the 1980s. May's mom focused her attention on her two daughters. She sewed many pretty dresses for May and her sister and helped them stand out like princesses.

May's parents happened to be visiting from China when Esther arrived. Her dad was working as a delivery man while her mom worked for a sewing company. Their income from these blue-collar jobs in the United States was so much more than their income as professionals back in China! They were happy to make good money during their visit. Meanwhile, May was working as a waitress at night and on the weekends to earn money for her school.

Esther could not believe that a tender girl like May could work as a waitress! More surprisingly, her father, a well-respected professor, was working a blue-collar job.

This country can change a person, Esther thought.

The two girls slept on the floor together because there was no extra bed for Esther. They talked for many hours every night.

"I will live the life of a middle-class professional in this country and have my own house and my own car," Esther declared. In the early 1990s in China, nobody owned a house or a car. It seemed like a quite ambitious goal for Esther.

"Sure, we will all have our own houses and cars," May responded with a sense of uncertainty.

Esther realized this dream just five years later. Now another three years had gone by, and her first son would be born in the United States as a U.S. citizen automatically! Esther could not help but be happy and content.

Kevin looked very happy, too! He may have been a little nervous, though. Just a couple of days earlier, he had serious diarrhea, and they ended up in the emergency room. While they sat in the waiting area, a nurse came to them and told Esther that they should go to another floor.

"The delivery room is upstairs," explained the nurse.

Esther suddenly realized that she must have looked ready to give birth.

"It's not me; he is the emergency," Esther answered and laughed.

It turned out that Kevin was allergic to some dried seafood Hua brought from China. It was a delicacy from Hua's hometown, and somehow Kevin's body could not tolerate it. It was a funny experience, and Esther thought it was a good rehearsal for the delivery. Esther heard some stories about how men were not prepared to become fathers.

It was probably the case with Kevin, she thought.

CHAPTER 3

Empty Palace

It was getting late. The blue of the sky in the west had faded away into a pink sunset, and night was falling like a thick mask. Esther, Kevin and Hua returned from their walk to their two-story contemporary house.

Inside, the house was spacious and comfortable. On the right-hand side of the front entrance was a dining room. An expansive redwood dining table occupied most of the room. The table was huge and beautiful; its edge was carved with patterns of flowers and leaves. Eight dining chairs had slim and tall backrests that were heavily carved with matching patterns.

The factory plastic wrappers for the seat cushions were still covering them. Esther wanted to remove them, but Kevin wanted them kept on. He had a weird habit of wanting to keep things so protected that they still seemed unused after years. His insistence on leaving the tacky covers on did not bother her much. Esther was easygoing when it came to the little things. After all, they did protect the seats from wear and smoke from the kitchen.

A monumental, elongated wall sculpture hung behind the dining table. It was an intriguing piece of art—more eye-catching than a traditional painting with pencil or oil brush. It was like a painting with clay. This sculpture featured a beautiful woman sitting sideways and

17

half-naked with her breasts shown. Her right arm reached out for an apple. Esther did not really know what the sculpture meant; however, somehow it attracted her when she first saw it. The figure's face reminded Esther of an angel in typical traditional Western paintings. Esther knew many of these artworks were religiously inspired. Although she was not religious, she liked such art. Kevin was indifferent as long as it was not too expensive.

Growing up in China, Esther was automatically an atheist. She was taught to believe in the Communist Party and to live for communism. What happened during the Cultural Revolution and afterward, though, made many Chinese people, including Esther, suspicious of this doctrine. As a matter of fact, Esther felt so cheated by the teachings of her childhood that she did not want to believe *any* doctrine anymore. Esther learned to believe in herself. Her successes so far validated her belief.

However, deep inside, she sensed a force out there bigger than herself. She remembered the first time she prayed. It was on an anniversary date of the Tiananmen Square event. She was waiting in line outside a United States embassy in Shanghai for an interview to get a student visa. She took so many tests and filled out so many applications for the privilege to study in the United States. She carried so much hope from her parents and her family on her shoulders for a better life. She could not imagine what her life would turn out like if her visa request was rejected.

I can NOT fail.

It was her motto then and after for a long time. But at this last step for her to walk on the new land of America, her fate was determined by a total stranger in the embassy. She felt powerless.

Esther prayed and asked God for help right in the line outside the embassy. It was a hot and humid morning, and cicadas were buzzing nonstop. Her sense of powerlessness disappeared and a strong sense of peace settled in her heart after she prayed. During the interview, a counselor met her with a warm and welcoming smile and approved her application right away after a few short questions. Esther was not sure whether her prayer helped. She was certain of the inner peace she felt after she prayed, though, and she liked the peace.

On the other side of the house's foyer was an open room that could be used as a living room but was still completely empty. After all, they had only moved in several years ago. This was their first house, and it was hard to fill it with only the two of them.

Next to the living room was the study, which was crowded with two desks—his and hers—and many stacks of papers and documents. Kevin was restless and always came up with ideas to make more money. These documents were evidence of his efforts. Esther liked his strong desires to be rich and successful.

The highlight of the house was probably the family room. It was two stories high; on one side were stairs going up to the second floor, and the entire back side featured a huge window from floor to ceiling. Another side connected to the master bedroom and had a well-organized entertainment center; the opposite side connected to the kitchen and breakfast room—it was a very open floor plan. Esther liked the appeal of grandness, although sometimes it felt empty with only a few pieces of furniture.

Kevin made very good money as an IT consultant while Esther also made decent money as an engineer. Money was not a concern; however, their humble start in the United States prevented them from buying expensive furniture. After all, they were still new immigrants in a new country. It was just hard to find good furniture at a price they considered reasonable.

They did splurge on some items, such as the curtains. Many windows were graced with custom-made curtains. The huge windows in the family room were covered by fancy curtains with valences that could open and close all the way. It was almost like the curtain on a theater stage—one that opened to their beautiful backyard. Many of their Chinese friends were very frugal and would never spend that much money on curtains. They either bought the cheapest blinds or shipped curtains from China.

Esther displayed many family pictures around the house, especially on the dining table. Pictures of her parents and brother and sister were quite prominent; those photos were taken around West Lake right before she came to the United States. One of the pictures was of just Esther and Ling. The gazebo by the lake in the background, with its fancy flying roof corner and carefully painted-on Chinese traditional patterns, made the picture stand out. Ling sat there with her typical sad yet sweet smile.

Ling was always viewed as the prettier of the two sisters, but Esther never envied her. As a child, Ling was very shy and submissive. She grew up to be a beautiful and gentle young lady. She had the most beautiful eyes, and her long lashes cast a shadow that added mystery to her demeanor. She also had the smoothest skin Esther had ever felt, like a thin piece of porcelain that could break if flicked.

Esther was standing behind Ling with her hands on Ling's shoulder. She still remembered that touch, which gave her a strange feeling. She did not know then that it would be the last time she would ever touch her dear sister.

Esther carried the burden of Ling's dream—actually, the whole family's dreams—when she came to America. She knew that her only choice was to go forward and find a way to settle in this new country.

Back in the house, Esther noticed that the picture of the two sisters was lying down on its face. Hua did this every day. Esther put the picture back in its standing position.

Of course, her and Kevin's wedding pictures were on display in the middle of the dining table. It was a dream wedding. Everything went as planned—the wedding dress, the bridesmaid gowns, the flowers, the food, the friends. It was quite exhausting, too! She spent months preparing for it. Kevin did not help much with the wedding, but he did not stop her from spending money, either. Esther appreciated the trust and freedom he gave her.

The wedding day was cloudy in the beginning, but the moment they exchanged their vows, the sun peeked out. A ray of sunshine fell on both of them.

It must be that God was smiling on us. Esther was quite sure.

One wedding photo captured the perfect moment. The sunshine had cast a warm glow around Esther's face, and she had to admit that she looked as beautiful as everyone said.

"You look like an American doll!" Kevin's mother, Feng, praised her when she saw this picture.

Why an American doll? Is an American doll prettier than a Chinese doll? Esther thought.

There was one little odd surprise during the ceremony. Hua was ushered in by a very tall groomsman; he made her look so short. The contrast was comically dramatic, and Esther could see it in the faces of some of the guests. This man was Kevin's friend, and the plan had been for him to usher Feng, who was much taller than Hua. Esther was told that Feng had requested this change at the last minute.

Why would she want to do this? To embarrass my mother? Esther had this suspicion in her mind long after the incident. She heard that Feng complained behind her back that Esther was a little short for Kevin.

Both mothers, Hua and Feng, came from China for the wedding and lived with the couple for half a year. The presence of both mothers almost ruined the wedding. It was fight after fight every day. The main cause of all the fights, or so Esther deduced, was that Feng thought herself superior to Hua. Feng was college-educated and had a professional career as an engineer. She looked down on Hua. Hua, on the other hand, was a strong lady and would never take any insult lightly.

Feng's arrogance was on full display every time they went out together in a car. Feng considered the front passenger seat to be a symbol of importance, and she wanted it. Every time Kevin drove, Feng took the front passenger seat as if it were her God-given right. Esther and Hua would sit in the back without any complaints. Whenever Esther drove, Feng would tell Kevin to take the front seat, and she never thought Hua had the same right as she did. Fortunately, Kevin always rejected her suggestion and let Hua sit in the front seat.

As a matter of fact, Kevin often seemed to be embarrassed by Feng's behavior, and he always backed up Esther. Esther was grateful that Kevin was willing to stand up against his mother. She was sure that she would not want to live with Feng ever again.

Many photos in the house also showcased the young couple's vacations around the United States and the world. They smiled in front of the Chinese theater in Los Angeles; they climbed to the top of Mount Rainier in Seattle; they took a picture with a handsome guard at Buckingham Palace.

Esther got a chance to visit Kevin in the United Kingdom when he was on a business trip, and the whole trip was paid for by his company. While Kevin was busy working, Esther enjoyed herself, visiting all the dream places she had only read about in books: Buckingham Palace, St. James Park, the British Museum, the University of Cambridge, and many more.

Esther really enjoyed walking on the streets of London. Unlike the widely spread-out Houston and most Texas cities where one had to drive to get anywhere, major attractions in London were within walking distance. Esther particularly liked St. James Park. It was a drizzly London afternoon when she went, and the whole park seemed to be surrounded by fog. The setting of the willow trees by the water reminded Esther of her hometown and West Lake.

What surprised Esther the most in the British Museum was the huge Buddha statue. It was still in good shape, and the colors were so vivid. This statue was from the Forbidden City, stolen by British soldiers during their invasion of China in the late nineteenth century. While it reflected a humiliating history from China's perspective, considering that its treasure was purloined, the Buddha statue offered Esther a moment of awe and a sense of pride for her native country.

The photos provided further proof of her successes in the United States. Esther was already living the middle-class life, which she had declared to May as her most ambitious goal on her first night in the United States. But she had to admit, sometimes she felt empty. If Esther argued with herself logically over her situation, she realized that she should feel extremely fortunate. All her friends in China were working so hard and earning so little. No one she knew there had a house or car yet.

However, something was missing; Esther just did not know exactly what it was. If this was the American dream, she often wanted to ask, just like in the Peggy Lee song, "Is that all there is?"

But now this new baby brought a new meaning and purpose to her life. She was so happy and enjoyed all the experiences of pregnancy even though she had to prick her fingers three times a day to check her blood sugar level.

"It is uncommon that you are so skinny and yet your sugar level is so high." Her gynecologist was really puzzled. "But it is more common in Asian women."

Interesting! Esther thought. She tried very hard to blend into the melting pot of the United States. However, her place of origin seemed to show up in many unexpected areas.

Her body changed every day, and her joy and hope grew. To her surprise, her pregnancy attracted so much attention and recognition. Strangers would stop and talk to her and share their stories everywhere she went, especially in public places like a grocery store or a shopping mall.

Esther used to always give the same answer when people greeted her and asked how she was doing: "I am pretty good." She never felt like she could share with others how she felt in this new land. This was probably the only answer most people wanted to hear anyway. Now she could joke with others about her ever-growing belly and talk about childbearing and life in general. Her life became so much richer with this growing new life inside her. She felt like she was finally taking root in this new soil.

Like a tree, she was going to grow big and tall!

CHAPTER 4

New Land

Esther moved five times within the first month after she landed in America. When she stayed with May in Dallas, she was able to get in touch with the Chinese Student Association of her school and arrange for the president of the association to pick her up. Three days later, she took a Greyhound bus and arrived in Houston. For her first night in Houston, she stayed in a motel in a rundown neighborhood where the president worked part-time to fund his education. The next day she moved in with a young Chinese family of which the husband was working on his doctorate degree in the same engineering department as hers. After a couple of weeks, Esther moved in with a young musician couple who recently went through a miscarriage of twins, so the mood in their place was lugubrious.

Finally, Esther moved into an apartment with a young lady whose husband had just left for Hong Kong to be a professor and whose young daughter was living with her grandparents back in China. It was quite typical for young Chinese couples to ship their young kids to their families in China to care for because they just did not have the time or energy for a young child while they both worked hard to survive in this new land.

Esther moved again to a popular apartment building after one semester, which was a government-subsidized building for senior African Americans. With central air, the place held the same wisp of death as did a hospice because many seniors spent their last days there. However, it was popular among poor international students because it was cheap and safe and close to the campus.

The area around the campus was not safe at all. Esther heard that shootings and robberies happened from time to time. A popular story among the Chinese students was about a robbery that happened in a neighborhood just a few streets away. A few Chinese male students shared an even cheaper apartment there. A robber kicked his way into their apartment one late afternoon, grabbed their TV, and ran out. A few minutes later, he returned and shouted, "Where is the remote control?"

The apartment building allocated a very small number of units to the college students; thus, its waiting list was usually very long. Esther was finally assigned a unit with two other female students. In the two years Esther stayed there, roommates came and went. Among them, Jean and Zia became good friends to her who later supported her during the darkest moments of her life.

Jean worked as a technician in a lab in a well-known and respected hospital and in her spare time studied for the medical board exam. She had the best education in medicine and worked as a doctor back in China. She was quiet and determined, and she vowed in her heart to become a doctor in the United States and achieve significant success before she turned forty. Later, Jean passed the test and was accepted into a residency program in Seattle.

Zia came one year later and enrolled in a graduate program in computer science. Zia was a very smart girl but usually did not act very confidently. Luckily for her, she had an older sister who had arrived a few years earlier and was already settled in the same city. Her sister introduced a young man, Sean, to her not long after. He was a Christian, and Zia started going to church with him.

For the first year, Esther walked to school during the day. The school was within walking distance, and she did not have a car. The Texas sun could be very tough; Esther often was covered with sweat from head to toe by the time she arrived at the Engineering Department building in the morning. She usually stayed quite late in her office after taking night classes and doing her homework and research. She would then call the school police department to request a ride back to her apartment.

Often Esther was the only one left in a very empty engineering building, staring at the darkness outside and waiting for the police car to show up. The wait could take an hour or more. She could have asked any single male student for a ride, and the young man would be more than willing to help. However, she never asked for help because she was afraid of giving any of them the false impression that she may be interested in a relationship.

By the end of the first year, Esther had saved some money and borrowed more to buy her first car. It was a secondhand Toyota Corolla, and Esther was so proud of her accomplishment!

Letters were the only connections Esther had with her family and her friends in China. She could not afford phone calls to China because they were prohibitively expensive, just like an international call from China; it was several dollars per minute at the time. In her letters, she shared with her family and friends her experiences in this new land at every step of her journey.

Esther told them how sparkling clean and comfortable the restrooms were in the airport, which impressed her the most on her trip to America. She could never understand why Americans considered toilets a place to "rest" and would name them in such a way until she used one in the airport. In China, toilets were not a place to rest. You wanted to get out of there as fast as possible. She talked about the restrooms so much that her friends protested in their letters back.

"You are so Americanized! I heard that the moon seems rounder in the U.S. Now for you, even toilets smell so good!" one friend joked.

She also told them about her first car she had bought. Nobody in her family owned a car in China yet. Her dad was so proud of her that he even bragged about her first car in his classroom to the undergraduate students. Her friends were envious of her accomplishments. Esther earned a small monthly salary of $900 (an equivalent of 7,200 RMB in China) as a research assistant in her graduate program. However, she was still way better off than her friends in China whose yearly salary was less than her monthly salary in the early 1990s.

Although Esther's letters might have been a window for her family and friends to peek through for a glimpse of this so-called promised land, their letters were a much-needed anchor for Esther during her first lonely years in the U.S.

For a whole year, Esther did not buy a single item for herself except food and necessities. Before her departure to the United States, she borrowed $2,000 from Ling. It was a huge chunk of money at the time! She spent more than a thousand on the airline tickets and had only about $800 in her pocket when she headed to the U.S. She also had two overstuffed suitcases, which contained everything she needed, including clothes, bedding, books, kitchen knives and other kitchenware. She almost ran out of money before she received her first fellowship payment.

Esther was well-prepared for Houston's weather, which did not require many different types of clothing. The weather had only two seasons, Esther joked to her friends in her letters: summer and non-summer. Thus, T-shirts and a few jackets were enough.

At the end of the first year, she rewarded herself by going to a mall for the first time and spending around a hundred dollars. Converted to Chinese currency, renminbi (RMB), it was about one thousand yuan, a significant amount of money in China back then. The average monthly salary was a few hundred yuan.

"Am I a little too loose with money?" Esther asked Jean. "I feel I just 一掷千金" (a Chinese idiom that refers to living a life of luxury, or spending one kilogram of gold per day).

"You are fine! You have worked hard!" Jean assured her.

American people were very nice and welcoming, especially Esther's American host family. Carol was a Caucasian lady in her early fifties and a member of a local megachurch who participated in an outreach program to care for international students. She worked for a big engineering contract firm for almost thirty years as an executive secretary. She had two failed marriages and a grown daughter. Later, she married for a third time to an engineer, Steve. The couple was so kind to Esther and treated her as their own daughter. They took Esther to restaurants, rodeos and many other events. Steve walked Esther down the wedding aisle because her dad, Qing, could not make it to the wedding.

Esther went to her first Christmas party at Carol's house. She was quite impressed by the holiday decorations and gifts, which were like the items one might see in an American movie. What she remembered the most clearly, though, was her embarrassment after she gave a wrong answer regarding the Chinese population. She was the youngest at the party and an obvious foreigner. When someone asked her about the current Chinese population, she got busy doing mental math.

The Chinese numbering system was different from the one used in the United States. Both systems were the same up to one thousand; after that, they changed. The Chinese system had an extra unit called "万," which was "ten thousand." Thus, one hundred 万 was a million. 万万 was one hundred million and was given another unit of 亿 in Chinese. Ten 亿 was a billion.

The correct answer was twelve 亿 in the Chinese system or 1.2 billion in the U.S. system. Esther knew the answer in the Chinese system by heart; however, she was not sure how to convert the answer to the American system.

She was taught to be proud of her mother country for being the most populous country on the earth. A national policy in the 1950s and 1960s promoted multiple children for every family. The logic was that "人多力量大," which meant the more people you had, the more powerful you were. Esther herself, as a third child of her parents, was a direct result of this policy. After the Chinese population exploded, though, a total opposite policy of one child per family started in the early 1980s.

It was amazing how government policy could swing from one extreme to another overnight and dramatically impact everybody's personal life. Most people were used to having their lives dictated by the government; however, many women and families suffered greatly between the policy and Chinese tradition of having a male offspring for a family.

"Maybe 12 billion?" Esther answered.

Nobody pointed out the obvious mistake. The whole world population was only about six billion at that time.

There were too many zeros for Esther to think through. She found a piece of paper and wrote down all the zeros. Steve helped her. They finally figured out that the two systems were off because of the additional unit of 万.

"It is 1.2 billion!" Esther corrected her earlier mistake and felt quite embarrassed.

A system, as well as a culture, is to a person like water is to a fish. You are not aware of its existence until you come out of it.

Esther once heard of this story, and she thought it was funny. An old fish was swimming with a baby fish and said, "You are swimming in water." The baby fish looked around and asked, "Where is the water?"

How naïve the little fish is! Esther once thought.

Esther now began to understand the story. She was the baby fish! Wait, she was also the old fish! With no family member around her, there was no old fish around. She had to figure it all out by herself.

The U.S. measuring system was different from the Chinese ones as well. China had both a traditional measuring system and an official metric system. The traditional system was still used in everyday life in almost all the farmers' markets and small shops. Esther's parents and their generation and older were still stuck in the traditional system. However, the official metric system was taught in every school for decades, with everything measured by meter and kilogram. Esther was proud of her knowledge of this new official measuring system. She was so used to the unit of meter for her studies and work and everyday life. She even set an ideal height for a future husband in the metric system: 1.8 meters.

Now she was all confused with the official imperial system used in the United States. The common measuring units in length were feet and inches. Esther had to convert between meter and foot and other units constantly in her studies as an engineering student and in her everyday life. Her requirement of height for a mate now was six feet!

How original, to use a human's foot to name a measuring unit! Esther thought. She found it very interesting, if not confounding. It did make sense that measurements were probably done using body parts a long time ago. However, those constant conversions disoriented her like a sailboat having to constantly change its sail.

Luckily, Esther had many Chinese friends to hang out with, which helped ease her loneliness and confusion. She was very popular in the Chinese student community where single female graduate students were a rare commodity. Having an opportunity to study and work in the United States was a dream for many Chinese young professionals, but only a very small portion of them realized this dream. Not only did they have to go through all kinds of hurdles in China for a passport, including the five-year service requirement after college graduation, but they also had to pass many difficult tests, such as the TOEFL and GRE, for admission to American colleges. It was even more difficult for them to get a scholarship. Only those who were superb in their studies and research—the majority of them male nerds—were able to overcome all the hurdles and come to the United States for advanced degrees. These men were usually well into their twenties or even thirties and married. It was rare for a young lady and a recent college graduate like Esther to gain admittance to a graduate school and get a full scholarship.

Right before Esther came to the United States, families and friends gave her much advice on the type of man she should choose as her future husband. A popular debate was whether she should choose a Chinese or an American man. Nobody had a good answer. A college friend who was also her not-so-secret admirer told her to choose a Chinese man.

He invited her to go for a walk around West Lake right before she left for America.

"You know my mom really likes you," he said. "My parents told me that they would reward me well if I convinced you to marry me."

He stole a quick glance at Esther and smiled. He had never told Esther this before. It was not embarrassing to disclose it now since time was running out and it really was not possible anymore.

"Keep yourself for a Chinese man," he added at the end.

He did not explain any further, and Esther never asked. Esther guessed it was a compliment. Somehow this suggestion stuck with her.

Many single males showed interest in her; most of them were fellow students from China and neighboring Asian countries and a few of them were Caucasian men. Esther was firm with her high standards and waited patiently for the right candidate. Soon she was introduced to a Shanghainese man a few months after she arrived in the U.S.

This young man was honest, smart and cute. He had already finished his graduate studies and worked as a software engineer. He was very enthusiastic about Esther and took her to dinner every week. He even taught her how to drive with his own car. More importantly, this young man was also very close to getting his permanent resident status in the U.S. (also called Green Card) through his employer.

The transition from student to working professional was quite a milestone in realizing the American dream. An employer usually sponsored a Green Card application for an international student with a job offer. A job meant legal protection and financial stability for an immigrant.

A marriage to this young man would provide Esther with a secure legal status and financial support. He also seemed to be a good candidate for marriage. He was more than ready to marry her, but Esther was not quite ready for a serious relationship at that point. She did not know exactly what she was waiting for, but she did not feel in her gut that he was the type she wanted to marry, although she could not pinpoint a reason.

One night after he took her back to her apartment, they had a pleasant conversation. Esther shared her album with him. He was so excited, thinking that it might be his opportunity to propose, and he did. Esther did not know why, but she decided to take him down a notch. She told him that he was not as ambitious as she wanted in a partner.

That was it! That was the reason she still had doubt about their compatibility. Esther wanted a mate who was strong and ambitious. Maybe she thought only such a mate could match herself, or maybe she thought the dynamics of her parents' marriage would have been much better if her dad, Qing, had these qualities. The young man disappeared from her life after that night. Esther was a little disappointed that he did not persist.

One year passed since her arrival in the United States, and it was a lonely summer. Esther was quite settled with her car, her roommates, her school and her work schedule. Her life became a little monotonous.

Houston seemed more like a gigantic countryside than a city to Esther. The downtown was quite modern with many skyscrapers, and there were some very nice neighborhoods in the area. However, driving away from downtown on the highways, Esther would see acres and acres of ranches with cows feeding on grasslands and even more unoccupied land. Growing up in the beautiful city of Hang-Zhou and going to college in modern Shanghai, Esther found Houston to be countrified and rough. Over time, she found that many Americans were quite straightforward and even simpleminded, like the farmers back home.

School was never difficult for Esther. She cruised through her master's program and a research extension. What made her school less difficult was that many of her professors were Asian. Their English was broken, but she could understand them perfectly.

Some celebrations were held in the Chinese community for Chinese National Day on the first day of October. Esther went to dance parties with Jean several nights in a row. At the end of one party, Esther was pushed to the center of a group of young students, and she led the group to dance.

Then a young man was introduced to her. His name was Kevin.

CHAPTER 5

Tragedy

It was love at first sight with Kevin. He was very tall, and he had a heavy beard that made him look somewhat older than his age. He had very heavy eyebrows, and his long eyelashes lent an intriguing mystery to his eyes. Yet, his eyes behind a pair of glasses were childlike with a glimmer of sensitivity. He graduated with a master's degree in computer science from the same university a few years ago and now worked as an IT professional.

Kevin made it obvious that he was interested in Esther. After the party began to fizzle, he continued talking to Esther and her roommate, Jean. They walked together down the stairs towards the parking lot and stopped in the middle. Kevin was a couple of steps above them. He had a strong athletic body.

Kevin told them that his sister, Leah, was working in the same engineering field as Esther and that his parents wanted her to come to the United States for an advanced degree.

He turned to Esther and asked, "Can you get an application package for a master's degree for my sister?"

"Sure!" Esther had no hesitation in helping.

He went on and talked more about Leah. "My sister has some

good connections." His hometown was a big city in northern China in which many government bureaus and officials were based. Connections may be important in the United States, but they were essential in China. From everyday life to career promotion to business development, good connections played a pivotal role for a good outcome in China.

He also suggested that he was planning to start his own business on the side.

He is boasting, Esther told herself. But he was ambitious! And he seemed to have big dreams and the persistence to go after them.

Kevin set up a time with Esther to pick up the application material from her and offered to take her to dinner as a token of appreciation. He took her to a fancy seafood buffet—a great first date—and took her out every weekend afterward. He drove her around in his red race car, which drew a lot of attention.

One month later, Kevin hosted a birthday party celebration for himself on a Saturday afternoon. He planned to take Esther to his office and show her around before the crowd arrived. He lived in a nearby city about an hour's drive from Esther's. He drove all the way down and picked Esther up early in the morning.

The office building was a magnificent high-rise, but his office space was a small cubicle. It was a standard setting for a software engineer like him. He was very passionate about his work and had already obtained several patents in his field. A crystal trophy that was an award for one patent sat very prominently in his office. Some of his coworkers, some Asians and some Caucasians, were working overtime in the office that morning. Kevin introduced her to each one of them.

Then he took her back to his apartment. His apartment was clean and spacious. There were quite a few boxes stacked in his living room, inside of which were samples of silk flowers and clothes from China. He was working with some relatives in China and planning to market these products in the U.S. Esther was impressed with his desire to become a business owner.

They watched *Pretty Woman* together after a simple lunch. From the side of her eyes, she sensed Kevin was watching her most of the time. The smile on his face told her that she was as pretty as Julia Roberts, if not more. Esther was quite flattered.

Many friends came to Kevin's birthday party. They made dumplings and had some lively conversation. Among the guests was a well-dressed young lady who came with one of Kevin's coworkers. She apparently was interested in Kevin, but Kevin made it clear that his affection was now only reserved for Esther. At the end of the party, a couple offered to take Esther back on their way home to save Kevin some time. Kevin insisted that he would take Esther back and that he did not mind the one-hour drive. Esther was again flattered.

The Sunday morning right after his birthday, Esther felt the urge to call Kevin. The phone conversation lasted through the whole day and the whole night until Monday morning. He told her all the interesting things that happened when he was young. She could even imagine how naughty he was when he was a young boy. The morning came, and it was time to start a new week.

He surprised her by saying, "I love you!"

He waited for her to respond. Esther felt it was a bit too soon, so she paused.

"Would you want to say something?" Kevin urged.

"I love you, too!" Esther responded. She said so under pressure because she did not want to disappoint him. She indeed liked him, although she was not sure whether it was love.

The next Friday afternoon, Esther responded to a knock on the door of her office. She opened the door, and it was one of her fellow graduate students. Just before she was about to talk to him, she saw Kevin standing across the hall at a distance. Apparently, he was waiting there for her for a while. The afternoon sun was shining on him, and he looked so handsome and sweet. He smiled at her with a little shyness.

Her heart was touched, and they became inseparable. Having him in her life made her feel like she finally had something solid to grasp in this new land. They were quite harmonious and had very few arguments. Esther was quite easygoing, and Kevin usually let her do whatever she liked. People told them that they looked like a perfect couple.

They had a great time on a trip to New York City during the Christmas holiday. Among all the attractions, Esther loved the Rockefeller Center the best. The holiday spirit was in the air, and the whole area was beautifully decorated with many Christmas lights and flowers with the world's largest Christmas tree as a centerpiece. The square was covered with ice and was a popular skating rink. Esther and Kevin came down to the rink and joined the crowd. Kevin was an amateur athlete in skating. He skated very well. Esther was just learning to skate. Kevin looked happy to teach her and was even happier to catch her when she was about to fall and screamed for help. Her scream and his laughter mixed with the cheerful Christmas music and people's laughter all around them. They took many pictures; their young and smiling faces were like the most beautiful flowers blooming in the holiday season!

They also visited Mr. Zhou, who was Esther's financial sponsor for studying in the United States. Mr. Zhou received much help from her dad, Qing, with his application of immigration to the U.S. in the early 1970s. He returned this favor by sponsoring Esther and Ling for their study in the U.S. in the 1990s.

Mr. Zhou's father was a sailor who jumped off a ship in Philadelphia and settled in New York City back in the early 1930s. He was not educated and could speak neither English nor Mandarin. He could only speak a local dialect of WenZhou. Yet, he worked hard and waited patiently for more than thirty years to become a legal citizen of the U.S. He finally met some people who understood his dialect and, through them, reconnected with his family back in China. He brought his wife to the U.S. first, and then the two of them brought all their children out from China to join them in the United States.

Mr. Zhou, the oldest son of his father, grew up not knowing whether his dad was alive. He was overwhelmed when he heard from his dad and knew that he and his young family could leave the countryside and go to the United States. Like his father, Mr. Zhou did not receive any formal education, and the only language he could speak was the local dialect of WenZhou. The emigration process was almost a "mission impossible" for him and his family, yet he was able to pull through with much help from Qing.

Upon Esther's visit, Mr. Zhou gathered all his family and threw a feast for Esther and Kevin. All his five children were married and working, and the third generation was growing fast. More than twenty people came to the gathering. The area of New York City where they lived in now had so many people from WenZhou that their local dialect was an official language. A person who spoke only this dialect could work and live comfortably without speaking a word of English or Mandarin.

It was amazing that an uneducated man like Mr. Zhou's father could bring his whole family to the United States and alter the entire family history! The whole family could thrive and multiply in this new land. This incredible immigration story was full of sacrifice and hard work; an earlier generation created more opportunities for the next generation who, in turn, built more successes.

"Does he have a Green Card?" This was the first thing Mr. Zhou asked Esther about Kevin. It was a very practical question for any immigrant. He seemed a little relieved after Esther gave a positive answer.

On New Year's Eve, Esther and Kevin waited in the freezing winter wind for hours in Times Square and witnessed the ball dropping. It was quite exciting to shout along with a big crowd to count down to a brand-new year! They kissed when the ball dropped. What a beautiful new year! Esther was not all alone in the United States anymore!

Shortly after she met Kevin, Esther noticed Ling was not writing to her anymore. Ling was pregnant when Esther left for America. She gave birth to a boy half a year ago and named him Joshua. Ling apparently regretted her decision to return to China and was thinking about coming back to the United States again. Her plan seemed quite unrealistic to Esther. Esther wrote a letter to her and told her it would be better for her to stay in China since she had a child to care for now.

"Let me realize your American dream!" Esther comforted her in the letter.

Months went by and she did not get a response from Ling. Then Jian's wedding had been postponed for a few months, and her family never gave her a reason for such an unusual change. In the wedding pictures Esther finally received, Ling was nowhere to be seen. Moreover, her parents did not seem that happy. There seemed to be suppressed sadness behind their smiles.

Why is that? Esther could not stop wondering. *Their beloved and only son has finally found the love of his life and is getting married. Why do they not seem to be happy in one of the supposedly happiest moments of life?*

She called her family on Chinese New Year's Eve and really wanted to talk to everybody. International phone calls were still very expensive but being able to hear the voice of her family mattered more. She wanted to talk to Ling in particular; Ling should have been there with the rest of the family. But she was not. When Esther asked why, Qing would not answer. The call was dropped.

Esther sensed something was very wrong.

"My sister may have died or gone insane," Esther started shaking while she told Kevin; she did not want to believe any of these possibilities.

She called her family again. This time Jian picked up the phone. She asked again where Ling was. After a long pause, Jian broke down and started sobbing.

"Ling died!"

These simple words shattered Esther's world.

"No!" She burst into tears.

On both ends of the phone line across continents and oceans, everyone was crying.

How can this cold "death" be associated with my young and lively sister? This thought screamed in her head.

How can such a beautiful life end so early? Esther would probably never know the answer until one day when she could ask God. Life showed its brutal side to Esther, and Esther had her first taste of tragedy.

Kevin embraced her and comforted her. "I lost a sister, too!"

As she drove back to her apartment, rain was pouring down. Esther was crying loudly, tears streaming down her face. It was almost like the whole earth was crying with her. Every time she emerged from under a highway bridge, rainwater dumped on her front windshield from the bridge and totally blocked her view. She was afraid she could lose control of her car at any time on that drive home.

Esther cried nonstop for days. She never imagined that she would never see Ling again. Ling was so young, so beautiful and so innocent! The time when the two sisters lived together in the same home was brief. Ling grew up in their Japanese grandma's home until second grade, and Esther grew up in her maternal grandma's home until before her elementary school. The two sisters lived together with their parents in HangZhou for only six years before Ling left home to attend college and graduate school. Esther went to college in Shanghai before Ling came home after her graduate school. Then Ling went to America before Esther graduated from college; Esther went to America soon after Ling returned to China. However, Ling, being her sister, was an absolute part of her life like the air she breathed. Esther always thought they would get together on the other side of the tunnel of time after they grew old. They would reunite then and talk about the joys and silliness of their lives in rocking chairs on sunny afternoons.

This dream was gone.

A few days later, a family friend called Esther from China and comforted her at Hua's request. "Your mom had a dream that you were crying nonstop for Ling. She is worrying about you. She wants you to be strong," the family friend explained.

This family friend worked in a high-ranking government office and could make overseas phone calls from his office. Through this conversation, Esther learned that Jian's wedding was abruptly postponed because of this sudden tragedy. She also learned more details about how devastated her parents were. They cried day and night for months after Ling's death. Qing could not get out of bed for one full month. Ling was very adorable from the day she was born, and she was Qing's first daughter and his favorite child.

Visualizing her gray-haired parents crying their hearts out at the sudden loss of their adored daughter, Esther was heartbroken. She vowed in her heart that she would pick up Ling's portion of caring for her parents.

From Jian's letter that came a few weeks later, she learned that Ling suffered badly from postpartum depression and struggled with mental health. Ling was extremely disappointed with her husband and wanted to get out of her marriage. Their parents did not support her. The end of her life became a vortex of despair. She died from an apparent suicide.

"We did not want to tell you since you were all alone. Now that you have Kevin, we thought it may be okay to tell you," Jian wrote. "Please take care of yourself. You are my only sister now."

"Women have two major hurdles in their lives, one being marriage and the other childbirth. I hope you prepare well for these two hurdles," Jian added.

Esther was heart-wrenchingly regretful over what she said to Ling about her American dream. It may have been the only hope that Ling was holding onto at that time. Esther thought she was just being truthful but now realized that she was cruel. How she wished she had encouraged Ling to try again instead.

She would pick up Ling's life and carry it with her, Esther decided. She would not only realize Ling's American dream as she had proposed but would also live her life also for Ling.

CHAPTER 6

New Marriage

The tragic loss of Ling seemed to inspire a stronger bond between Esther and Kevin. They decided to let their families know how passionately they felt for each other. They jointly wrote letters to their parents. In their letter to her parents, Kevin expressed his affection for Esther and asked to marry her. In their letter to his parents, Kevin praised Esther extensively and especially bragged about her money-making capability; although she was the youngest graduate student in the engineering department, she was making as much as other Ph.D. male students! Esther was flattered and yet felt such a compliment to be a little odd.

In his parents' response, Feng stated, "Welcome to our highly educated family!" and went on to brag about her family.

What does this mean? Is your family in a higher class than my parents? Esther was troubled. Maybe Feng considered her own family to be in a higher class because Esther disclosed that her mother worked in a factory.

My dad is a college professor. All the children are college graduates. My family is highly educated, too! Esther was not happy, but she did not say anything.

Kevin sensed her discontent and talked to his mother on the phone.

Later he told Esther that he rebuked his mother harshly and his mother was left speechless.

"I feel guilty that I was so harsh on my mom," Kevin sobbed.

Kevin attributed every good thing in his life to Feng. His dedication to his mother was wholehearted, like a little child's. It was strange to Esther; he never acknowledged that Feng had nothing to do with her being in his life! It was a very difficult thing for him to go against his mother's will or wishes.

It was a huge red flag! However, Esther dismissed it since Kevin seemed to care more about her feelings and was willing to stand up to his mother. Besides, his mom lived on the other side of the planet and would not likely have much impact on their lives.

In her parents' response, Jian wrote the letter and congratulated them and wished them well in their relationship. Esther was a little disappointed that her father, Qing, did not write the letter.

Maybe he is still mourning Ling's death, Esther thought. Her heart ached again for her parents.

One Friday night, Esther could not reach Kevin. His phone was turned off. She tried to contact him throughout the night and into the next morning, but he never answered the phone. Esther was scared that something bad might have happened to him. Then Kevin called her on Saturday noon and told her that he was in a detention center.

After Esther picked up Kevin from the center, he told her about the incident. He was caught shoplifting in Target.

"What? Why would you do that?" Esther was shocked.

"I was in a bad mood because somebody scratched my car, and I did not know who did it. I went shopping, and I do not know why I did that. I will never do that again." Kevin lowered his head. He took a shower as soon as he got home as if he wanted to wash off his dirtiness.

Esther was really disturbed by this incident. She did not know how to process it.

Was it immorality or immaturity that caused him to break the law?

She wanted to discuss the issue with somebody, but she could not find anyone she could trust with such information. Jean had already left for Seattle. It seemed too embarrassing to tell anybody that her very successful boyfriend was arrested for shoplifting! How did she even bring up such a subject with her family in China?

It was a major red flag that she should have heeded. Instead, Esther chose to believe it was Kevin's immaturity and that he would outgrow it.

Soon after, Kevin showed up with a big diamond ring in his hand. It was designed just as Esther wanted. Esther said yes, and they married in the city hall. They decided to hold the wedding ceremony the following year after she earned her master's degree and their parents could come and attend the wedding.

It was very difficult for a foreign student to go back home and visit family at that time, not only because the exorbitant cost was usually too high for a student who lived on a meager scholarship but also because the legal process for reentry to the country was quite complicated. Esther did not feel too guilty about deciding to get married before they met each other's parents. Esther was always very independent, and she had to make many decisions on her own. People said that marriage was the most important decision in one's life. For her, it happened so naturally, and Esther figured she was just fortunate.

She continued working on her master's degree. Mike, a part-time student in the same master's program as Esther, was a manager of an oil company called Pride Oil. He offered her the internship.

"Should I accept this offer? I plan to spend the summer finishing up my thesis so I can graduate in time," Esther asked Kevin.

"Of course, you should take the offer! It may lead to a permanent position!" Kevin said.

He was right, and a job meant the first step toward achieving the American dream for an immigrant!

"You can work on the internship and your thesis at the same time," Kevin added.

He had done both, as well. He held a full-time job before he even graduated. His work was more than an hour from the school; he traveled between those two places almost every day. He hid his employment from his advisor, who was still paying him fellowship money. His advisor later found out about his employment and was mad at him. "You should have told me this. I could have given this fellowship to other students who really need support," his advisor said.

Kevin told Esther this story before and laughed without feeling any embarrassment. Esther had mixed feelings about it. On one hand, she was impressed with how hard he was willing to work; on the other, she was not sure it was right for Kevin to take money from both sides.

Esther decided to take the internship and put her graduate study on hold for one semester. She would take some of Kevin's suggestions, she decided, but not all. She worked hard during her internship throughout the summer and then went back to school and finished her master's program. As expected, she was offered a permanent position from Mike right away.

Kevin switched jobs and started working as a contractor for Disney. He had to travel quite often. Esther was willing to put up with it, not only because he was making jaw-dropping hourly rates, but also because she was busy with her own study and work. Esther visited him in many different cities, including Seattle and London.

Esther met Jean while visiting Kevin in Seattle. Jean had started her fellowship residency in psychiatry. She was dating a young man she met on the internet who was a software engineer for Microsoft. The internet was getting popular at this time, and online dating was in its infancy. This young man majored in biology back in China; however, he switched to computer science as soon as he came to the United States. His job at Microsoft paid very well, the corporation's stock options making him and his coworkers instant millionaires.

In the mid-1990s, high-tech became such a booming industry that seemingly every young Chinese immigrant in the States switched to that field. Many of them, like Kevin, might have worked in technical fields such as engineering or science, so the transition was quite natural. However, for anyone who worked in fields on the opposite side of the spectrum from high-tech such as journalism or arts, the transition could be very painful. Indeed, survival was always the priority of an immigrant. Furthermore, ample job opportunities and the high income offered by the high-tech industry were so enticing that this transition seemed less painful and more glorious than mere survival.

It was amazing to see so many people abandon their dream careers and tolerate all the pain to survive in this new land!

Kevin was almost a perfect husband to Esther except for one thing she noticed early on. He was quite a miser with money even though he made very good money. One time, Zia asked Esther to donate some money to a newly built Chinese school in Houston. The Chinese community was growing fast in the mid-1990s, and many people wanted to have a place for their children to learn the Chinese language and culture.

"Your name will be permanently carved on the wall of the entrance!" Zia's suggestion was quite attractive. Esther wanted to donate one hundred dollars. Kevin balked, and Esther did not insist. Esther regretted later that she did not persist.

Another time, Esther wanted to sign up for a gym membership for them both. Sitting behind a desk all day was not only a little boring but also not the best thing for the body.

"Why go out to a gym in the darkness after a whole day of work?" Kevin was strongly opposed to it.

"How about we go to the gym just a couple times a week? You do not have to go if you do not want to," Esther compromised.

"I just want us to relax at home." Kevin would not budge.

Esther could not figure out the true reason for his objection. *Was it because he just did not want to spend money on a membership? Was he not interested in the obvious benefits of exercise?* She withdrew her proposal nevertheless. For a long time, it troubled her that he stopped her from joining the gym.

Maybe he did not like exercising after all? Kevin trained intensively for professional skating from the time he was around four years old. Esther later found out that his training was for a very important benefit, should the Cultural Revolution continue. The benefit was that his special skating skills would enable him to stay in the city and exempt him from being deported to the countryside. A whole generation of youth was denied opportunities of education and wasted their lives in physical labor in the most remote and the poorest areas during the Cultural Revolution. Not surprisingly, it was Feng's idea for Kevin to be trained for this benefit. Kevin may not have enjoyed being trained so intensively in his youth.

Another time, Kevin embarrassed Esther greatly with a lie. He wanted to return a suit after he wore it. The salesperson pointed out that it could not be returned after wearing it.

"I never wore it!" Kevin lied.

"The sales tag is gone," the salesperson gently pointed out.

"I did not wear it!" Kevin insisted.

Esther wished she could vanish from his side. She did not want to be his ally in this situation. Her conscience was very upset at this moment, but she did not speak up. They never discussed this event, and it seemed to be an isolated one. He kept the next suit that he bought, and an incident like this one did not happen again.

Most of the time, their relationship was very harmonious. On a few occasions, they talked about their parents' marriages.

"How was your parents' relationship?" Kevin started this conversation.

"They argued all the time," Esther sighed. If there was one thing in her life that she felt hopeless about, it was her parents' arguments. It seemed that they were eternally stuck in a vicious cycle, with the same arguments replaying again and again. Sometimes she felt she left China just to escape her parents' arguments.

"Argue? My parents fought all the time! Physically!" Kevin was a little excited and continued, "My sister and I always helped my mom and fought against my dad!" He seemed proud of his standpoint.

Kevin told Esther he hated his dad, Liu, while growing up. His relationship with his mom seemed to be a closer one than his parents' relationship with each other.

"My mom wanted to know everything that happened in my college. I would fall asleep with her during my summer breaks when we talked for a long time every night." Kevin looked very innocent.

Esther was shocked upon hearing this, and Kevin stopped talking on the subject immediately. Not surprisingly, Feng suggested she sleep in the same bed with Kevin to talk with him for the first night when she came to the United States. Thankfully, Kevin said no this time.

Kevin's sister, Leah, finally came to the United States for a graduate program after ten failed visa applications. It was Feng's determination and dedication that brought Leah to the States. Feng was able to find help for her daughter from every willing person from pastors to neighbors in both China and the U.S. Kevin and Esther also helped a great deal; however, their efforts were barely acknowledged. Feng claimed all the credit for this success.

Leah was close in age with Esther and the two got along well. It was apparent that Leah was a second-class citizen in her family and that Kevin was the favored child as the firstborn son. Leah liked to hang out with people who, from her parents' perspective, were seemingly below their class.

"Do not let my mom help you with 'sitting a month.' My mom does not know how to care for the house or cook. We ate dumplings all the time when I was growing up, whether fried, boiled or steamed, but all dump-lings," Leah laughed. What she said seemed a little terrifying to Esther.

"She is not well, physically, also," Leah added.

This was not news to Esther. She knew Feng was a cancer survivor. Her illness happened when Kevin was in seventh grade. According to Leah, Kevin matured instantly.

Leah told Esther that Feng was hospitalized for a month another time after Kevin had already come to the United States and Leah was in college. When Leah asked Liu why her mom was not home, Liu hid the fact and lied, saying that Feng was on a business trip.

"Why did he do that?" Esther was really puzzled.

"He said he did not want us to worry," Leah answered. "But he did not go to the hospital to take care of her, either. He just went to work like nothing happened."

One night in the hospital when Feng was still hooked to an IV, she had to go to the restroom. She went alone and slipped and fell, cutting herself with the IV stand. The cuts became infected, and she developed a high fever.

"It took a long time for my mom to recover. Her health has been deteriorating ever since," Leah sighed. Although Leah was not happy about how her parents treated her, it was clear that she genuinely cared about Feng.

Leah was very aware of her mother's character. Once Feng gave a bottle of wine to a professor as a gift and asked him to write a reference letter for Kevin for his applications for graduate study in the United States. After she received the letter, she came up with an excuse and asked for the bottle of wine back.

"My mom is the kind of person who will tear down a bridge while she is still halfway across it," Leah laughed. A famous Chinese idiom "过河拆桥" refers to those who are not grateful. Esther had already witnessed Feng using people for her own agenda again and again without giving anything back.

It is also stupid if she cannot wait to tear down a bridge while she is still crossing it, Esther thought.

After Leah came to the States, Feng acted more and more as if Kevin and Esther's home was her own home and she was the matriarch. She started to look for a husband for Leah. One night, Hua and Esther came home to find a room full of people who apparently came for a dating arrangement. Feng introduced Hua as her sister and did not even bother to introduce Esther. Esther felt awkward but did not say anything.

The more Esther found out about Feng, the more uneasy she became. This was another major red flag to appear early in her marriage, but one she figured she could ignore because she was not getting married to Feng but to Kevin. As long as Feng did not live with them under the same roof, Esther believed that she could manage, or tolerate, Feng. The chance that Feng would live with them seemed very slim to her.

Esther and Kevin had a few years to themselves after both moms went back to China. Life was peaceful. They soon accumulated enough money and bought their new home.

"It's a mansion!" Her boss Mike commented when he saw a picture of the new house.

"It's a palace!" Jean wrote in her letter. She was very busy in her fellowship residency program. She married the young IT engineer.

The only big fight Esther had with Kevin happened when her dad, Qing, came to visit them in the United States. Qing had just retired, and he wanted to come and visit Esther. It had been five years since Esther left China, and it was such a happy reunion. Qing was very proud of Esther and her achievements. After the initial excitement was gone, life in the States for a visiting parent was quite limited. Esther and Kevin were working through the week, and they took Qing to Chinatown and restaurants on the weekends.

What Esther did not know was that Feng was jealous of Qing because he was ahead of her and enjoyed the new house first.

"Why does he need to be there so long, doing nothing all day?" Feng complained on the phone with Kevin.

Kevin became more and more impatient with Qing. Esther was not happy with his disrespectful attitude but did not address it right away. Instead, his attitude started influencing her.

One Saturday afternoon, Qing was mowing the lawn. He not only did all the cooking for them, but he also learned how to do all the house-work and did as much as he could. Kevin stood in the living room and looked out at Qing from the big window, complaining that he was not mowing the lawn correctly. Esther stood next to Kevin up against the beautiful curtain and watched her dad. She could see that Qing was not good at maneuvering the cumbersome mowing machine but was making a huge effort. She knew she should speak up and defend her dad, but she did not. She noticed her dad getting angry, sensing their criticism.

Qing soon changed his plans and decided to go back to China. The night before Qing's departure, Esther became very angry with Kevin. She felt ashamed over how they treated her dad and was probably angrier with herself for not standing up for him. She could sense her dad's disappointment with her, which really hurt her. He had lost his favorite daughter Ling and now might have felt he was losing his other one.

"What do you want me to do?" Kevin blinked his eyes and pretended to be innocent.

"Apologize to my dad! He raised me, and he deserves better treatment!" Esther shouted.

Kevin apologized.

Qing looked a little comforted at the end. But he told himself in his heart that he would never come to the United States again.

CHAPTER 7

American Dream

———— •◆• ————

Soon after her dad went back to China, Esther fell into a serious depression. It was triggered by antibiotics that were supposed to cure her duodenal ulcer once and for all. Esther unconsciously knew there had to be deeper reasons for her malaise, though. But she could not quite figure it out. Esther was also plagued with ingrown toenails for a while. The nails grew into the flesh of her toes and would cause extreme pain if she did not trim them in time. She spent a lot of time on quiet Sunday mornings trimming her nails.

A feeling of loneliness lingered around even after the depression went away. The Chinese community was still small in Houston in the late 1990s. There were very few activities for young Chinese professionals on the weekends. Most of their Chinese friends were older than them and very busy raising their kids. On the other hand, it seemed very difficult to make real friends with coworkers or neighbors of other races. Esther spoke very good English now and mingled with people from different background very well. However, there always seemed to be an invisible wall blocking her from making a true connection.

Families and friends were so far away! Mountains and waters were far away, too! The water in the Gulf of Mexico was nice; however, it could not be compared to the silky water in West Lake. She could only see her beloved West Lake in her dreams.

Another feeling of frustration about her legal immigration status was much clearer and stronger. It took forever for her to get her Green Card. Without a Green Card, Esther could not go back to China to visit her family and friends because she risked being rejected for a reentry back to the United States. It was the real reason that they did not go back to China to meet their parents before they got married. Without a Green Card, she also had a huge limitation on her career mobility. If a new company wanted to offer her a new job, it would have to first commit to sponsoring her for a working visa and eventually a Green Card. It was a huge burden for any company; seldom was a company willing to make such commitments.

There were different application categories for the Green Card: employment-based and family-based being common ones. Each category had a quota, and the process time differed dramatically. The quota for employment-based applications was more abundant relative to the number of applicants and may take only a couple years of wait. On the other hand, the quota for family-based applications was a lot less and would take many more years of wait—sometimes a decade or more. Houston, with its ever-growing immigration population, was probably one of the slowest cities to process an application even after a quota was available.

Esther started a family-based application for her Green Card right after she married Kevin since he was already a permanent resident. The application did not move forward much at all for more than five years. Many Friday afternoons after her coworkers left the office, Esther would call the hotline of the immigration office to check out the status of her application. The progress was slower than a thousand-year-old turtle, and her case was always years away from being even processed. She felt helpless after each call.

Nevertheless, Esther still believed in the American dream despite all these negative feelings. Her great joy with the pregnancy pushed these feelings even further away. Her new baby represented the promise of a future that she could not wait to discover!

A few baby showers were held for Esther and her upcoming baby. One was hosted by Zia, her graduate school roommate. Zia was working in a big company called Enron, which was making headlines almost every day. Enron had many innovative and sometimes bizarre business ideas and made tons and tons of money. Zia was also a mother now. She also became a devoted Christian like her husband, and they regularly attended church.

Then, one day, her coworkers at Pride Oil hosted another baby shower for her. Esther had worked for Mike since she finished her master's program. The oil industry took off in the middle 1990s after the terrible 1980s. Located in the capital city of global energy industry, Pride Oil was expanding rapidly by acquiring many smaller oil companies left and right. Esther was at the right place at the right time in terms of her career.

The party was held in the big conference room, and almost the whole department came. The room was crowded with thirty-odd people. It was blue everywhere—blue balloons, blue ribbons, blue cakes. A huge cake was in the middle of the table, and it read, "Welcome, David!" Gifts were piled on the table; Esther picked up each gift and read every card. It was overwhelming to experience such an outpouring of love for her and her new baby.

Michelle, the secretary of the department, organized the shower. She and Esther had become good friends over the years. She was a vibrant, young blonde woman from a small city in Texas. Her mother was a German and came to the United States after she married Michelle's dad, an American soldier stationed in Germany. For Michelle, it was quite a struggle to leave her parents and establish her life in Houston. Her first boyfriend came with her initially but went back to their familiar hometown after he tried the big city life for a little while.

Esther thought that Michelle had a domestic immigration story. What Esther gradually found out was that there were very few native Houstonians around. Behind the Western façade that was so different from hers, there was often a similar story of immigration, which resonated with Esther.

Allen, manager of the maintenance group, also showed up to the baby shower. He was a typical Texas cowboy; he owned a big ranch where he raised hundreds of cows in addition to working full-time for the company. As always, he joked with her. "What's cooking?" He signaled to her abdomen, which looked ready to explode.

Esther could understand his jokes much better now. Five years ago, when she had just started this job, she usually got lost very quickly in a casual conversation, although she could discuss any technical issues in reasonably good English. Allen's cowboy jokes were the most confusing to her.

To Esther, like many immigrants, life in a foreign land is like seeing flowers through a fog. Behind an obvious language barrier are much bigger barriers of culture and tradition.

Esther never felt discriminated against by her almost all Caucasian male coworkers, and she really appreciated them. She felt the casual ethnic slurs elsewhere from time to time, though.

She once was told by a flight attendant that she could not sit by the emergency exit, although the plane had an open seating system. "You have to understand English, and you need to react quickly if there is an emergency," the flight attendant explained.

Do I look like I do not understand English? Esther thought.

Her puzzled look probably made the flight attendant more convinced of her own guess.

Kevin came to Esther's rescue and told the flight attendant, "What are you talking about? She is an engineer!"

The flight attendant left her alone but never apologized.

George, supervisor of the engineering team, also came to the shower. He was from Louisiana and was just recently promoted to the supervisor position. He was a kind yet slightly hot-tempered boss. He attributed his temper to the heat of the bayous where he grew up. His biggest weakness, in her mind, was his lack of control over his anxiety, evidenced by the way he constantly gnawed on his fingernails. It was quite amusing to see a grown man biting his fingernails all the time. He was struggling to balance a family with two young kids and growing work responsibilities.

Michelle often passed messages from his wife: "George, phone home!"

One time, George held the men's restroom door open for her. The restrooms for men and women were next to each other.

Esther was a bit surprised and pointed to the other door. "I am going to this one."

They both laughed at the incident. Being the only female engineer in the department, Esther's identity at work was often as muddled to herself as it was to others in the male-dominated oil industry.

What moved her quite a bit was that Mike also showed up at the baby shower. He was already the vice president of the whole department. She would never be able to thank him for all he did for her. Esther felt forever indebted to him although she did him right by excelling in her position. Mike seemed satisfied with her performance as well.

Esther had to admit, however, that the first few years of her job were quite routine and boring. She really wanted to change jobs, but her legal status made this change very difficult. Besides, Esther had already started a lengthy Green Card application process through the sponsorship of her current employer, Pride Oil; a job change would forfeit all previous efforts and require her to restart the process all over again with a new company. It could mean more years of wait. Not long ago she had spoken up and asked Mike to expand the scope of her current work. Mike listened and assigned her to a huge rig conversion project where she supervised the main contractor's design work. Her work became more interesting.

Sometimes she would visit shipyards to check on the status of the construction work. It was quite a scene; she was the only female engineer, and an Asian woman to boot, who showed up at the shipyard. Workers would stop their conversation and follow her with their eyes as she passed by. Later, Esther was assigned as a site engineer and worked on a shipyard full-time. Field experience was essential for promotion in the company. Her engineering career looked quite rosy. However, she found herself pregnant shortly after she worked on the construction site. Esther was allowed to move back to the office because of the potentially hazardous environment. She guessed she would have to put her career on the back burner for a little while.

"As a boss, I will say 'never have kids,' but as a friend, I am happy that you are having a child," Mike joked with her at the baby shower. Esther was so grateful that he considered her to be a friend.

Her only regret with the baby shower was that Kevin was not there. Kevin worked downtown, almost an hour away. He usually stayed up late and got up late. Esther thought it might be too much trouble for him to take time off right after he showed up for work. She did not even ask Kevin to come. Esther regretted this decision even more as she moved the mountain of gifts to her car by herself and then unloaded them all by herself again at home.

Finally, the big day was looming. Her first child would be born. Esther went to the hospital the night before her child was scheduled to be delivered.

"He is getting too big for your little body, although your uterus still looks like a green banana," her doctor told her.

Esther guessed her son would come into this world just like she had: begrudgingly. Esther was three weeks late from the due date. And, indeed, David was a difficult delivery. After rounds of anesthetics to numb her, her body finally gradually opened the next afternoon. Kevin was by her side the whole time, and he took many pictures of Esther. Her doctor and the nurses praised Kevin for his attentiveness.

"Some men would go in and out of the delivery room like it's not their business!" they said. Esther was so happy that she had a loving husband!

It was ten o'clock at night when David arrived. It took a total of thirty hours to deliver him! David was such a cute and healthy baby. He caught the nurses by surprise. They were cleaning him on the little table before wrapping him with a clean blanket when he peed for the first time. His first pee presented the most beautiful arc that Esther, his engineer mother, ever saw.

She was totally exhausted when David was put in her arms. But what a miracle! A new life! Her son!

Her American son!

CHAPTER 8

Family Tree

Esther and Hua enjoyed the rare opportunity of staying together all day long while taking care of David during her three-month maternity leave. They had many conversations, and Esther learned more of her family history. They grew much closer, and Esther became more appreciative of Hua.

Esther's dad, Qing, was very handsome and extremely smart. He had thick hair and a delicate face. He always stayed fit and slim. Qing had only two years of formal education in elementary school since his parents were very poor and could not afford to send him to school. He started working as a mail delivery man in his teens. Later, he worked for a court as a secretary shortly after the Communist Party came into power in 1949. The party took an interest in this intelligent young man, and he was sent to college for further development. Qing became a college professor afterwards.

Qing's mom, Esther's grandma, was a native Japanese. Qing's dad, a Chinese, went to Japan in the early 1920s and ran a successful grocery business for many years. He met a young Japanese lady there and they soon married. The young couple had their first child, Qing's older brother, before Japan's brutal invasion and subjugation of China, in which war crimes and other atrocities against the Chinese people became commonplace.

Qing's dad decided to return to China before the war broke out, given the change in the political climate. However, his wife's dad locked her up in a house because of his obvious concern about what was happening. Going to a different country in the 1930s probably meant a final farewell, which sadly turned out to be true. Qing's dad waited outside the house holding the infant in his arms for the whole night.

On a dark night in a little town of Japan in the 1930s, a baby's cry echoed on an empty street and tore at a mother's heart. Qing's mom escaped from her father's house and boarded a ship to China with her husband and her baby. The young couple planned to live in Shanghai when they first arrived in China. However, Qing's dad lost all his fortune due to gambling. They went back to his hometown and settled down in WenZhou.

In Esther's fuzzy memory, her Japanese grandma was a quiet and beautiful lady with very pale skin. She was so nice that everybody in the village liked her, even though the Chinese people naturally built up great resentment against the Japanese after the invasion. She was also very smart and quickly became fluent in the local dialect. For her whole life, however, she longed to go back to Japan to see her family. After the two countries finally reestablished diplomatic relationships in the early 1970s, almost four decades later, she had all the paperwork ready to return home and visit her family in Japan. Unfortunately, she was stricken with cancer and never made the trip.

Qing stayed at her bedside during the last moments of her life on a cold winter night. He put his hands under her skinny body and tried to warm her up but instead watched her drifting away. Qing burned paper and cried bitterly afterwards, feeling sorry for his mother's life-long regrets.

Esther could not imagine the depth of emotional pain her grandma had on her deathbed—she followed her baby to a totally strange country out of a mother's love, but she could never go back home and see her family ever again. Yet, it was her sacrifice that brought Qing to this world and thus Qing's family, which included Esther. Esther was forever grateful to her grandma.

Qing was very mild-tempered and slow to anger. Hua was quite the opposite and was hot-tempered, and as a child Esther quickly learned to stay out of her way and keep her distance. Hua was petite but had a big personality. She had a sweet smile, yet she was mostly grumpy while Esther grew up.

Hua was very ambitious and smart; however, she could barely read and write since she had only a few years of education in night schools. Her limited education hindered her from any significant career advancement, which her ambition yearned for. This conflict contributed greatly to her constant frustration.

Hua started working in a paper mill at the tender age of fourteen, right after the Communist Party took over control of the country in 1949. She was very proud every time she recounted how efficient she was as the youngest worker in the factory, one who could always out-work other workers and make more money. For Hua, work meant recognition. In Esther's childhood apartment, Hua decorated her bedroom wall with all kinds of certificates and awards from work.

Qing and Hua met and married in their hometown of WenZhou, and Hua followed Qing to HangZhou and settled in the city in the early 1960s. They were the only people out of their respective families who moved away from their hometowns. They departed from their ancestors' lives as farmers and took up a brand-new metropolitan life in the city of Hang-Zhou. It was uncharted territory for them! HangZhou was the capital city of the province and thus had all the state government offices and many universities. Nevertheless, it was still more like the countryside since its infrastructure was barely developed back then. Bus routes were few and did not cover most of the city area. Personal vehicles were unheard of.

Esther's parents were modern and hip before the kids were born. With two salaries, they became relatively rich. They were among the first who bought a radio and a nice watch, which were considered lux-ury items. They would bring back goodies from the city to their families that nobody saw before, such as tasty cookies. Hua saved these cookies, which were her compensation for night shifts, so that she could share them with her parents and her family. In their hometown, these goodies were like trophies, highlighting their great city life.

With the births of their three children, money became tight and life became rough. With neither family nor relatives close by, they had to send their infant children to daycare and juggle their schedules between work and family. Hua stayed in her factory dorm and took care of little kids during the weekdays. On weekends, she would take the kids and go back to Qing's college dorm.

For a long time, the family's only mode of transportation was a twenty-eight-inch bicycle. It carried the whole family back and forth between their dorms. Esther's brother Jian sat on the top tube in front of Qing, and Hua sat behind Qing on a back seat with Ling in her lap. Later, Esther was also there in Hua's abdomen.

When the kids were a little older, they were sent to the grandparents' homes in Wenzhou and lived there for a few years before the kids started school in Hangzhou. When the kids started school, Hua took the kids and moved into Qing's college dorm. The grade schools around the college were of a much higher quality. From what Esther could remember, Hua left for the factory before daybreak and returned home after dark, day in and day out. She worked six days a week. The factory was almost a one-hour bicycle ride away, a grueling commute for her every day. The family bicycle, at twenty-eight inches high at the saddle, was a little too big even for an average-sized man. Her feet could hardly reach the pedals on the lower turn, but she managed with the tips of her toes.

Everything was scarce in China in the 1960s. Most everyday necessities, including rice and cooking oil, were distributed by a national quota system. A bicycle was also distributed through the system and was a particularly hot commodity. After obtaining a quota, Qing waited in line for two nights before he could buy the new bicycle. It was the family's only mode of transportation for years.

Because Qing had a flexible schedule as a college professor, he took care of most of the housework, including cooking, while the kids were growing up. He was the ever-present parent for the kids. Since Hua's work was so far away, she was barely home during the day. Sunday was the only day of the week when she did not need to go to work, and then she usually was busy washing and cleaning. Life made Hua grumpy in general, but now and then she showed her happy nature—very briefly.

Qing tolerated Hua's bad temper and constant complaints. Hua's complaints were mostly about a lack of money and his affairs she imagined in her mind. Qing usually remained silent. He did explode at the end, but it always was a little too late, failing to interrupt Hua's harangues. A fight between them would break out almost every other day. It was a constant recurrence while Esther was growing up.

Sometimes Esther thought Qing was too weak. If he could have spoken up for himself earlier and sooner, it would have put a quick end to the big fights that always erupted. Sometimes Esther felt pity for Qing because she felt the marriage was more of a burden to bear for him. More often, she sensed a deep and hidden helplessness in Qing's attitude. For a long time, she did not understand it, and she even lost some respect for him back then.

As she grew older, Esther gained more insight as to why her parents argued so much. It had to be very stressful and difficult to work full-time and raise three kids all by themselves without friends or family close by. Traditionally, the entire Chinese family lived close to each other and pitched in to help with child-rearing. But those who moved away from their hometowns lost this support.

Throughout Esther's childhood, her family was always busy with visitors from her parents' hometown of WenZhou, which was famous for its people's spirit of entrepreneurship and desire for emigration. Some of the visitors came seeking government approval for emigration; some looked for resources and business opportunities; and some searched for chances for their kids to enter a college. Her parents would always host these visitors with great hospitality and help them achieve their goals with many selfless efforts. Her parents were honored in their hometowns because of their good deeds.

Looking back, Esther realized that these visitors probably helped her parents more! They helped her parents stay connected with their roots and, probably more importantly, connected with each other by distracting them from their own problems.

The college dorm where they lived for many years was surrounded by rice fields. A big fishpond was not too far away. Esther's family even raised four ducks for a while.

Many years later, Esther could still see her sister, Ling, walking among the rice fields memorizing English words, her eyes filled with joy and hope. HangZhou began to open to the world in the late 1970s after the Cultural Revolution. The American president at the time, Richard Nixon, visited China and established relations, and English was introduced in all the middle schools and sometimes as early as elementary school. Ling loved English, and the American movie *The Sound of Music* was her favorite.

The dorm where they lived was a plain, three-story building with two entrances. Esther's family had two rooms next to one entrance. The college clinic was next to the other entrance. The entrance was comprised of two old wooden doors with a few panels missing. Esther often used the doors as a swing and happily climbed on and swung back and forth. On every floor, a long hallway in the middle ran from end to end, with rooms on both sides. There was a common washing room and restroom.

Most of the families used a portable charcoal stove to cook. The stoves were placed outside the doors in the hallway. Qing took advantage of a little area outside their rooms and under the stairway and built a brick stove. That stove was quite grand compared to a common portable stove. It was a little bit too high for Esther. She remembered it was quite a struggle for her and Ling to make a fire with the briquettes. During mealtime, the hallway would be filled with smoke and the smell of meats and vegetables. How the families managed their daily living in the dorm was a mystery to Esther when she thought back on it years later.

These families came from all over China. It was a very common domestic immigration story in those days. Most of the parents came from agricultural backgrounds and were the only ones in their extended families living in the city, just like Esther's parents. The young adults were usually the smartest and most ambitious ones in their families. They came to the city to pursue higher education and a better life.

Some parents, on the other hand, came from more prestigious backgrounds. You could define the family's status by how they dressed and talked. For instance, a few families came from Shanghai. Their kids wore clothes with laces and had American Barbie dolls. They spoke Shanghai dialects among themselves and had an attitude of superiority that would show up from time to time, particularly when they needed to prove they were of allegedly superior stock.

Still, even with these social divisions, there were quite some happy moments living in the dorm. The kids gathered around grey-haired grandparents on summer nights and listened to fairy tales. The best time was New Year's Eve, one of the rare moments when Esther felt spoiled. Like many kids, she would get a set of new clothes, and dinners were abundant. Esther's parents spent one whole day preparing the dinner; eventually, dishes would be spread all over the entire table. All the delicacies they did not get to enjoy for the whole year would be there, such as 贵妃鸡 (Houdan chicken) and 八宝饭 (eight treasures rice).

Esther and Ling were usually assigned the job of making egg dumplings, which were different from regular dumplings because the wrappers were made of eggs. They would get a small stove and put a steel spoon on the fire. Then they would set a small piece of pork fat in the spoon, and the lard would start sizzling, filling the room with a delicious aroma. The two sisters would then turn the spoon around to make the lard spread evenly. After placing a little bit of beaten egg on the spoon, they would turn the spoon slowly until the egg wrap was formed. Finally, they would put some ready-made fillings in it and wrap it up, ultimately creating an eye-pleasing and mouthwatering egg dumpling! These dumplings were usually dunked in a big soup. It was so satisfying to find an egg dumpling in the soup and bite into it!

Egg dumplings happened to be a favorite among many of the kids. Many families made the same egg dumplings at the same time on New Year's Eve. Kids would borrow pork fat from each other. The mouthwatering smell filled the whole dorm.

CHAPTER 9

Red China

Esther was born during the height of the Cultural Revolution, one of the most devastating and disruptive periods in the country's modern history. Hua took a maternity leave for six weeks. She returned to her hometown of WenZhou before giving birth and stayed in her mom's house, hoping to receive more care for herself and her newborn. Qing stayed in HangZhou, working and taking care of Esther's two older siblings, Jian and Ling. Esther was two weeks overdue, leaving Hua very anxious. Hua went hiking in the mountains for three days before Esther was finally born.

Because of the late delivery, Hua did not finish "sitting a month" and had to return to work before the month was up. The trip between WenZhou and HangZhou was a one-day rough bus journey. There were no trains or airplanes between the two cities in the early 1970s. Many roads were not paved and were very bumpy. It was during a freezing cold January, and there was no heating in the bus. How Hua handled it right after childbirth with a newborn baby in tow was really a mystery to Esther. Although Esther may not have liked her mother all the time, she always admired Hua's courage and inner strength.

The Cultural Revolution erupted in 1966. Qing and Hua, like any loyal members of the Communist Party, participated enthusiastically in the beginning. Qing took many students with him and

69

went to Beijing to visit the great leader Chairman Mao in Tiananmen Square. He talked about the exciting moment when Tiananmen Square was covered by red national flags and a sea of young people wearing red armbands. They all held a little red book full of the chairman's quotes. Those young people were called Red Guards. The entire Tiananmen Square was covered in red. The young Red Guards all shouted, "Ten thousand years, Chairman Mao," when Mao made an appearance and waved his hand to the crowd in the main building.

The entire country fell into total chaos when loyalty to Chairman Mao became the ruling criterion for everyday work and life. Many political campaigns were initiated by Chairman Mao to persecute his potential enemies, most of whom were his would-be successors and highest-ranking officials and generals in the nation. These campaigns were trickled down and carried out at every level of the Communist Party throughout the country, twisted and manipulated by whoever was in charge.

Organizations were assigned a quota for "enemies" of Chairman Mao, and they were required to meet the quota. Many people could not wait to step on others to claim themselves as the most loyal; some people gladly got rid of their own enemies in the name of this seemingly noble cause. Subordinates were encouraged to turn over their leaders; students were encouraged to turn over their teachers; and children were encouraged to turn over their parents. Everybody needed to tread carefully even at home; otherwise, they risked being denounced as an enemy overnight. The revolution quickly turned violent and even deadly in many places.

It was estimated that hundreds of millions of people were wrongly persecuted. Many accusations were fabricated and a lot of evidence was manufactured. Many couples divorced and many families were broken during the Cultural Revolution. When one spouse was persecuted, the other spouse, while trying to remain separate from the accusations and protect the children, would then pile on more accusations voluntarily or under pressure. Many of those wrongly persecuted chose to end their lives out of total desperation.

The Cultural Revolution did not end until ten years later when Chairman Mao died in 1976. It devastated the whole nation and left profound damage on the thoughts and minds of the Chinese people.

Qing and Hua moved to the sideline very quickly since they did not quite understand the warring factions. Endless meetings were held to study Chairman Mao's new thoughts and new campaigns. Women would weave sweaters, and men would read the newspaper or play chess in the meetings.

Qing's life took a dramatic downturn right after Esther's birth. During yet another long and boring meeting, Qing was scribbling on a piece of paper mindlessly and threw it away afterwards. Later at night, an emergency meeting was called, and everybody needed to show up. They were asked whose writing was on one particular piece of paper. Qing raised his hand and admitted it was his paper. Suddenly, he was labeled as an anti-Maoist (反革命分子) and became a target of the collegewide revolution. On that piece of paper, the writing of "打倒毛主席" ("overthrow" and "Chairman Mao") was seen as treason! Qing explained over a million times that it was just a coincidence that the two words were next to each other, nothing else, but to no avail.

Qing was immediately arrested and then, after a while, placed under home arrest and ordered to confess every day. Meeting after meeting was held to get at all his wrongdoings and anti-Mao thoughts. Under pressure, Qing even confessed to mutual admiration with a female teacher that could possibly lead to an affair. The confession ended the relationship, which was probably good for his children and his family. However, the short-lived relationship took root deeply in Hua's mind and fueled many arguments throughout their lives.

Qing rarely talked about this painful experience. When he mentioned it, he always showed deep gratitude to many of his colleagues who acted righteously during the meetings, then patted his back and comforted him secretly afterwards.

Hua was really concerned about Qing's state of mind at the time and decided to leave Esther under his care in his dorm. Qing would carry Esther on his back as he wrote endless confessions day in and day out.

No wonder my dad was my favorite parent!

Esther guessed their bond grew much stronger while Qing carried her on his back as he wrote his confessions. He may have been at the lowest point of his life, but what could be better for an infant girl than to have her dad carry her all day long? Maybe unconsciously she felt the momentousness of the situation because she was helping Qing persevere through the toughest time of his life.

Qing was grateful for Hua because she was on his side the whole time. Now, when Esther thought about it, she admired Hua for her dedication to Qing and her wisdom to put a little child in his care and keep him busy. It was probably why Qing tolerated Hua most of his life. In some ways, he must have felt that he owed her this kind of devotion.

As Esther grew up, she liked to find the logic behind everything and loved to reason and debate. She even dreamed of becoming a lawyer. But things never went well between Esther and Hua. At the dinner table, Esther usually was the one who kept talking about the news and her opinions. Her siblings were quiet.

"Do not speak this loud!" Hua would interrupt.

"Why? What is the matter? Why can I not speak loudly in my own home?" Esther responded, puzzled.

Was there someone outside the door listening to our conversations? Why all the fear and paranoia? Esther found her mom's reaction ridiculous.

"Would you speak in public this way?" Hua asked.

"We're not in public; we're in our home." Esther could not understand her mom's reasoning.

Esther was still little when the Cultural Revolution ended. She only heard and read about what happened then. The more she learned about this part of Chinese history, the more she understood Hua's logic. Personal trust was destroyed at every level during the revolution. Everybody was on high alert all the time; they had to constantly watch out for themselves and protect themselves against betrayals even from within the family. This damage was probably the most fundamental and left scars on nearly every family throughout the whole nation.

A famous Chinese idiom "祸从口出" ("disaster comes out of your mouth") warned every Chinese person to be careful with his or her words. The Cultural Revolution enhanced the warning and made it more of a command. It was safer to hide your thoughts and feelings. It was widely accepted not to mean what you say and not to say what you mean, especially in public surroundings.

The devastation caused by the Cultural Revolution ended when Chairman Mao died. Deng Xiaoping came to power in the late 1970s and directed the focus of the country toward economic growth and opened the country to the outside world. Life became richer and more colorful throughout the 1980s. Food and merchandise became abundant. Rice fields quickly disappeared and were paved over by concrete, and steel-reinforced concrete buildings were erected one after another. Foreign movies poured in from Hong Kong, India and later the West. Pop music came into fashion; a whole young generation fell in love with Teresa Teng's sweet voice and heartrending love songs. More universities sprang up all over the country, and more young people went to college.

Qing was finally cleared of the wrongful conviction. His salary finally caught up with Hua's, which gave him some confidence. Intellectuals were persecuted under Chairman Mao's era, and their salaries were often below that of industry workers. It probably contributed to Qing's low self-esteem.

Because of Deng's new policies that encouraged free enterprise, some people became rich very quickly, including Esther's relatives in WenZhou. For a while, WenZhou dominated the small family goods' markets in the country. Her parents, who used to be relatively rich as employees of state-owned organizations, became poor in comparison to their relatives in this round of economic reform. This change fueled more of Hua's complaints and uneasiness.

Esther was always a happy girl. Her first memories were of times spent at her grandma's house. Her parents sent her to her grandparents' home for care before she started school. It was a common practice in China for many busy working parents to leave their young children with the grandparents. The same practice was repeated with many Chinese immigrants in the United States.

Esther still remembered walking in the rice field to deliver lunch to her uncle. Esther would always stop at a water lily pond; she loved to watch waterdrops roll around the fat, green leaves of the water lilies. They were like pears enhanced with a mystical twinkling light, beautiful and shining. When a light breeze blew, those waterdrops would rush to one side and then the other like a bunch of playful kids. Esther was amazed by the roundness of the drops. It was not until her middle school years that Esther learned about surface expansion and could understand scientifically some of the things that fascinated her as a curious little girl.

As her grandma's favorite grandchild and knowing she would go back to her family in the city later, Esther developed a sense of superiority—that she belonged to a better place. She was never intimidated, even though she was the youngest among her cousins.

The summer before Esther started elementary school, she went back to her parents' home in the city. She had to face an opposite reality because now she was an outsider and more of a peasant girl with tomboy manners. She looked and talked and behaved like a peasant, and she felt instantly inferior compared to fashionable and advanced city girls. To make things worse, Esther had a flat nose and was quite an ugly duckling among them. Some kids would call her "猪八戒" (a pig character in the classic *Journey to the West* novel). She always felt grateful for those who did not look down upon her. May and Lan were two of them.

A few days after she arrived back at her parents' home, Esther was offered her first piece of watermelon. Not knowing any better, she ate the whole piece, including the peel. Qing felt pity for his little daughter and regretted their decision to leave her in the countryside for those few years. He later took her with him to many gatherings and parties to make up for it. Esther's brother, Jian, welcomed his little sister heartily.

On the other hand, Ling was not happy at sharing her parents' attention with this little sister. It took a while for her to get used to Esther.

Qing took Esther with him during the summer to a 五七干校 (Five Seven Cadre School) for college professors. The site, like many all over the country, was set up during the Cultural Revolution to reeducate and tame the intellectuals by making them do farming and labor work. Chairman Mao's hatred and fear towards the intellectuals was the reason behind these sites.

The site on a beautiful mountain, however, was like a paradise. The intellectuals, who mostly grew up in very poor peasant families, had great times farming, fishing and relaxing. After years of development, the site was self-sufficient and had plenty of food, of vegetables and fruits. Fruit trees were bent with ripe fruit ready to pick and eat right there in the gardens. The men stayed up late and caught wildlife, such as frogs, for late-night meals.

Esther received her first toy ever in her life there. It was a wooden monkey that flipped on a string every time you squeezed a bow-shaped handle. It was handmade by Uncle Wang, who was a Christian and hid this identity at the time. Esther was amazed by the toy.

Western movies were the best part of the paradise. A huge screen was set up for movies in the open every Friday night. All the people, young and old, enjoyed the movies under the starry sky. Among the first movies Esther watched was *The Count of Monte Cristo*. Esther could not remember the story much; however, the movie opened her eyes to a very foreign and fascinating world.

CHAPTER 10

Number One

Right after Esther started elementary school, Chairman Mao passed away, which marked the end of the Cultural Revolution. Memorial services were held all over the country, including at schools. On a very hot September afternoon, all the teachers and students lined up on the running track and stood for hours, listening to one eulogy after another. All Esther could remember were a few distractions; one kid nearby farted loudly at this serious event, and the kids started giggling.

Esther was quite an outsider when she started school because most of her classmates went to kindergarten together and knew each other. Slowly, she blended in and made a few friends. Lan, with whom she later went to the United States together, was her first friend. The two little girls shared their dreams and crushes on boys as they grew up.

What also made Esther's transition harder was her Chinese teacher in the third and fourth grades. Teacher Li was very good at teaching Chinese, and she assigned a heavy load of homework. Esther built a solid literature foundation and developed beautiful handwriting through her teaching. But Teacher Li could be very harsh on the students.

Chinese characters are pictographic and very beautiful. A character evolved from the image of its content and usually implies its meaning and great insight. For instance, the Chinese character for "brightness" was 明, which put the sun （日） and moon （月） together. Calligraphy by itself was a very popular art in China. There were so many beautiful ways to write a single Chinese character.

Teacher Li was also big on helping kids set up plans. In the beginning of every semester, she requested the kids to write up a new plan. Esther often questioned the effectiveness of these plans in her head since the plans were soon forgotten. She nevertheless developed a habit of making plans, a skill that she would later appreciate.

Teacher Li loved bees and hated butterflies, like many adults. One essay in the third-grade Chinese textbook explained her reasoning. The essay claimed that bees worked diligently all day long, but butterflies just flew around and showed off their beauty. This lesson was to teach all the girls not to pay any attention to physical appearance, as if beauty and diligence could not coexist.

What a misconception! Years later, Esther could only find this kind of doctrine absurd.

Teacher Li was very strict and could be a little hysterical sometimes. One day she could be the nicest person in the world, giving out candies or dessert to her students. The next day she could be the nastiest person who got angry and rebuked every student. One day she was so mad that she threw all the homework out of a window of the classroom in front of all the students. Esther and all the kids were stunned and speechless by her rage. Sometimes Teacher Li made fun of kids and gave them belittling nicknames. She called Esther "old lady" for a long time because Esther was late in physical development and lost her two front teeth in the third grade.

Another time, Teacher Li called Esther a "fly." At the time, a boy and a girl usually were paired up and shared one desk. The logic behind this arrangement was probably that girls usually matured early and could help discipline boys. The boy with whom Esther shared a desk was not good with his schoolwork, and Teacher Li often called him a "fly." One day out of the blue, Teacher Li included Esther and called them "a pair of flies." Esther felt so humiliated and cried her whole way back home.

According to Teacher Li, Esther was too spoiled and prideful and needed to be corrected. Esther never agreed with Teacher Li's reasons for all the harsh rebukes. As a matter of fact, she could not make sense of Teacher Li's many behaviors and remarks even after four decades. She guessed Teacher Li may have had bipolar disorder and that the Cultural Revolution may have been a reason. The topic of mental health remains a cultural taboo in China even till this day, let alone in the 1980s.

Esther would go with her fellow classmates to visit Teacher Li with gifts during the holidays. It was a Chinese tradition that expected students to show great respect to their teachers just like children to their parents. The kids praised Teacher Li like she was the best teacher in the whole world. Esther never felt comfortable with these visits, but she felt obligated to go along with the tradition. She hid her feelings and pretended to be happy and grateful.

Esther's life totally changed in the fifth grade with a wonderful Chinese teacher, Teacher Yang, who remained her favorite teacher throughout her life. He was a kind and gentle man in his mid-thirties. He always smiled and had a very calm temperament; he was the total opposite of Teacher Li. Teacher Yang was recognized as the highest-ranked Chinese teacher in the nation and later as one of the best principals in the nation.

Teacher Yang was very good at drawing. He would sketch a picture on the blackboard while he taught an ancient poem or a Chinese idiom. The chalk in his hand seemed to have magic; just a few lines would tell a story and even convey an emotion. The famous poem "静夜思" was about longing for one's family and hometown when a traveler watched a beautiful moon on a lonely night far away from his home. A famous idiom, "四面楚歌," reflected an ancient story in which a defeated general was surrounded by his enemies at night who sang a song in the general's mother tongue. He thought his people surrendered and joined his enemies and thus felt desperate. He killed himself shortly afterwards.

The school also hosted quite a few events. A few of them were still marked by the influence of the Cultural Revolution. The kids were required to taste pig food and were taught that this would have been their eternal reality if the Communist Party did not liberate the people in 1949. Fortunately, more events were related to new social and scientific developments. One of the parents participated in an international scientific exploration of the South Pole and was the first man from China to put his feet on the continent. He came to the school and gave a few presentations about his experience. The kids were all so proud of him and felt a connection to greatness through him. Esther became so interested in all the new developments that her dad subscribed to a well-known magazine, 新华文摘 (*New China Abstract*), just for her benefit. The magazine became her favorite reading material for a long time afterward.

HangZhou, being one of the most beautiful cities in China, was often used as a setting for film productions. One night, Qing took Esther to a movie shooting site for *Shaolin Temple*. The scene was about a bunch of monks who broke the rule of abstinence and drank and ate for a whole night. One monk was so drunk that he did a Kung Fu practice with stumbling feet, which was famously called Drunken Kung Fu. The monks came up with an excuse for their drinking: 酒肉穿肠过，佛祖心中留 ("wine and food go through your body, only Buddhism teaching remains inside your heart"). Esther was totally amazed when she saw the scene on the big screen—it was how a movie was made!

Esther fell in love with reading and writing. She wrote many essays about the parks and sceneries of her beloved hometown, HangZhou. One of her essays was published in a famous nationwide elementary student magazine. She earned eight-yuan RMB, roughly one U.S. dollar, for the publishing! It was a significant amount of money in the early 1980s of China. The average monthly salary was probably fifty yuan. She bought a photo album for her family, which was their very first one. She also bought herself a set of Chinese classic books, *A Dream of Red Chambers* (红楼梦). It was then she dreamed about being an author in the future.

Esther was usually ranked number ten in academic records in her class and much lower in the whole grade. It was even questionable whether she could even make it to the best middle school in her town. Teacher Yang warned that Esther had to perform exceptionally well for her to have a chance to get in. Esther was not happy about his warning because she thought Teacher Yang underestimated her abilities.

The admission test had two subjects, Chinese and math. She knew math was her weakness, and she thought about how to improve. She took the initiative and bought a book that collected many past middle school admission tests and practiced every day. She almost achieved a perfect score in math on the actual admission test. Her excellent writing skills helped her a great deal on the Chinese test. The topic of the essay was "I like my Chinese textbook." Esther really enjoyed the Chinese class and liked the textbook. Who would not like Teacher Yang's Chinese class? The writing was easy, and she scored 100.

A few days later after the entrance test, Esther went to school to find out her score. May, who was already back from school, met her along the way.

"You were number one!" May smiled at her, with a sense of disbelief and admiration.

"What number one? Number one in my class?" Esther was puzzled. She was so used to being number ten in the class that being number one made her feel dizzy.

"You were number one in the school!" May told her as if she herself needed to be convinced.

"Me?" Esther felt lightheaded.

By the time she arrived at the school, the news of her being number one in the school had already spread. Everybody was so surprised. It was almost like a miracle—the number one position in the admission test went to somebody unpopular and unknown! Esther was the most surprised.

Esther rushed home and delivered the hard-to-believe good news.

"Dad, I am 状元in my school!" Esther shouted from two blocks away.

Qing's face lit up. He always said it was one of the happiest moments of his life.

"状元" meant the number one student in an imperial test. The imperial test was used by many Chinese ancient dynasties to find talents for government positions. Ranking number one on the test meant big potential in power and wealth, not only for the individual but also for the whole family.

Jian did not believe it. He looked at her in disbelief and questioned, "You?"

This success was quite a monumental achievement for Esther because it hinted at a potential for greatness in her that she might not have even recognized otherwise. This realization stayed with her in her heart and always encouraged her.

CHAPTER 11

Incredible 1980s

Since China switched its focus to economic growth in the late 1970s after the Cultural Revolution, everyday goods and electronic gadgets became more available. More and more apartment buildings were built. Families moved away from dorm buildings and into apartment buildings. Esther's family was among the first families who were assigned an apartment, thanks to Esther. The government housing system considered the size of the family—the more children a family had, the bigger chance they were assigned an apartment. The professors usually had two children or less; having three children gave Esther's parents a little advantage.

Esther liked the new apartment; her family finally had their own kitchen and bathroom. Although it was more convenient for everyday life, it also felt a little isolated. Esther missed the environment of the dorm where she felt more connected to other families and being part of a community.

Her parents bought their first sofa and a color TV in the late 1980s. A TV used to be such a luxury; only those who had overseas relatives could afford one. May had many uncles and aunts in Indonesia who ran a big family business. Her family was among the first families who bought a big color TV in the early 1980s. Esther still remembered how May's home was packed every Sunday afternoon when middle school kids gathered and watched the Hong Kong TV series *Shanghai Society*.

Esther and her brother, Jian, loved Disney cartoons, and they watched and laughed together. Donald Duck was their favorite character; the duck's silliness resonated somehow with them. It was almost like the pig character 猪八戒 in the classic Chinese novel *Journey to the West* who was easily tempted and got into trouble. Disney cartoons were so lively and humorous, and they began to draw Esther and her generation toward American culture.

One time, Esther became mesmerized while watching figure skating in the winter Olympic games on TV. The athletes wore so little, and they looked almost naked to Esther. They danced so close to each other, and the male athlete kept pulling his female counterpart through his two legs and then throwing her up to the air before catching her.

"What are they doing?" Esther could not believe her eyes.

The scene was so remote from Chinese reality, where gender and sex were never mentioned in any conversation; it was a cultural taboo to do so. The public display of physical beauty and affection between male and female shocked Esther.

Although such Western influences enriched everyday Chinese life, core beliefs of the young generation were not only shaken but also lost in the process. What they were taught before always turned out to be total lies.

They once believed people in South Korea lived miserable lives while North Koreans lived happily. A famous North Korean movie portrayed a family who was separated by the Korean war. All the Chinese people cried their eyes out for a sister who was sent to South Korea and deeply worried about her fate. However, just a few years later when China opened its door to the world, they realized that that sister was likely far better off than her siblings left behind in North Korea.

They once were taught that capitalism was all about exploitation and was an outdated system that would soon be replaced by socialism. Yet, they soon found out capitalist countries were much more modern and advanced. People seemed happier and freer in those countries. Now her country of China needed to learn from capitalism and catch up to it.

Esther tried to find something more solid to grasp and searched for a deeper meaning in life during her middle school years. Esther liked to collect quotations that she found inspirational. Not surprisingly, many of them were from Western leaders and philosophers.

Peace Pilgrim, an American activist, offered this famous quote: "Life is like a mirror. Smile at it and it smiles back at you." Esther decided that she would smile as often as she could.

Another famous saying that she liked was, "If you want to walk fast, walk alone. But if you want to walk far, walk together," by Ratan Tata, an Indian industrialist and philanthropist.

Esther found the first half of this quote so true, but she did not quite practice the alleged wisdom of the second half. She made many decisions on her own, and she walked alone on her journey all the way to the United States. She walked faster and farther than most of her friends. Her plans were all carried out successfully so far.

She also loved poems by the Indian poet Rabindranath Tagore, although she did not quite understand their full meanings. The words were just so beautiful: "The world has kissed my Soul with its pain, asking for its return in Songs," and "The day is near when thy burden will become thy gift, and thy sufferings will light up thy path."

Unbeknownst to her, many Chinese philosophers had a more profound influence on her than those from the West. She thought she was rebellious against Chinese culture, which put much emphasis on tolerance and obedience and a collective experience of the world. After many years in the United States, however, she came to realize that she was much more a product of Chinese culture than she ever imagined when she was young.

"三人行，必有我师." ("Among three people, one must be my teacher.") This proverb taught the Chinese to be humble and learn from others.

"宁静以致远，淡泊以明志." ("Be calm and you can go far; get rid of desires so you are sure of your ambitions.")

"枪打出头鸟." ("A gun will target a bird that sticks out its head from the herd.") This proverb served as a threat to many Chinese people, including Esther, and discouraged them from standing out or being their best. It taught that blending in was the safest way to avoid an attack. It agreed quite well with the Chinese philosophy of being moderate and reserved in behavior. Its influence was dramatically enhanced by the recent Cultural Revolution. Many times, Esther ended up being the second best in many competitions and chose a second-best option for major life decisions. Now, thinking back, it was probably her subconscious mind that believed in this philosophy and tried to protect her.

A particular Chinese one-liner caught her attention, however, and became her motto: "修身养性，兼济天下." ("Cultivate self-improvement so that you can benefit yourself and the world.") Esther thought it summed up well the purpose of life. It offered the usual focus on individual improvement of Chinese culture, but it was balanced with social obligations.

When she began high school, Esther had to choose between liberal arts and STEM for her future career path. Esther's English teacher wanted her to choose liberal arts because she thought Esther would thrive in the field. She believed this so adamantly that she put Esther's name on the list for the liberal arts class. However, Esther knew a career in liberal arts would be quite difficult, especially in Chinese society. Her dad, Qing, had to change his class material quite often depending on who was in power. She switched herself to STEM without consulting anybody.

China was advancing quickly in the mid-1980s and had a huge need for talents in science and technology. A very popular quote at the time was, "Being good at math and science, you can conquer every land on this earth!" Liberal art students were the minority in the school and almost considered inferior because they were not good at science.

Esther did well in math and sciences and ranked around number three in her class. She was nowhere near the top ten in her grade, which had six classes and more than 300 students. One day when Esther passed the running track, a boy whom she secretly admired was practicing for the one-hundred-meter race. The sun was shining on the boy from the back; his youthful body was like a black bullet from a huge golden light.

A question came to her mind suddenly: *Why can you not be in the top ten of the school? What makes those top ten so different from you?*

At that moment of revelation, Esther committed herself to being at the top of her grade. Soon she excelled at school and ranked number one among 300 students! She was exempted from the nationwide admission test and admitted to the best engineering school in China. Esther was also the class president of her high school class at the time of graduation.

Physically, she became prettier every day. Her skin looked soft and smooth. Her eyes were so bright that grownups could not stop praising them. Interestingly, her nose was not round and flat anymore; it became finer and longer. Nobody called her the pig character 猪八戒 anymore. The Chinese idiom "女大十八变" ("when a girl grows up, her appearance changes eighteen times") proved true in her case. No one considered her the ugly duckling anymore.

Her college years were marked by her efforts to prove herself academically. Her engineering major was probably the most popular but also the toughest in the university. It was often ranked number one in the nation and in the world. It took quite an effort to stand out amongst the most talented youths from around the country. It was not until her junior year that Esther first claimed the number-one spot in her class.

It was a bigger personal success since Esther also had to overcome being distracted by her first love. Yong was a kind and handsome young man, but he did not have much ambition. Esther passively accepted his love, and their romance instantly drew attention across the campus. Esther enjoyed the thrill and sweetness of first love, and she liked the smell of his body, like licorice, when they hugged and kissed. More often, however, she was burdened with caring and protecting his feelings. It was quite a struggle to handle the heavy study loads and first love all at once.

Then, in 1989, the Tiananmen Square protest erupted. Although Shanghai was not at the frontline of the activities, all college students felt obligated to support their fellow students in Beijing. They went on a school strike and held marches for many days. It felt quite exciting walking on fashionable Shanghai streets in the middle of the day with tens of thousands of other college students. Many adults soon participated in the strikes, and many businesses and even government organizations supported the protest. Soon all public transportation stopped and every street was empty.

Esther remembered Yong took her for a bicycle ride in the very middle of an empty street right before the Tiananmen Square event. Esther sat on the top tube in front of him. The pleasant breeze of early night kissed their young and smiling faces. They felt so happy and so close to each other.

Then they heard about the tankers and gunshots in Beijing on the fatal night. Everybody was shocked, and everything went deathly still. College students were sent back home, and things were back to "normal." People did not know what to think or say or what might happen to them in retaliation, so they simply shut up.

Her junior year started, and everything seemed to go back to the old routines. They had to participate in official group learning and discussions about the Tiananmen Square event. They were told how to think about the event, and that was it. It was wise to shut your mouth and hide your feelings and thoughts as always.

Esther did well at school, but her relationship with Yong began to deteriorate. Yong informally introduced her to his parents, but his parents were dismissive towards their relationship. A prevalent thinking of the older generation was that campus romance was short-lived and could not stand the test of real-life challenges. Yong's mother did not seem to be satisfied with Esther, though she did not know why. It was an experience that she would relive years later as well with her mother-in-law, Feng. As a young college student, Esther was insecure.

Am I too skinny? Am I not feminine enough? Is it because I am not a native Shanghai girl?

Then Esther was in an accident. It was right after a morning class when Esther found out she was finally ranked number one in her class. She did very well with two very tough courses when most of her classmates failed. At the end of the class, Yong walked toward Esther against the crowd of her classmates when they rushed towards the exit. He was so tall and so handsome, and he was smiling at her.

Esther felt like she was on top of the mountain and said to herself, *I have everything I want in my life!*

An hour later, Esther was struck by a truck as she rode a bicycle back to the college from a nearby flea market. Esther went to the market to buy some yarn, which she planned to use to weave into a scarf for Yong. Esther woke up in an emergency room. She could not move at all; her whole body was numb. All she could tell was that she was in a big room and there were many noises.

What happened?

She had no memory of the accident. Her memory was truncated at the moment when she left the flea market. She was hit on the left side of her face, so her cheek was swollen like a blue egg. Luckily, her body and her limbs were intact. Hours went by; then the hospital finally was able to find her identification and locate her college counselor. The news of her accident spread.

Yong rushed to her bedside right away. He held her hands and told her, "I love you!" He never expressed his love so clearly before.

Am I so badly wounded? Am I going to be paralyzed? Will I die? It was a moment of great uncertainty. However, she was preoccupied and touched by Yong's expression of his love for her.

"I love you, too! And even more!" Esther said.

"I know." Yong grasped her hand even tighter.

Esther stayed in the hospital for three weeks, and her body slowly recovered. She was moved by the outpouring of love from her family and friends who came to visit her and care for her. Her college roommates took turns and came every day and helped her to eat and go to the restroom. Her childhood friends, Lan and May, took a four-hour train ride from HangZhou to Shanghai to visit her. Her parents also came from HangZhou and stayed for a few days until they knew she would recover for sure. They also met Yong's parents and thanked them for their care. Esther felt sorry that she had to put her parents through such worries and stresses. It was certainly not the best timing for the parents from both sides to meet for the first time; Esther felt uncertain of her future with Yong.

Her brother, Jian, came to Shanghai a few times to negotiate with the truck driver's company for compensation because it was the truck driver's fault that caused the collision. Esther heard about the protests held by her college classmates outside the company, led by Yong, on her behalf. The company agreed to pay for all the hospital bills and some more. The company even sent two ladies to take care of her during her entire stay in the hospital. At the end of three weeks when Esther was ready to leave the hospital, everything was settled. However, Yong did not show up to help her go back to the dorm.

"Why do you want to leave me?" Esther asked. She was still physically weak and naturally lost some self-confidence. The idea of him leaving her at this difficult time was almost unbearable.

"I need to focus on my future and plan for it," he answered. She knew it was an excuse, but she could not fight back.

The Chinese residential system was always very strict, to say the least. Every person had to register with the city of his or her residence to be eligible for all government benefits, including employment. It was extremely difficult to change a person's residence. As a college graduate, Esther was supposed to go back to her hometown. If she wanted to go to a different city, she had to find a local company that was willing to hire her and sponsor her for the residency. The process was much like the one for permanent residency in the United States, though even more difficult. Yong was a resident of the city of Shanghai. Shanghai was the most populous and modern city in China; getting a residency for Shanghai was almost impossible for a college graduate. The accident made clear the many challenges and difficulties they could face if they continued their romantic relationship. Yong was not ready to make a commitment to help Esther achieve residency for Shanghai. So, he absconded from her life like a coward.

During her senior year, Esther struggled to find a direction for her future. She could have easily stayed at the same college and pursued a master's degree. But why stay in this same city when her first love was already gone? She wondered if she should go back to her hometown and settle into a common job. Somehow her disappointment over the Tiananmen Square event and the loss of her first love piled up in her heart and urged her to come up with an unconventional solution.

During this time, more and more young college graduates and professionals pursued a higher education overseas in popular countries such as the United States. Her sister, Ling, was in the middle of her application for a Ph.D. program in the U.S. Her best friend, May, was already in the U.S. and continued her college education there. It opened Esther's eyes to the possibilities.

Maybe I could also go to the States and continue my higher education there! How hard could it be?

As it turned out, it was extremely hard! It was hard to get a passport in the first place for a new college graduate. The five-year service requirement after college graduation, to be fulfilled before applying for a passport, was in place at the time. Esther was among a very small group of lucky people who did not have to follow that rule.

It was difficult to achieve the requisite scores on the tests (TOEFL and GRE) to qualify for an accredited program in the United States. It was almost impossible to get a scholarship for an international college graduate. Without a scholarship, it would be almost impossible to get approval from the U.S. embassy for a student visa. Even if the visa was granted, the prospect of having to support herself financially while working on an advanced degree in English in a totally different country was almost too scary to pursue.

Nevertheless, Esther was able to overcome all these obstacles and set foot on this promised land with a full scholarship in the beginning of the 1990s.

CHAPTER 12

Bubbling Hope

It took a good while for Esther to recover from childbirth, which completely drained her strength. She even slipped and fell the first time she went to shower. Hua truly stepped up and took excellent care of Esther during this time. Although Hua was not school-educated, she had a broad knowledge and experience with everyday life. She made all kinds of soup, congee and other dishes to help Esther recover and produce milk. Gradually, her body began to regain its strength.

Esther could not believe she was a mother now. She was such a tomboy growing up. Excelling at school and in social interactions made her a stronger and often winning competitor among her fellow male classmates and friends. The idea of having a child did not even occur to her as a possibility until a few years prior, when her biological clock finally started ticking. Esther finally felt feminine when she got pregnant.

Breastfeeding David was such an amazing experience, although it was not a smooth process in the beginning. During the first month, Esther could not produce enough milk. But soon enough, she was producing more than enough for David. It was a miracle to see her body provide for this new life. Often, at the beginning of nursing, David would struggle to get enough. Then suddenly, milk would gush through her and into his tiny mouth. Sometimes Esther felt as if the milk had to come from some mystical place above, which gave her a sense of awe.

David would try so hard to keep up with the pace of flowing milk, but often he would get overwhelmed and choke, causing him to cry. Esther would then pat him and slide him over to the other breast until he was full. It did not take long for a well-fed baby to fall asleep. Many times, by the time Esther sat him up on her lap to burp him, he had already dozed off, his big head resting on her hand with his eyes closed and his baby face looking so content.

David was such a perfect child, always happy and content. One time Esther put him on the big sofa in the family room. It was a long, black sofa, and his little body was in the middle of a small white blanket. A ray of sunlight peeked through in between panels of the gorgeous curtain and shone upon him. Esther was in awe of the beautiful scene.

Esther often felt awestruck watching David grow and change almost minute by minute. Such a tiny life brought her more joy and happiness than she ever experienced. Kevin also fell in love with David. It was apparent that he became immediately attached to his son, which was not true of all fathers, Esther knew. David brought the new parents even closer to each other. One day after Kevin and Esther watched their baby fall into a sound sleep, they turned their eyes toward each other and burst into laughter.

"Your face is huge!" Esther giggled.

"Your face is gigantic, too!" Kevin could not stop laughing.

For this day on, they called each other "big-faced." Their marriage gave the young couple each other to count on in this foreign land. Now it was David who gave them hope and opened a window that looked out on the future.

Esther also started preparing for a GMAT test to apply for an executive MBA (EMBA) program during her maternity leave. This part-time EMBA program had just become available to working professionals. Esther always wanted to enroll in an MBA program; it would equip her for more career advancements. But she did not have the courage to quit her good paying job and pursue another full-time degree. Kevin was supportive of her taking on this part-time program. Esther studied for the test between nursing and resting. She did not need to worry about cooking or anything else; Hua took care of all of those chores. It was truly a perfect life!

Esther's perfect life ended when she had to go back to work after the three-month maternity leave. On her first day back, work had already piled up on her desk. The computer needed to be replaced, and her office was in desperate need of a good cleaning. Nevertheless, she needed to turn in a report by the end of the day. Nobody seemed to remember or care that Esther just had a baby and this was her first day back to work; it was just another hustle-and-bustle business day. Esther had to stay late to finish the report, and her milk started to leak. It was quite embarrassing when it became visible from the outside of many layers of clothes.

Transitioning to her new role as a working mother was not a complete horror, thanks to Hua. During lunchtime, she would rush home and feed David. Hua already had David ready by the time she arrived home, and Esther would just start nursing. She was probably more ready to nurse than David needed it. Her milk always seemed ready to leak out at any moment.

Soon after, work became even busier; she could not find time to go home during lunchtime. She brought a breast pump with her to the office so that she could pump milk out. She felt like a cow when she hooked the bottles and machine to her breasts. She would so much rather have been feeding David directly.

Three months after Esther started working, Hua had to leave the country because her six-month visiting visa expired. Before she left, Kevin's parents arrived to take care of David. Esther did not totally forget the vow she had made to herself that she would never live with her mother-in-law again. However, it seemed in David's best interest that his grandparents take care of him. As a matter of fact, Esther and Kevin never talked about possible choices for the care of David before Hua left. His parents seemed to be an automatic choice.

It was a common practice in Chinese culture to—if health allowed—have the grandparents babysit for young families. For Chinese immigrant families, it was usually an opportunity for the grandparents to visit their new grandchildren for the very first time! The grandparents also could spend time with the young couple who were so far away for years. Theoretically it could be a great family reunion. However, many problems often arose because the grandparents from China usually have very different values and habits from those of their children who may have already been "Americanized." Moreover, the grandparents would stay with the young family under the same roof for months, or years, or sometimes forever.

Esther wanted to discuss childcare options with Kevin, but he never seemed interested. As a matter of fact, he was dismissive of any discussions about his parents. He sponsored his parents for permanent residency in the United States without any discussion with Esther. Esther did not know about the sponsorship until she overheard Kevin's conversation with his parents on the phone. She did not like the fact that Kevin did not include her in the planning; it was as if the planning had nothing to do with her. Although it may take years of waiting for his parents to become permanent residents, still, it meant that they could live with her forever!

"Where are your parents going to live if they settle down here permanently?" Esther carefully brought up this sensitive topic to Kevin.

"Oh, they will live with my sister," Kevin looked very certain. To further prove his point, he added in a joking tone, "Who wants to live with you?"

Esther hoped that would turn out to be the case, but she felt uneasy. She felt an urge to round up Kevin and Leah to discuss this matter. Kevin did not seem to be interested in having the conversation, though. As always, Esther pushed her concerns aside and chose to believe his words. Years later, Esther found out that Leah had the same question for Kevin.

"Oh, they will live with me," Kevin casually answered Leah.

This time around, Esther did not even feel like she could bring up a discussion about choices of care for David. A discussion seemed to be an objection against this automatic choice of his parents taking their turn to take care of David.

The day came, and Kevin and Esther picked up his parents from the airport. Esther was stunned when she saw her mother-in-law again. Feng was very weak; she could barely walk. She was still as heavy as before—probably heavier. It was the first time Esther saw her father-in-law, Liu. He was stone-faced and seemed devoid of any emotion.

After arriving home, Kevin and Liu carried Feng to the main bathroom so she could take a bath. Kevin then asked Esther if his parents could sleep in the master bedroom, which was downstairs, so that Feng did not have to go upstairs. The request caught Esther off guard.

"How can we stay upstairs?" Esther asked. David slept in a crib in the master bedroom with them. All their stuff was downstairs, too! Liu looked at her when they talked. That was the first time Esther saw him giving her a look that scared her.

Hua prepared a wonderful dinner with many dishes to welcome his parents. Feng regained her strength after the bath and, as usual, talked the most. The first thing she said to Hua was, "You are so good at cooking. How am I going to match?"

Esther saluted her mother Hua secretly for her kindness; Feng did not really deserve it, considering the way she treated Hua when they lived together the first time.

Several days later, Kevin and Esther drove Hua to the airport. Esther felt so lost when Hua disappeared into the passageway that led to her plane. Esther wanted to see her mother again so badly that she begged the security personnel at the door and came up with an excuse. They allowed her to board the plane for a moment.

Esther found her mother on the plane. She stood before Hua and started crying. She did not know why she cried. Of course, she was grateful for Hua and for all the love and care she showered her in her first childbirth. She did not want to see Hua leave. She probably felt uneasy thinking of her life ahead with her parents-in-law in the house. Or was it more than unease?

Was she frightened?

Life nevertheless reached a measure of stability after Hua's departure. Her parents-in-law seemed to really enjoy their first grandson and took good care of him during the weekdays. Esther was grateful for their help.

As soon as Esther came home from work, however, it seemed that the duty of taking care of David was hers and hers alone. Esther did not mind, though; it was such a pleasure to be with her son. Kevin and his parents, on the other hand, spent hours sitting together by a computer and going through many dating sites for Leah. Leah was close to thirty and did not yet have a boyfriend, and his parents were anxious. It was quite awkward to see the three of them discussing different candidates for his sister when she was not there. However, from previous experience, Esther knew they did not want her involved. She was more than happy to stay out of it.

The highlight of her day was always David. He was growing bigger every day and was so happy and strong. He had long, heavy and very neat eyebrows that almost connected in the middle. His eyes were so clear. His smile could woo any heart.

He soon became more and more engaged with his surroundings. Often, when they were out in a restaurant, he would wave his little hands at the people at the next table. Pleasantly surprised, they would instantly respond with something like:

"Hey, little fellow, I would vote for you if you ran for the president of the United States."

It was a new adventure every day. He started talking. He could roll over and then sit up, and soon he was crawling all over the place. The sweetest treat in her life was to see his smile and have him crawl to her after a long day's work.

One day when Esther came back home from work, David was in his crib playing with the toys. Esther stood by his crib eating an apple and watching him play. David stood up and put his little hand on her hand which was holding the apple. Apparently, the apple tempted him. Esther let him take a bite. He did not have teeth yet, but he rubbed the apple against his gums and managed to get a little bit of flesh off. He licked his lips and seemed to really enjoy the taste. He smiled like an angel. Esther took another big bite to expose more flesh of the apple, and he rubbed some more off. They went back and forth, and quickly they finished the apple. It was the best-tasting apple Esther ever had!

Another time when Esther arrived home, David was sitting next to the sofa on the carpet and biting on Kevin's shirt. He was facing the window, and the afternoon sun was shining on him. He was wearing a little T-shirt and a diaper; his butt crack was showing. He was so concentrating on biting that he did not notice Esther entering the room.

"David," Esther whispered.

Little David turned around and gave her a smile that was worth the whole world! He immediately dropped Kevin's shirt, crawled to her, giggling, and climbed up to her arms. Embracing this bundle of joy, Esther could not be happier!

CHAPTER 13

Falling Darkness

Shortly after his parents arrived, Kevin told her a comment Liu had made. "My dad thinks I am treating you TOO good."

"What does 'TOO good' mean? Isn't it the way it is supposed to be?" Esther was confused.

Kevin seemed really bothered by this comment. The air was getting a little heavy. Esther wanted to lighten it up and she joked, "I am treating you even better!"

"I wanted to believe it was my immaturity that caused me to hate my dad when I grew up." Kevin tried to push down some emotions.

What is the real reason then? Esther looked at him and wondered.

Kevin stopped and did not talk anymore. Esther did not insist because she did not want to embarrass Kevin by talking about his dad's problems.

Why would a parent speak this way about his son's treatment of his wife? Esther was troubled by the motive behind this comment. She pushed her concerns away because she trusted that Kevin's love for her would never change.

Besides his earlier comment, another thing that Esther did not like about Liu was that he did not seem to care about their privacy as a young married couple. One Saturday morning, they were still sleeping with David between them. Liu opened the door of their bedroom without knocking and walked straight to their bed. He stood right next to her and wanted to take David out for a walk. Neither of them asked him to do this; they enjoyed sleeping in with David on the weekends. It was so rude that he came into their bedroom like this! But he insisted on taking David out like it was non-negotiable.

Does he think he is doing us a favor? she thought. Esther reluctantly picked up David and handed him over to Liu. She felt so awkward and uncomfortable that Kevin must have seen it on her face.

The next Saturday the same thing happened. Esther regretted that she did not lock the door the night before. She did think about locking it but was afraid that Liu would be offended.

Kevin told Liu, "Can you come to my side of the bed?"

Liu did, although he seemed to be put upon by the request. Kevin picked David up and handed him over. Esther felt bad after this incident but did not complain to Kevin at all. Esther thought that he must know how she felt. Liu stopped doing this afterwards.

What Esther did not know was that Liu told Feng, and then they told their daughter and all her friends about the incidents.

"What was she thinking I would do? Rape her?" Liu angrily shouted.

Years later when Esther heard about this accusation, she was shocked by the malice of the remark. Esther did not feel comfortable with Liu's presence by her bed in her bedroom, but she never thought about rape. *Rape* was not a word Esther would even think of in association with her own family.

Was it what he *was really thinking about? If not, why would he say such a thing?* Esther felt a chill rising on her back.

Esther stayed very busy with her work. Pride Oil was upgrading a few drilling rigs for deep water operation. With her new family status as a mother, Esther was not considered to be a candidate for site representative anymore. Although this role could boost her career towards becoming a lead design engineer, Esther did not fight for the role, either. It was much more important for her to be able to go back home after work every day and take care of David. Her daily life was getting so busy with ever-growing responsibilities at home that such a position was clearly not a good fit at this point.

However, she still wanted to pursue the part-time EMBA degree program. After she passed the GMAT test, she informed Mike about her plan and tried to get his support. Mike did not like it at all.

"Why do you need an EMBA degree?" he asked. "The job I gave you is that of an engineer, and it doesn't need an executive MBA degree."

Although astonished by his response, Esther did not confront him. He was her boss, and he gave her the very first job she had in the United States. As an immigrant in this country, she always felt like she owed someone else something for her success. Esther did feel belittled, though.

Can I only be an engineer for my whole life and nothing more?

The secretary, Michelle, was even madder than her. "This is BS. He has no reason to prevent you from bettering yourself."

Esther went to the human resources department and checked out her company's policies. She was pleasantly surprised to learn that Pride Oil encouraged employees to pursue further education and reimbursed the employee for part of the costs. She went ahead with her plan, and Mike approved it reluctantly because of the company policy.

At the end of the application process, she had an interview with a director of the executive MBA program. Everything went well until the last question.

"What can you contribute to the whole class?"

Esther was caught off guard by this question. *Of course, I will contribute!* she thought. *But what will my specific contributions be?*

Her English was usually much slower than her thoughts. If she had a clear answer, it may still take her a little time to articulate. For this question, she did not even have a clear answer. Under pressure to respond in a timely manner, Esther gave a most obvious answer with a pretended confidence.

"I can do the number-crunching as an engineer!"

Esther did not like her own answer at all because she knew she had so much more to offer. Furthermore, she felt she voluntarily jumped into the typical stereotype of Asian women. Esther was later informed that the class was already full, and she would have to wait for another year.

When her initial disappointment dissipated, she started planning, which she was trained to do in elementary school.

When should we have another child? The program took two years, so should I wait until the program ends before having another child? If I want to change my job after the program, should I wait a couple years more until I am adjusted to the new job?

Esther worried that she might already be too old to have another child if she had to wait that long. The older a pregnant woman was, the higher the chance her baby may have chromosomal abnormalities. She heard that an amniocentesis was usually required for a pregnant woman over thirty-five years old.

It was such a struggle for female professionals to have both career and family!

She figured she could use this one year to have her second child before the program started. She had, at most, a two-month window to get pregnant for this plan to work. Kevin went along with her idea. In those days, he was very set on keeping her happy. Esther did not ask anybody else, including her family, about the idea, just like she did not discuss with anyone about her decision of getting married. Life was so busy and her family so far away. She just had to make decisions, one after the other, on her own. They both were surprised when she conceived right away. It took her years to get pregnant with David but only one month with Joseph!

Her parents-in-law became more and more difficult. They often argued fiercely between themselves, but they always covered their anger in front of her. It was obvious that they did not want her to know anything about themselves or their family. Frankly, Esther did not have the will, time or energy to get involved with them. But their behaviors were often disturbing and impossible to ignore.

One Sunday morning in late August, they were going out for brunch as usual. Esther dressed David up in a sleeveless coverall that did not even cover his knees.

"That is too hot for David," Feng claimed.

Esther was extremely puzzled.

How can this sleeveless outfit be too hot?

Kevin, however, changed David's clothes despite her objection. Esther could not make sense of the whole thing. She did not know why they always had to be so against her.

Have I said something to make them act this way? she wondered.

At the brunch, his parents looked in such high spirits while she looked depressed. They talked and laughed while Esther remained befuddled by their behaviors and mad at Kevin for ignoring her feelings. Kevin looked uneasy, not knowing which side to take. Esther had to walk away and look elsewhere for a while.

When Esther sat in another corner of the restaurant holding David and another baby growing in her body, a strong sense of helplessness erupted in her like a poisonous cyst.

Later, the young couple planned a cruise with his parents in the Gulf of Mexico. They wanted to show their appreciation to his parents for their care of David. Unexpectedly, Leah also joined them on the cruise. Nobody even mentioned this arrangement to Esther until Leah showed up at her house on the day of departure. Esther felt like a third wheel in their special family vacation. His parents seemed to make many decisions and deliberately hide these decisions from her. More disturbingly, Kevin did not tell her, either! Though displeased over the situation, Esther suppressed her anger and went along.

What use to argue with Kevin and his parents? They will label me as small-hearted!

During the cruise, his parents and his sister seemed to enjoy all the activities, and they left David all to her and Kevin. One morning, as Esther took care of David for several hours before eating breakfast, she almost fainted. Kevin grew angry with his parents; he had to argue with them before they would agree to share some of the responsibilities of caring for David. It would have probably been better if Kevin and Esther had just stayed home with their son because they would know they were supposed to babysit and could plan accordingly.

Shortly after they came back from the cruise, David became sick. Liu called her at work and told her that David had a fever. Esther told him to give David some Tylenol and water and dress him lightly. He did not agree.

"Dress lightly?" he responded. "No, I dress him heavily so that he can sweat and then the fever will go away."

Esther told him that wearing too much could be bad for a little kid with a fever, but he would not listen. Esther told him she would call the doctor. One thing about parenting, Esther found out soon enough, was that every sickness felt like the first time, and you were never sure what to do. Esther called the pediatrician and was told what she already knew. Esther called Liu back and told him what the doctor said.

When Esther arrived home from work, Liu looked furious. He shouted at Esther, "What did your parents do when you got sick as a child?"

Esther was totally confused. *What did this incident have to do with my parents?*

Esther did not remember what her parents did; furthermore, she did not have to follow what they did if their practice was wrong. Esther did not know what to say and was really surprised at his anger.

"Eh? It was David's doctor who gave this instruction," Esther murmured.

His parents were so mad at her that they went on strike the next morning. When Esther needed to go to work, they stayed in their room and did not show up to help with David. Esther decided to stay home with David and let Kevin go to work. She would take care of her own son, no matter what. It was a mother's instinct. In her heart, Esther secretly hoped that her own parents would come soon and save her from all these difficulties. Thinking back, Esther guessed she was not proactive in handling the situation; in the end, Esther paid for their anger and unreasonableness, which she never did understand.

Things did not get better. Her in-laws were still mad. Kevin also became mad at Esther and would not talk to her. The atmosphere in the home was growing suffocating. A few days later, Esther asked Kevin to meet outside the house to talk matters over. Esther really did not know where to start. She could not begin to understand why things were always so difficult. Kevin would not say anything to her. They sat there silently for a long time. In the end, he looked at her accusingly and, with a sense of pity, insinuated that it was her fault. He then suggested that Esther apologize to his parents.

"What? Why?" Esther asked.

"No reason. Just to make them happy. After all, they are taking care of David for us, right?" he said. "Besides, I apologized to your dad last time for no reason."

Esther knew there were plenty of reasons Kevin apologized to Qing last time, although he might not recognize them. She was surprised that Kevin was keeping score. Nevertheless, he apologized after Esther was so angry that she began to consider leaving him. Esther just wanted peace this time, so she agreed.

The next night, Kevin and Esther went to his parents' room and Esther apologized. His parents seemed happy. Feng said that they considered this family their own and that was why they did everything for them. In Chinese tradition, people said this to show their dedication. But deep inside, Esther knew Feng really wanted to take over this family and make it her own. Esther did not want to think about it too much; anyway, the older couple would not be with them forever. Her parents would come soon. Liu still could not get over the issue of whether to dress a kid lightly or heavily when he had a fever. He insisted he was right until Feng stopped him and said that he should listen to the doctor.

They also mentioned something Esther did that hurt them. They said one day when Esther came home from work, she pulled a garbage can away from the window and all the way to the edge of the patio next to the grass. Esther could not understand why they made such a big deal out of this. She just put the garbage can back to its usual place; she did not want the stink of garbage in the house since the windows were open at the time. Liu explained that he washed the garbage can very well, and he left it there to get dried. Esther found their accusation to be nothing but nonsense.

What kinds of people are so sensitive anyway?

Still, Esther let it go. After all, if they were happy and Kevin was happy, there would be peace. Several days later, Esther received a phone call from Leah who praised her for her efforts at making peace and told her that Kevin felt sorry that she had to apologize for no reason. Esther felt much better since at least Kevin knew the truth.

Feng probably felt a little guilty, too. She initiated a conversation with Esther a few days later. It was about Esther's plan to enroll in the EMBA program.

"Your life is just too busy with two kids. You do not have time for your own development," she insisted.

How is this any of your business? Esther thought.

Working as a fellow female engineer throughout her life, Feng probably felt justified in saying that because she was speaking from experience. But Esther was determined to follow through with her plan.

Another time, Feng told Esther about one experience in her childhood. Her dad was a small-business merchant, and he and his fellow businessmen delivered products from place to place. Feng was told to join them sometimes to help. During nights when they went through thick woods where many wolves wandered around, the businessmen would put her at the front of the group.

"You see how they treated me! They put a little girl at the very front!" she said in a condemning tone.

Esther could feel Feng's fear and pain as a scared little girl. Esther almost felt sympathetic toward her then, a rare moment of camaraderie.

Feng must harbor many miseries and bitterness inside.

Feng often dressed like a beggar and walked around the house in a big T-shirt and baggy underwear. The big T-shirt did not cover an ugly scar from her breast removal surgeries due to breast cancer. The baggy underwear did not cover her very deformed legs and knees. A few times, Esther even spotted Feng going out to the driveway to fetch something in such an outfit. Esther was so embarrassed at the scene.

When Feng took pictures with Liu, she would put her hands around his arm. Liu's stone expression did not hide his contempt. It was almost like he would pull his arm away any second. Esther knew that Feng did not like Liu at all and was puzzled why she would want to hold onto him this way.

Was she so physically weak that she could barely stand on her own? Or did she just want to paint a fake picture? It was weird to see that oft-repeated scene.

David remained the sunshine of her life while her life got heavier and darker. Almost a year old now, he could crawl and was trying to walk. He had a big head, and his arms and legs were like fat lotuses. At nearly thirty pounds, he was beginning to get chubby. He was such a bundle of joy, and his smile was the light of her life.

One night, he was practicing walking along the sofa, holding onto the edges. He looked ready to walk on his own but could not muster the confidence. Esther stayed about two feet away from the end of the sofa and opened her arms.

"Come, David!"

Encouraged, David left the sofa behind and wobbled into her arms. Esther caught him and joy overwhelmed her. She forgot all the looming troubles and falling darkness.

What could make you happier than to witness your child's first step?

CHAPTER 14

Impossible Visas

Esther had to make a trip back to China as part of the process of getting her Green Card. After almost ten years in the United States, finally Esther was about to get her permanent resident status. The little Green Card provides a solid proof of the realization of the American dream!

Her employer, Pride Oil, decided to sponsor her for a Green Card and switched her application from family-based to employment-based several years ago. It was like a light finally peeking through the darkest tunnel! After she finally got a quota, it would take another two years of waiting for her to get the Green Card in Houston. Her lawyer moved her application back to China so that she could get her Green Card instantly through an immigration visa that could be issued by a U.S. embassy in Guangzhou.

At last, Esther was able to go back to China ten years after she came to the United States. How things changed! Ten years ago, Esther came to the United States as a single and naïve girl who had only hundreds of dollars in her pocket and a dream of becoming a middle-class American. Ten years later, Esther had achieved the dream and was the mother of a one-year-old, with another one on the way. But she lost Ling! She would never be able to see her dear sister again.

Esther hoped that Kevin could accompany her on this trip. She was six months pregnant. Her stomach was growing so big, and she often felt physically exhausted. She needed his support on this twenty-four-hour journey back home. She also wanted him to finally meet the rest of her family. She would love to show him around her hometown, especially her beloved West Lake. She also wanted to share her happiness with Kevin at the very moment when she would finally become a permanent resident at their reentry to the United States. What a significant milestone it was, for which she waited for a decade!

Kevin refused her request. "I need to stay here and help take care of David. What if David becomes sick?"

"We will only be gone for two weeks, and the chance of David becoming sick is very little. He is such a healthy boy! Even if he does get sick, Leah could help, right?" Esther responded. She was a very responsible mother. She would never put her son in any possible risky situation.

"Leah has a job! My parents can't handle David all by themselves," Kevin insisted.

"How about we shorten the trip to one week?" Esther asked. She was never this needy for Kevin's support!

"It is still too much for my parents." Kevin would not budge.

"How about we take David with us?" Esther was desperate. Taking a one-year-old on such a long journey could offset all the help that Kevin could provide, but she was willing to do it if this was the only way for him to agree.

"David is too young for such a long trip." Kevin was not willing to negotiate at all.

"Is this about money? You do not want to let go of two weeks' pay?" Esther asked, wondering whether this may be the real motive. He still worked as a contractor and his hourly rate was even higher now. Money was very important to Kevin.

"No. I just need to be around to take care of David!" Kevin seemed very justified with this reasoning.

Esther felt lonely when she stepped out on her first journey back home. Nobody in the house, including her husband, seemed to care about her permanent residency or her journey or her.

It turned out to be a great trip for her, though. Her family was so happy to see her and showered her with much love. Her brother, Jian, accompanied her to the American Embassy in Guangzhou where her interview was scheduled. She was approved for an immigration visa right away.

She reunited with many of her old friends. Around age thirty now, everybody seemed settled and busy with work and family. If the future seemed uncertain ten years ago, it was certain by then. They all seemed to be doing well and made good money with their college degrees while opportunities were abundant and accessible. Most of them were married and had young children like Esther. May and her husband, Ming, were the first among her friends to have bought their own house in a suburb and own a car.

May's life in the United States took a dramatic turn after she was diagnosed with a brain tumor. She underwent surgery and had to take many medications afterward. She gained quite a bit of weight and looked swollen. All the young men who lined up to get her attention before the diagnosis disappeared. A possible marriage prospect was in such a rush to get out of their relationship that he stopped taking her calls altogether. It was a huge disappointment to May and her family.

It was also difficult for May to achieve her bachelor's degree. She left China in a rush before she finished college to avoid the mandatory five-year service requirement. She had to start all over as a college freshman in the States. It was very difficult for a foreign student to learn all the core curriculum such as American History since English proficiency was expected. Luckily for Esther, all she needed to study for her master's program were major-related courses, which were very technical and did not require English proficiency. As a matter of fact, more than half of her professors were Asians, and their broken English was quite easy for her to understand. When Esther finished her master's program, May was still working on her bachelor's degree.

During one summer break to visit her parents in China, May married Ming, who was her admirer for many years. Ming was seven years older than May. The parents of May and Ming were close friends for decades. He studied English in college and worked first as a translator and then as an assistant to the city mayor. Esther knew about Ming and met him a few times before. Among all of May's admirers, he looked the most ordinary. He was short and stubby, but he looked like a big brother who was trustworthy.

May's parents encouraged the speedy marriage because Ming remained affectionate to May even after he found out about her health condition. Although May was not sure about her feelings for Ming, as an obedient girl she agreed to her parents' arrangement. Her parents were hoping that Ming would go to the United States and settle there with May. Ming tried, but he found himself useless in the States since his mastery in English language was of no value. He decided that his future was in China, and he would stay in China. May went back to China to be with Ming after she finally graduated from college.

Ming had started his own business a few years earlier, which provided an integrated commercial bidding platform for overseas projects. May was working for a prestigious five-star hotel as a manager of foreign affairs. Her college education in the United States helped her tremendously in this role. Her health improved, and she looked almost as beautiful as before. They had just had a baby son.

Esther also visited Shanghai and her friends there. The change in Shanghai was stunning! Shanghai had two major parts, the West Bank and the East Bank of the Huangpu River. The West Bank used to be considered the real Shanghai and was a symbol of wealth and fashion in China. Its famous and beautiful waterfront area along the river was called "the Bund" and was packed with European-style buildings and top restaurants. The East Bank, on the other hand, was always an ordinary countryside until the 1990s. The people of Shanghai used the real estate principle of "location, location, location" to its extreme. A popular philosophy stated that it was better to have a tiny room on the West Bank than a house on the East Bank. A major development plan for the East Bank was initiated and sponsored by the national government in the early 1990s. Now, right after the turn of a new millennium, the East Bank was packed with high-rise office buildings. High-end communities and pricey single-family houses were booming like bamboo shoots after a fresh spring rain. The East Bank was now more modernized than the West Bank!

One huge disappointment for Esther on this trip was that her parents were denied visitor visas to come to the United States. With her second child on the way and increasing difficulties in her family life, Esther was so ready to have her own parents come to the U.S. and help her. But the U.S. embassy would not issue visitor visas to her parents on the suspicion that they intended to immigrate to the States.

A counselor in the embassy held incredible power; his decision of pass or fail was like a judge's verdict that determined an applicant's life trajectory. Yet, with hundreds and hundreds of applicants waiting in line every day, a counselor gave no more than five minutes to review an applicant's case and made this critical decision right on the spot. Just like ten years ago when she was waiting outside the U.S. embassy to be interviewed for her student visa, the only thing Esther could do was again pray to God for help. Yet, her parents failed to get the visas. All they could do afterwards was go through the application process again and try their luck later.

At lunch with her parents afterwards, Esther felt so disappointed that she stepped out of the restaurant for some fresh air. Suddenly she saw her college boyfriend, Yong, coming out of an apartment building across the street and walking toward her. She must have looked funny with her eyes and mouth wide open. Yong did not see her or maybe did not recognize her since her hair was much shorter and she was indeed very pregnant. Her heart was in her throat; she could just barely mutter "Hi" to him. He then turned and disappeared. Esther was not sure whether it was Yong or her imagination. She could not shake off this image for a very long time. She told May about this incident.

"You may be still in love with him," May said.

Her comment surprised Esther even more. She thought her love for Kevin should have been so strong that it erased her feelings for her college boyfriend. Was this incident telling her otherwise? She carried this puzzle in her mind for a long time.

Esther returned to the United States two weeks later. Her belly was getting bigger, and the baby she carried was becoming heavier. Every day on the way home from work, Esther walked up a ramp in the garage to her car. The fetus sat right on top of her bladder, and Esther felt really exhausted. While in the car, Esther often wondered where she could go to get a few hours of sleep. But, without exception, Esther would drive to the clubhouse and pick up David, who was playing around, and Liu, who was looking after him, and take them home with her. Her small frame was not equipped to handle the weight of a thirty-plus-pound baby in her arms and another twenty pounds in her abdomen. Nevertheless, she often carried David in her arm, although her body told her not to. David was the only joy Esther had to hold onto.

Kevin became so involved with his parents that he did not have much time for her at all. On weekday nights, he spent countless hours with his parents on the web absurdly looking for a boyfriend for his sister. On the weekends, he would take his parents to eat and grocery shop. The couple did not have much alone time. He became more distant with each passing day.

Her life was like a train that had long since left the station; the landscape changed so much that she forgot where she started. And nobody seemed to care where this train was heading!

One Saturday afternoon, Esther was working around the house. Kevin took his parents and David out to eat and shop for groceries as usual. Esther stopped going out with them altogether after the incident about David's outfit. Kevin called her and told her that he forgot to bring his wallet with him and did not have money to pay for the meal. He asked her to bring his wallet to him. The restaurant was more than forty minutes away. Esther agreed and drove all the way there feeling exhausted.

Before Esther sat down and took a breath, Feng told her, like a master talking to a servant: "Go get milk for David! He needs to drink milk." The milk was in Kevin's car.

Why cannot any of you get milk? You have been here sitting and eating for several hours. Esther looked at her in astonishment and her anger was aroused.

Esther wanted to respond with this question, but she knew it would start an argument. Feng was very good at arguing, and she would lie under a bright daylight in order to win an argument. Anything Esther said would just give them more reasons to accuse her. Esther became more and more silent around them.

"I will get it," Kevin said right away. He obviously noticed how inconsiderate his mother's request was.

Esther and Kevin never talked about this incident, just like they never mentioned all the other problematic incidents. Anger and loneliness overwhelmed her, yet Esther pushed them aside and tried not to let them bother her. But the dark clouds continued to gather around her heart and saturate it with sadness.

Her parents went back to the U.S. embassy four more times to apply for visitor visas and were denied every time. It was like a prison sentence for life—once you were denied one time for the visa, you seemed destined to be denied forever.

How do you prove to them that you have no intention of immigration when you come to beg them for a visa every month?

For every interview at the United States embassy, her parents had to take a train to Shanghai the day before and stay for one night. They got up early the next morning to get in the long line and wait for hours. They had to pay somebody to fill out the extremely detailed applications in English ahead of time. If they were lucky, they might be able to get an interview the same day and talk to a counselor for a few minutes, only to be rejected again. Then they rode a train back to HangZhou and started planning for the next application.

For the last visa application before her second child was born, her parents decided that Qing would apply for the visa alone and Hua would not apply. They hoped that this arrangement would be enough to show that Qing would return to China soon and had no intention of immigration because his wife was still in China. Qing went through the whole process one more time and went into the embassy alone for an interview in an afternoon. Chinese time was fourteen hours ahead of U.S. Central Time. It was early morning in the United States.

Esther was woken suddenly as if somebody punched her hard in her stomach. Esther knew something was wrong—Qing probably failed again. It was indeed true. A visa was granted to Qing, only to be taken away minutes later because the counselor suddenly discovered previous records of rejections that she overlooked. Qing was never so upset in his life.

What a painful cost of immigration this was! She could not have her parents with her when she needed them the most.

At home, there was little joy or excitement about bringing a new baby into their family. Kevin had gained a lot of weight and lost a lot of hair. Maybe Esther was not the only one completely stressed out by her in-laws. He was still working long hours and would not come home until dark. His parents did not talk to her much, and, frankly, Esther did not talk to them much, either. Whatever words were exchanged were about perfunctory matters, and their only connection was David. Kevin mentioned to Esther more than once that his parents wanted to go back to China. But they did not seem to do anything about it, so Esther did not know whether it was a threat or their actual intention.

What she came to realize was that her parents-in-law usually did not mean what they said, for their actions were usually totally different from their words. More often, they deliberately hid their true intentions from her. Esther could only guess their true intentions by their actions.

They did not even seem to be happy about their upcoming grandson. From the few things Feng talked about, Feng seemed to be afraid that their love for David would be divided because of the newborn. Esther thought that was so ridiculous.

Is love limited?

But Esther could not reason with her. Like many things Feng said and did, Esther had to push them aside and not let them bother her.

Even the older couple's friends were kind of odd. One Friday morning when Esther happened to be home, one of their neighbor's parents came to visit. Liu rushed out and met them in the backyard before they came in. When the elderly couple arrived, they ignored her when Esther smiled at them. Esther was really puzzled and wondered, *Do they know that this is my house?*

Esther wanted to greet them and remind them of this fact, but, somehow, she did not speak up. Her words seemed weightless, and Esther became more silent every day in her own home.

Near the end of her pregnancy, she wanted to be pampered. Esther craved seafood, but her parents-in-law would never cook it. One time Esther bought a fish and told them about it, and the same fish was left in the fridge for a month till it rotted. Esther told Kevin about her cravings, but he did not want to upset his parents by honoring her request. He suggested that Esther go out and get seafood for lunch. From then on, Esther often visited a Chinese restaurant near her office on her lunch breaks to get seafood.

Esther did not like the dinners served at home. The food was neither healthy nor tasty. Potatoes were often among the dishes served because they were very cheap. Esther did not like the conversations at the dinner table, either. The discussions were always superficial. A few times, his parents had a lively conversation about some past events in the family, then the three of them would break into laughter, leaving Esther again feeling like quite the outsider. One time Liu talked about his experience when he was little and Japan invaded China.

"They raped many women," he said from out of nowhere.

In his voice, there was neither rage against the invaders nor sympathy for the women. He said it like it was a mere fact. He even seemed to enjoy retelling some of the horrors.

Esther was astonished at his statement and the way he said it. Feng gave her a quick look; obviously, this statement rubbed her the wrong way, too. Liu changed the subject right away.

What became clear to Esther was that she could not count on her in-laws to take care of her and her newborn. Not knowing when her parents would be able to visit, Esther knew she needed to come up with a contingency plan. While Esther grew up, she heard many personal stories about "sitting a month," which always ended with the same advice: make sure you rest in bed for the whole month. While Esther did not fully understand the reasons behind this custom, she did not want to work against the wisdom of a thousand-year-old tradition.

"We need a nanny!" Esther told Kevin.

Kevin never said no to her proposal, yet he did not get involved in the search. His parents were strongly opposed to the idea of having a nanny, which Esther found odd. They said they were physically tired of taking care of David and wanted to go back to China. As a matter of fact, Feng could barely take care of herself as her physical health seemed to be deteriorating. Having a nanny would free them from taking care of David and allow them to go back to China. Esther did not quite understand how they seemingly had no idea what was involved in bringing a new life into the household. Or were they just pretending not to know?

Esther put ads in local Chinese newspapers and interviewed many candidates. Finally, Esther found a lady who seemed nice and capable. Esther invited Kevin to come with her and meet the candidate for an interview, but Kevin declined. It seemed that having this new baby was a matter she would handle all on her own; nobody seemed to care, not even Kevin. Esther shook off her disappointment and went to the interview. The nanny agreed to start her work right after Esther gave birth and came back from hospital.

Finally, the day came when her baby was ready to arrive into the world. While Esther was packing everything to take to the hospital early the next morning, Kevin prepared a rib stew for her. It was probably the first time he did any cooking; he looked irritated and tired. Feng was sitting next to him and talking nonstop. This was so typical of her—she could talk forever!

Esther asked Kevin afterward to take a family picture with David as a memory, but he refused. It was almost as if he did not want to show any excitement about his upcoming second son in front of his parents.

It was quite a disappointment to her, and Esther was getting used to disappointments by now.

CHAPTER 15

Battlefield

Early the next morning, Kevin sent Esther to the delivery room. While the nurses set things up, to Esther's surprise, Kevin suggested taking a picture. Apparently, he felt guilty about rejecting Esther's request the previous night. David was not there, so it was not quite the family picture she envisioned. Still, it was better than nothing. When Esther put her arms around Kevin's shoulders, Kevin's face pushed up against her very extended belly. They smiled at the camera. Esther felt somewhat relieved that at least Kevin still seemed to care. What she did not understand was why he rejected her request the night before.

Joseph's delivery was a breeze compared to David's. After a few pushes, Joseph was born. He looked just like David, but he was much redder and a little heavier and longer. He came out of the womb with a full shock of hair. Throughout the delivery, Esther could not stop coughing. She was drained physically; her weak body could no longer resist even a minor virus. She had to ask for cough syrup in the middle of labor.

Kevin's mom and sister came to visit afterward. They brought a huge bag with several pots and bowls. However, there was not much food in there—just the rib stew Kevin made the night before and some leftover bread and rice. Esther did not want to eat any of it, so Kevin ate the stew.

Kevin drove back and forth between the hospital and their house. He was physically exhausted; at one point, he almost fainted. At home, David kept asking where his mom was. Both of his parents looked tired. The next day when Kevin arrived home from the hospital, Feng told him that she received a phone call from the nanny.

"She sounds uneducated. I told her not to come. Waste of money. Why do we need a nanny when we can do everything?" Feng claimed.

"What's the big deal with having another child?" Liu agreed.

"How am I going to tell Esther?" Kevin was surprised by his mother's action.

He knew that his wife had good reasons for insisting on hiring a nanny, but he didn't want to argue with his parents. Besides, saving a couple of thousand dollars always sounded like a good idea in his book.

"Just tell Esther that the nanny decided not to come. I will take care of her," Feng said.

In the hospital, Kevin told Esther the lie.

"The nanny called to say she would not be coming. My mom said she would take care of you."

Esther felt another blow to her stomach. She was mad at the nanny, but she could not get hold of the nanny to reason with her. Personal cell phones were very rare at the time. She did not have a cell phone or the nanny's contact info with her. Furthermore, where could she find the energy or strength to find a nanny now? She knew Feng's offer to help was a joke. Even if Feng had the will to take care of her, she simply lacked the knowledge and skills to help.

Esther was speechless, just as she had been in many previous instances. She knew it would not work out well without a nanny. She had no idea just how bad it would become.

Soon enough, Esther and baby Joseph came home. Esther could not get much rest at all with around-the-clock nursing. At night, Esther got up every three hours to feed Joseph. It seemed like just when she would lie down, Joseph would start crying for milk again. During the daytime, David was so excited to have his mom home that he wanted to stay with her. He was also very curious about the little baby and enjoyed looking at his brother and touching him. Esther felt exalted taking care of her two sons. At the same time, she was not getting any additional food for nursing; she was like a fountain that quickly dried up. Her cough grew worse. Kevin went back to work, although he helped at night. He soon complained that he had a sore throat and felt exhausted. It was like their bodies were staging an insurrection against them.

Five days after Joseph was born, he was due for his first checkup. It happened that David also needed a checkup. The young parents were getting ready to take their two kids to their pediatrician when an argument broke out between Kevin and his parents in the kitchen. Esther stepped into the kitchen after she heard the argument. Kevin looked quite upset and angry. Feng sat there silently, and Liu was shouting.

"What do you mean by not enough care? She looks just fine!" Liu turned to her.

Esther could not keep silent. "Am I doing fine? With both David and Joseph around me, how can I get any rest?"

Liu became more enraged. He pointed at Esther's face: "Why do you have to 'sit a month'? Other women have eleven kids and never need to 'sit a month'!"

Esther was never rebuked so severely by anyone in her life. She stood there, shocked and speechless.

Did I invent "sit a month"? Isn't this a thousand-year-long Chinese tradition that has the wisdom of generations? Why can I not "sit a month"?

Kevin came to her rescue and asked Liu, "Isn't it because Mom did not have 'sit a month' that she has such bad health right now?"

Liu became even more fierce. "No, it is not because of that!"

Feng stood up and walked away. "I will live in a nursing home when I get old."

Immediately, Kevin looked guilty, and he withdrew from the argument. Returning to their bedroom, Kevin blamed Esther.

"Why do you have to participate in the argument?"

"What do you mean? How can your dad be so unreasonable?" Esther was puzzled.

"It does not matter whether they are reasonable. As long as they are happy, it's okay," Kevin responded.

What about my happiness? Esther asked in her heart, and she felt a chill run down her spine.

Though still upset, they both managed to get ready to take the kids to the doctor's office. Liu insisted on going with them.

"I can help take care of David. It is too much for you two to have to take care of two kids," Liu said.

Kevin told Liu, "It is not necessary. We can do it."

It was as obvious as the plain daylight that the young parents could manage the two children. As a matter of fact, Esther was often left alone to take care of the two kids during the day. Esther knew Liu had some hidden intention, but she could not figure it out. She guessed Liu may have wanted to make up for the earlier argument. She was still so upset with Liu's early rebuke—Liu was the last person she wanted to see in this world at this moment! But she did not say anything since it did not seem to help a bit for her to speak up. Kevin finally gave up, and Liu went with them.

Nobody said a word on the way to the doctor's office, and the air in the car was still and heavy. Esther felt suffocated. Years later, Esther realized that Liu's real objective was to stop a private conversation between the couple. He wanted to make sure that they would not be able to discuss matters between themselves and come up with any plans against him and Feng.

While Kevin and Esther waited in the doctor's waiting room, Liu took David outside. He held David outside the glass door in the hallway and smiled at the upset young couple. He pointed at Esther and said to David, "This is Mommy."

Esther felt nauseated. Apparently, Liu knew how she felt but was just pretending that nothing happened. Maybe even worse, he was pretending that he already forgot the earlier argument so that Esther would look like the one holding a grudge. Esther was even more shocked by his smile than his earlier rebuke.

Kevin's sore throat became worse, and his neck swelled. It looked like a bag was hanging down from his chin. Leah came over after work to help Esther at night, which allowed Kevin to rest in another bedroom for better sleep. Shortly after midnight, Kevin came to the master bedroom and told Esther that he had to go to the emergency room because he could hardly breathe. Although Kevin insisted that he could drive on his own, Esther sent Leah to go with him to help. Kevin was admitted into the ICU right away. The doctors could not figure out what caused his lymph nodes to swell so dramatically.

Esther had no help. Dirty clothes piled up, and Esther could not find clean pajamas to wear. It was always her job to wash clothes for the family. Feng did not even know how to use the washer or dryer. Although she worked as an engineer, Feng refused to learn any new technology in everyday life. The only time she helped to warm up a bottle of milk for David in the microwave, she ended up blowing up the bottle because she did not loosen the lid.

"She told me just to put the bottle in," Feng pointed at Esther, blaming her. Esther simply shook her head and did not bother to reason with her.

Esther often had cold sweats. At this point, she knew that she was reaching her physical limit. She drank a lot of milk, which was pretty much the only thing available.

Now David started coughing. Esther was afraid that he would spread his germs to young Joseph, so she had to lock him out of the master bedroom. Little David did not understand his mother's actions, so he kept crying outside the door. Esther was heartbroken. What enraged her even further was that Feng seemed clueless with what was going on. A few times when Esther had to open her bedroom door, Feng would put David right inside the crib with Joseph while David was coughing and sneezing. Esther felt like she was in a battle to protect Joseph.

What else can go wrong? Esther could not help but think.

Over the phone, Kevin urged her to find a nanny. After a few days, Leah brought a new nanny, Dong, for her. Dong was a middle-aged woman and looked kind. She was quite sympathetic regarding Esther's situation and shared many of her own life stories. Like many Chinese women, Dong was not happy with her marriage. She put up with it merely because of her daughter. Dong was a great help to Esther; she stayed with Esther through the nights and helped to take care of Joseph.

Leah took their parents to visit Kevin in the hospital. He could not utter any words because of his swollen neck, so he wrote a note down on paper and gave it to Feng. The note stated: "It is all your fault."

Feng cried all the way back. His parents blamed each other for their decision not to let the first nanny come in the first place. But in the end, they decided that it was Esther who caused Kevin's sickness and all their troubles.

Esther's fear became reality. Little Joseph also caught the virus. He started coughing more and more. At night, Esther could hear his heavy breathing, and she worried that he could not catch his breath. It became such torture for Esther that she decided to take Joseph to see his pediatrician the next day.

Leah drove Esther and baby Joseph to the doctor since Esther was still too weak to drive. They left the house at noon and did not come back until midnight. The pediatrician doubted that little Joseph had a serious upper respiratory infection. He ordered a CT scan, which revealed that Joseph had pneumonia. Esther was told to send Joseph right away to the Houston Children's Hospital for further examination.

In the exam room, a few doctors and a nurse held two-week-old Joseph down and got a bone marrow sample. Little Joseph screamed and cried. Esther cried in her heart with her baby! Finally, the results came in and confirmed the pediatrician's suspicion that little Joseph had pneumonia and needed to be hospitalized.

The night fell, and the doctors left. Esther wanted to be with Joseph a little longer, but she was so weak that she could not even sit anymore. She climbed into the little bed Joseph was resting in and scrunched up her body around him. Tears ran down her cheeks.

What has gone wrong? Why has life become so difficult?

CHAPTER 16

Thunderstorm

For the next week, Esther's daily job was to check in on Joseph and Kevin by phone. She kept the phone next to her pillow. Her life was broken into pieces, and those pieces were scattered in the hospitals and only connected by the phone lines.

Esther wanted to visit Joseph and hold him in her arms, but no one could take her to the hospital. The hospital was a one-hour drive from her house, and she was still too weak to drive. The nanny could not drive. Leah also became sick and developed a fever, so she could not take her. All her friends were busy with their own young children and a few just had newborns. She went through her entire address book but just could not find a friend whom she felt comfortable enough with to ask for such a favor.

Kevin finally was released from the hospital. The doctors had to make a cut in his neck and drain all the pus, but they could not figure out the cause. Yet, they found that Kevin had a bigger sickness: diabetes! It probably explained his weight gain and hair loss.

On the first night when Kevin came back from the hospital, Esther saw Feng lying on their bed while Kevin sat resting up against the headboard. As usual, Feng only wore her sleeveless shirt and baggy underwear. Feng looked very content talking to her son. The whole scene looked so awkward and inappropriate to Esther. Feng sensed

Esther's uneasiness and sat up and left the room. Kevin did not seem happy about Esther's reaction but did not say anything. After all the trauma, he felt quite sorry for what Esther went through.

What Esther did not know was that Kevin's bouts of guilt really made his parents angry at her. Feng was furious when she left the room and immediately vented to her husband about it.

"Who does she think she is? I raised my son for all these years and cannot talk to him? We are all wrong and she is always right!"

Liu did not show any empathy for his wife, as always, and simply said, "You are wrong and deserve it!"

Feng shouted back, "You fart!"

They both believed it was all Esther's fault. "She is the one who spread the germs!" It was their mantra, and they told all the neighbors about it. Sometimes they seemed to think that all the illnesses had all been a part of Esther's scheme; somehow Esther orchestrated the whole thing just to prove them wrong.

It was a very long week for Esther while Joseph remained in the hospital. Finally, his doctor said he was well enough to come home. Kevin took Esther to the hospital to pick up their baby. When they stepped into the room, they saw Joseph lying in a crib, his face turned toward the door like he was waiting for them. His hair was getting so long that the strands stuck out everywhere. His face was a little rounder, but he appeared very pale and helpless. He looked rejected and given up like an orphan.

"My poor baby!" Esther picked up Joseph and held him close to her chest. Her heart ached. She felt horrible for leaving him there all by himself for an entire week.

How terrifying it must have been for him to be left in a totally strange place! There was no familiar scent or voice of his mother and family! How lonely he must have felt!

Esther regretted that she did not come to visit Joseph even once. She could not hold Joseph any closer; the sadness just overwhelmed her. Kevin stared at them silently, looking sad and regretful.

Upon their arrival at home, Feng was waiting for them in the family room. She waved a little red flag like a Red Guard did in Tiananmen Square while waiting to be visited by Chairman Mao during the Cultural Revolution.

"Welcome home! Welcome home!" she shouted enthusiastically.

Esther felt disgusted by her action and went straight to the master bedroom, holding Joseph in her arms.

"Are you insane?" Kevin looked at his mother with much anger.

His mother shut up and left quietly. Now she hated Esther even more.

One Saturday night shortly after that, Kevin did not come home until very late because he was out talking to a few potential partners with whom he planned to open his own business. Why he had to start another business venture at this crazy time was a mystery to Esther. The nanny was on her weekend break and not in the house. Right before Kevin came into the house, Feng came to the master bedroom and said, "Let me sleep with you tonight so that I can help you. Kevin needs to rest upstairs and get better sleep."

Esther was shocked by her mother-in-law's ridiculous request. Kevin sleeping in his own bed seemed a big burden to his parents. During the week, the nanny slept with Esther and helped take care of Joseph at night. The arrangement was made to allow Kevin to have better rest for his work. The weekend was the only time Kevin and Esther could spend some time together.

"I do not need your help!" Esther tried to control herself.

"Kevin needs rest!" Feng shouted.

"Is my bed now your bed?" Esther was so angry that Feng would not accept that fact.

Kevin stepped into the bedroom right in the middle of the argument.

"Go back to your room!" he told Feng impatiently. However, he did not talk to Esther for the whole night.

On a late morning a few days later, Esther was talking to Dong in the kitchen when her parents-in-law came back with David from the playground. Esther moved quickly back to the master bedroom before David could catch her, but it was too late. David ran quickly to her and held on to her legs. It was hard for this little boy to understand why his mom always stayed behind a closed door; he wanted so much to be with his mom.

Esther knew once she played with David, her parents-in-law would disappear into their room for hours. She would be very happy to play with David if she had the energy and time, but she did not. More importantly, Joseph was still weak and needed protection from any sicknesses. She could not afford the risk of bringing David close to Joseph.

Feng was sitting on the sofa nearby and looked a little tired. Liu was cleaning out the wheels of the stroller. Esther did not understand why he needed to do that.

Esther looked at Liu and pleaded, "Can you take David away?"

Suddenly, Feng started cursing. "Why did your parents not get visas? Just to anger you to death!"

Esther felt struck in the gut by a sharp blade; it was her great sorrow that her parents could not be here with her.

Dad and Mom, if only you could come! Everything would be so much better!

Esther, astonished by Feng's cursing, was also confused. She asked Feng, "What benefit would it be to your son or your grandsons if I died?"

Feng kept shouting, "You are a serpent! You are a poisonous serpent!"

Esther was caught off guard by so fierce of an attack and her body started shaking. Liu came over and took David. Esther went back into her room and tried to not go crazy. She thought a little and said to Feng before closing the door, "It is all your fault; you are handicapped!"

She did not feel right calling her mother-in-law handicapped, but she did not know what else to say. She had to say something, otherwise the anger inside her would burst out of her. She picked up the phone and called Kevin. "Can you send your parents home? I cannot take it anymore."

"Why?" Kevin asked.

Before she could say anything, the phone sounded a little weird, like someone else picked up another line. There were a few phones around the house connected to the main line.

Liu shouted angrily, "Why are you complaining to Kevin?"

"Why are you listening to our conversation?" Esther could not believe that Liu would do something like that.

"Hang up your phone, Dad," Kevin said.

Even more mystified, Esther hung up the phone herself. Kevin called a few times, but she would not pick up.

How could I know whether Liu was listening? She did not know what to think or do. *Why did Feng hate me so badly that she wished me dead? How could Liu be so low that he would listen to our conversation without feeling ashamed? How would Kevin react if he knew I called his mom handicapped?* She spent the whole afternoon confused about the whole situation and worrying about Kevin's reaction.

Finally, Kevin came home. He entered the master bedroom with steam coming out of his ears. Apparently, his parents told their side of the story to him.

"I swear I will not treat your parents well even for one single day; otherwise, I will change my last name!"

Esther was shocked at the hatred in Kevin's remarks. "How come you are like your parents?" she burst into tears and cried out.

She wanted to explain, but now it was already too late since Kevin believed whatever his parents told him. She started to realize how bad her situation was.

"I want a divorce!" Kevin shouted.

"What are you talking about? When I just bore a second child for you?" Esther was even more shocked. She almost fainted, not believing her own ears.

Kevin looked at her with a sense of guilt, but he visibly tried to shake it off. He stormed out of the master bedroom.

Esther could not stop crying. Her world turned upside down; she did not understand why everyone turned against her.

What did I do? Did I do something wrong by bringing a new life into this family?

She regretted saying "handicapped," but why would Feng call her a serpent? Esther lay on her bed with tears running down her cheeks. She still needed to get up and feed Joseph. She was still on antibiotics for her coughing. As a side effect, Joseph had diarrhea and was filling his diaper constantly.

Dong was very sympathetic to Esther's situation and told Leah about the whole incident. Leah came to the house and talked to her parents. Leah was very angry over what they did and started shouting at them. Later, she came to Esther's room. Esther begged Leah to send her parents home, and Leah agreed. As a result, Kevin's parents grew angry at Dong and looked for any opportunity to get rid of her. Dong stopped coming after a week.

Kevin still would not talk to Esther. He would come over to the master bedroom after work, looking enraged. He still mentioned divorce from time to time. Esther had no strength to argue anymore or defend herself.

She begged Kevin, "Can you take pity on me since I am still within a month of childbirth?"

Upon hearing this, Kevin stopped talking and left the room with a guilty look.

For a long time, she did all she could not to get physically sick. Everybody else in her family was sick, but she could not afford to be sick. The sky would fall and crash if she fell sick! Now her biggest fear was that she might lose her mind. Everybody turned against her, including her husband. Esther felt like she could not think too hard about it; otherwise, she would just go insane.

CHAPTER 17

Utter Desperation

Finally, Joseph turned a month old. It was the longest month of Esther's life. The night before, Kevin mentioned going to a studio to have a family portrait session. They had done this for David—how happy they were then! It almost felt like a past life. Nevertheless, Esther felt a little comfort. At least Kevin still considered them a family, even after all his threats of divorce.

In the morning, she started dressing Joseph and David. She was wondering whether Kevin would take his parents. She did not want them involved with the family portrait at all. Kevin would not say anything. In the end, she asked, "Will your parents be going?"

He answered, "Of course."

Esther stopped her preparation, but nothing else was said between them. Kevin went outside the room and called his parents. "Let's go take family portraits."

Liu answered, "We are not going. Let Esther go."

Kevin said, "Oh, she is not going."

Feng was standing on the second floor near the stairway, and she seemed thrilled by this. "Okay, we go. How can she not go and take care of the kids? We will help!"

Esther wanted to come out of her room and say, "I want to go." But she was afraid that they would also go. She feared she would start crying if she had to take a picture with them. She did not say anything. More and more, she felt that silence was her only option.

They left without her, and the door was shut. Esther still thought Kevin would come back and ask her to go at the last minute. But he did not.

Esther burst out with a loud cry in the empty house. She could not believe what had just happened. In the last month, she labored, nursed, worried and cried. She feared losing Joseph many times. She put her own needs aside and fought so hard to protect Joseph. And now, they were celebrating this new life without her! The sky crushed down on her.

In this moment, she thought about ending her life.

What is left for me in this world?

But Ling came into her mind.

No, I cannot! My parents already lost my sister. They will not survive if their other daughter dies.

She turned to her address book and tried to find somebody to talk to. Her teardrops fell onto the address book until she could not make out the names and numbers. She felt desperate like the ancient general surrounded by enemies closing in on him. The famous ancient story "四面楚歌" that she learned in fifth grade became her reality. What Teacher Yang drew on the blackboard became her life.

She knew she had to talk to someone; otherwise, she would die.

She went through her list of relatives in China. It was midnight in China, and she did not want to bother them. Besides, how worried her parents would be if they learned about her situation! How mad Jian would be! But what could they do?

Through her tears, she scanned through her list of friends in China. They had all grown distant, and it would take forever to try to explain the situation. Plus, they must surely be tired from taking care of their own toddlers and young families.

She then went through her list in Houston. Zia had two young kids; surely, she had to be overwhelmed as well. Zia's parents-in-law were also living with her right now. Besides, it would be kind of embarrassing to tell Zia all her family troubles, especially the issues she was having with her own husband!

"Do not let the outsider know the ugliness of your household." It was an old Chinese proverb. Esther did not want too many people around her to know all the ugliness going on in her household.

Finally, she decided to call Jean, who was living in Seattle. Jean picked up the phone right away. Esther cried for a long time before she could start to talk. Jean was furious, and she could not believe what she heard.

"Kevin is taking advantage of you! Such a bastard! How can he treat you like this?" Jean was so mad. "I would not have let you date him if I had known that he was this kind of person!"

Her words brought some clarity to Esther. Esther was so confused over how things had turned out. She just assumed it was all his parents' fault. Now she started to see the other side of her seemingly perfect husband.

What was his position? Did he ever try to protect me?

All these times, Kevin left her to stand against his parents and chastised her when he thought she was out of line.

Whose home is this?

She always thought this home belonged to Kevin and her, but more and more, it became his parents' home. He had no problem living in his parents' house and following their thoughts and ideas. What about her?

Who am I to his parents—a slave?

After she gave birth to their second grandson, they showered her with blame, curses and hatred. What Esther did not understand was the depth of the hatred they had in their words and actions towards her.

Do they want me to die?

Their harsh treatment of her during her most vulnerable time made her think more deeply about this chilling question. Yet, what troubled her the most was the change of Kevin's attitude.

What happened to him? How can he step on me like his parents?

After hours of crying and talking with Jean, Esther finally calmed down. Jean listened patiently and was totally supportive and understanding. Esther's disappointment and anger against Kevin mounted, and her heart turned cold toward him. Any sense of warmth she once felt was gone when she thought of him now.

When they came back home, Kevin walked into the master bedroom with a sense of unease. He looked a little surprised when he saw that Esther was calm and under control. He may have expected her to be crying hysterically.

He asked, "Do you know how tough it was to make Joseph sit still to take pictures?"

Esther did not want to respond, but she could not keep quiet this time. As usual, he wanted to muddy up the facts. He was the one who lied and did not give her a chance to go to the family portrait session. Between his parents and his wife, he chose his parents as his family! Now he wanted to make her feel guilty for not going.

She could explain why she did what she did as she had many times before. All she used to want from him was an embrace and a few kind words of understanding. She was so used to taking all the bullshit and swallowing all the pain, but not anymore.

She could start shouting and mocking and throwing the bullshit back at him. She used to look down on women who looked hysterical, and she swore in her heart that she would never behave like them. However, nowadays she felt that she could lose control at any time and become such a woman. So much anger and bitterness had piled up inside of her that she was ready to explode. But she was better than that.

Instead, in a cold voice, she snarled, "It was your choice!"

The coldness in her voice astonished Kevin, and he left with a sense of guilt.

Esther could not wait for her parents-in-law to leave her house. She sent David to daycare and looked for a nanny for Jospeh. In the afternoon of the first day when David started daycare, Esther got ready to pick him up. She found both Feng and Liu sitting by the back door.

"I am going with you to pick up David," Liu declared, holding a water bottle of David's.

Esther almost vomited. She would want to crash her van into a tree if she had to sit inside it with Liu.

"No. You do not need to go," she rejected calmly.

"Is the van too small for one more person?" Feng asked sarcastically.

Esther ignored them and left the house. However, Liu followed her to the garage.

Esther knew she could not stop Liu. He would get in the vehicle regardless of what she said. She called Kevin and asked him to stop his dad. She gave the phone to Liu, and Kevin told him not to go.

Liu stopped following her and then cursed her. "You asshole!"

"You asshole!" Esther cursed back to him calmly. She got into her van and drove away.

After she picked David up and drove home, his parents stayed in their room upstairs and would not come out to help. It did not bother Esther at all; she knew she would take care of both of her kids. Not only had she almost regained her physical strength, but she also was determined to not take any help from her parents-in-law anymore. She would not take any bullshit from them anymore, either! She put little Joseph in a baby bouncer and rocked him with her right foot. She put David in a high chair and fed him some fruit. Both boys looked content and happy. Esther felt peaceful.

Kevin showed up early at home, surprisingly. He usually came home very late from work after all the cooking was done and the kids were well-fed. It was unusual for him to come home in bright daylight. He looked nervous when he stepped into the house; he may have been afraid that another fight broke out between his wife and his parents. His anxiety quickly turned into anger towards his parents when he saw the scene. He went upstairs right away to their room. Esther did not know what they talked about, and she did not care, either.

Leah finally bought the airline tickets for her parents. A new nanny was coming right after they left. At last, Esther felt some hope in her life. On the afternoon before their flight back to China, Feng went to the master bedroom and took Esther's blanket. She saw Esther on the way back to her room upstairs with the blanket in her arms.

"We have put our blankets in the luggage. Can I just borrow yours?"

Esther did not say anything. She had no strength to deal with this woman and did not really want to. She knew Feng would not have even told her if she had not been caught. That night, Esther felt cold and woke up. Kevin had wrapped himself up with the only blanket on the bed. Esther pushed Kevin and said, "Give me some blanket."

Kevin did not respond. Esther pushed him again. Kevin jumped up and threw the blanket at her.

"What are you doing?"

Esther was so angry that she threw his pillow at him. Kevin caught the pillow and started beating Esther on her head.

"I will beat you to death!" he kept yelling.

Esther was shocked; she could not believe her own husband would hit her.

"You monster!" she cried out.

Kevin stopped. Esther cried the whole night until she ran out of strength.

The next morning, when his parents were about to leave for the airport, Kevin still sat on the bed and did nothing. Guilt was written all over his face. Esther busied herself with her everyday duties: nursing Joseph, changing his diaper, getting David ready for daycare, and more.

Was there any time for me to sit around and feel sad? No.

She swallowed all her pain and sorrow. Her strong sense of responsibility compelled her to keep going and take care of her kids. As his parents were leaving for the airport, Esther even forced herself to say good-bye to them and wish them a good trip.

She hated herself for her extreme efforts to be perfect. Chinese traditions taught her to be respectful to the elders, the teachers, the people in higher positions and everybody else except herself! It was destructive for her to neglect herself and follow the so-called traditions.

One and a half years had passed since Feng and Liu first came. Her home turned into a battlefield, filled with dueling cannon fire, raining down ridicule, lies and isolation from all sides. Her parents-in-law attacked her as their worst enemy, and her husband also joined them. Worst of all, she still did not know that she was their enemy, let alone know why she became their enemy. She was totally confused.

The home was saturated with sadness and pain after the battle. Their marriage was wrecked. The joy in their household was all gone.

CHAPTER 18

Small Light

When Liu and Feng left, they took all the strife with them. The house became very quiet. Esther wanted so much to talk to Kevin about the events and make sense out of them. But Kevin killed her every attempt to start a conversation. He simply wanted to pretend that nothing happened.

Life became even busier. Her executive MBA program started when Joseph just turned three months old. Her maternity leave also ended at the same time. It was frightening to start work and a new EMBA program at the same time. Esther made an exhaustive effort to search through the employee benefits and found one additional month of leave without pay from work. The additional month gave her a slight relief.

She still coughed constantly; often she coughed so hard that she would throw up at the end. It seemed like a tap inside her body was continuously dripping cold water that irritated her itchy throat and caused her to cough. When she had to resume work one month later, life became heavy and overwhelming. Esther was not satisfied with the new nanny; however, she still kept her because she needed help desperately and could not afford to be picky.

Kevin was very busy, too. In addition to his full-time IT job, he worked on his new business idea: a home remodeling store. Not sure when and how he came up with this idea, Esther was supportive as usual; it seemed a good idea to be your own boss in this land of opportunity. Kevin likely would not listen to her even if she wanted him to stop. Kevin was determined once he made up his mind. She once thought it was his great strength, but was it indeed? He talked to suppliers and potential customers in and outside of Houston. He just didn't have time to talk to Esther. The only thing he helped with was taking David to daycare every morning.

The bright side of her life was always David, who was now getting used to daycare and enjoying it. He learned so many things every day and constantly surprised Esther with his new knowledge. He was also very talkative. Picking him up from daycare became the highlight of her day; she just loved listening to him as he talked about everything he saw and learned, from birds to airplanes. David also started to enjoy his little brother, Joseph, more and more.

Joseph was getting better every day. However, his earlier sickness affected his immune system, leaving him susceptible to colds and coughs. He was always the first in the family to catch any virus and develop a cold and start coughing. He became a frequent visitor at his pediatrician's office and had to see all kinds of specialists. It was always Esther who took the time off from work to take Joseph to the doctors. The car seat felt so heavy at the end of a doctor's visit that she could barely put it back into the car.

The pediatrician later prescribed a nebulizer for Joseph to get rid of his lingering cough. It became a torturous process for both mother and son. Little Joseph did not understand the noise of the machine or the mouthpiece that was held up against his lips. He cried, screamed, and kicked. Esther would have to hold him tight while keeping the mouthpiece in place and trying to comfort Joseph at the same time.

The nanny did not stay long. She found a marriage prospect in a Chinese newspaper and decided to go to California to try her luck. She did not give any advance notice. Again, Esther and Kevin scrambled to find a new nanny. In half a year, they had to switch nannies six times.

Esther was not prepared for the executive MBA program, either. She did not even have a backpack to carry her schoolwork on the first day. In a rush, she took a suitcase and stuffed it with all the baby bottles and the breast pump along with notebooks and textbooks. One time, she accidentally dropped her suitcase, it popped open, and all the bottles and the pump rolled out. She was so embarrassed! It took a few months before she was able to equip herself with a backpack and all the necessities for the program.

It became unbearable for Esther to juggle the kids, a weekend EMBA program and a full-time job. Her worries for Joseph also grew; he was still so weak. She could not imagine Joseph growing up with twenty different nannies.

What could I drop?

Not the kids, for sure! Not the EMBA program, either; she had already waited a year. She had the second child beforehand just to make sure she could successfully complete it. Maybe she could drop her job temporarily at this point? One night in the study room, she turned around and asked Kevin, "Can I quit my job? I am so exhausted."

"I also want to quit my job. We would then have nothing to eat but the northwest wind," Kevin responded. He opened his mouth wide, pretending he was eating the wind. Esther did not think it was funny at all.

"Many women just stay home and take care of their kids. Why cannot I?" Esther insisted.

"Who? All the Chinese women go to work and take care of kids at the same time!" Kevin said as if it was the easiest thing in the world to be a working mother.

What he said was almost true. Amongst almost all their friends, the wives were like super women. They took on all the family duties while working a full-time job. Some even became managers. The realization almost made Esther angry at her friends.

Why did you all have to work so hard and excel at everything? Now I look bad when I want to quit my job and be a stay-at-home mom, even for just a little while!

She felt so disappointed.

Where can I turn? she often wondered. *If only my parents could come and help!*

Her parents applied for a visitor visa one more time. On the night before they went to the U.S. embassy for another interview, a thief broke into their apartment and stole their bags, one of which had all their passports and application forms inside. When they woke up in the early morning, they were shocked to see the bags were gone. They soon found all the paperwork scattered around outside the apartment. The thief may have found the papers useless, or he had a pang of guilt knowing how devastating such a loss would be for two elderly parents. Her parents, close to seventy years old by then, shook off the shock and went on the trip to Shanghai. They were rejected again.

The chance for her parents to get visitor visas was almost completely diminished. Esther's determination started to kick back in. Now that she was a permanent resident, maybe a local government representative could help. She contacted the district congressman's office and wrote a letter begging for help. The efforts turned out to be successful. Seven months after Joseph was born, Hua finally was approved for a visitor visa! She was able to return to Esther's side to rescue her and Joseph.

Hua came to the United States right after the 911 terrorists' attack. The media still offered endless coverage of the event and the victims. On September 11th, an ordinary peaceful morning turned into the worst nightmare in one blink of an eye. More than 3,000 people lost their lives. The images of burning towers and people running away from collapsing buildings haunted every soul in the U.S. and around the world. Esther could relate to the shock and fear in the hearts of those who were at the site.

My home was attacked not long ago. Although nobody died, we were all wounded severely. And the terrorists were my parents-in-law! Esther shocked herself with this realization.

With Hua's return, Esther finally felt hopeful for herself and Joseph. Esther argued with Hua all through her youth, but now her mother became her savior. With her mother on her side, she was confident she could hold her life together.

A few months after Hua arrived, Esther had enough of her lingering cough and decided to do something about it. Western medicine turned out to be very limited in her situation; each new round of antibiotics she took became increasingly less effective. Instead, she went to a famous Chinese herb doctor in town and spent hundreds of dollars on acupuncture, cupping and traditional medicine. When she smelled the herbal medicine for the first time, she knew it would heal her. Not surprisingly, before the month ended, her coughing stopped. The dripping faucet was finally turned off!

Esther wanted to restore her marriage, but Kevin remained cold and distant. She bought movie tickets for the two of them, but she ended up going to the theater alone. In a restroom stall of the movie theater, she cried for hours. Her tears poured down, and she had no idea how to go on with her marriage. The hurt grew exponentially inside her.

She finally found a marriage counselor for therapy. She used to doubt why marriage counseling was even needed; now she needed it desperately! She went to the counselor alone because Kevin was not interested at all.

"How long have you been married?" the counselor asked.

"Seven years," Esther answered. She could not believe her once-perfect marriage broke apart so badly.

"Have you heard of the seven-year itch?" the counselor asked.

It was a relief for Esther to know many couples went through similarly difficult times in their marriages. Regardless of race and nationality, all marriages seemed to have this common difficult period.

I am not all alone!

The loneliness dissipated a bit. But she desperately wanted to know how she could fix the problems.

The counselor lent her a book, *You Can Heal Your Life* by Louise Hay. It was such an eye-opener for Esther. The book revealed how mental thoughts impacted physical health. Furthermore, the book explained profoundly why life happened the way it did. From her own experience, she knew the principles were very true. Now all her coughing made much more sense!

A cough was a desire to bark at the world, "Listen to me!"

She felt ignored and suppressed for a long time by the people around her, especially her husband. Thus, she coughed and coughed and tried to get some attention. But still nobody listened to her. The coughing only stopped when her mom came and attended to her needs. She finally was heard!

Esther could not wait to find a thought pattern for the duodenal ulcer that had bothered her for years. According to the book, the associated thought pattern was a feeling of inadequacy.

Do I think I am not good enough? Esther asked herself.

In her youth, she secretly thought her mother, Hua, was not good enough—not educated enough, not patient enough, not graceful enough. But Esther never thought herself inadequate. Or did she?

Esther turned out to be better than expected by the people around her and even by herself. She grew up to be smart, pretty and very accomplished. It was a huge blow to her confidence, though, when her college boyfriend, Yong, left her. She decided to come to the United States partially because of this disappointment. Yong showed huge regret when they met again in Shanghai right before her departure to the United States. It was also his dream to come to the U.S., and he would have realized it if he had not ended their relationship at a most vulnerable time in her life.

"You are more capable than me." These were the last words Yong said. Esther agreed in her heart and was very proud of her own capabilities.

Did I still think I was not good enough for Yong for all these years? Unconsciously? Did I punish myself for him leaving me? Esther may have figured out the root cause of her duodenal ulcer.

Esther also was surprised at the explanation in the book for an ingrown toenail: worry and guilt about the right to move forward.

Do I feel trapped? By what? Is it my marriage? Esther asked herself. She thought she had a perfect marriage until her parents-in-law showed up.

Maybe it was not a perfect marriage from the very start? Maybe my body knew it all along? She was in awe that her body probably knew more than her conscious mind. She was also surprised that her conscious mind was likely not conscious of the truth for a long time!

CHAPTER 19

Deep Cry

M onths went by, and there was no sign of any improvement in her marriage with Kevin. Nothing seemed to be able to catch his attention. He was like a block of ice. Finally, Esther told Kevin, "I want a divorce."

Kevin did not say much but looked a little surprised. The next thing Esther found was that tens of thousands of dollars were moved from their joint account to Kevin's retirement accounts. She was furious and confronted him about it. Kevin said it was just a normal yearly contribution. But it was clear to Esther that he was already thinking about the financial side of splitting. Esther opened an individual account and moved over the same amount of cash. Once Kevin found out about it, a big fight broke out between them. Kevin demanded that Esther move the cash back. Esther refused to back down.

Leah called Esther a few times to talk her out of this course of action. Leah claimed her parents were so worried that they could not sleep well and that Liu almost got in a car accident. Frankly, Esther did not really want to divorce; the possibility of raising two young sons by herself was really frightening. Kevin did not seem to be on the battlefield, so she withdrew her fight quietly. All she wanted was just to talk things through!

Not long afterward, Kevin was fired from his job because he spent too many working hours on his own business. When he told Esther the news, she felt the need to protect Kevin and comfort him. She told Kevin, "Do not worry, I'll take care of the home. You just start your business."

What she did not know was that she would have to take care of their family finances from then on; Kevin would never bring one more penny home.

Hua was like a mighty warrior, carrying on the duty of taking care of Joseph and every household task. She did whatever Esther asked her to do and more. She even washed Esther's underwear. There were only two people in this world Esther trusted to wash her underwear: herself and Hua. Esther knew well that one day she would miss Hua greatly, if maybe just for that. The house was finally in order.

Esther felt guilty for putting Hua in such a position. After all, she was in her late sixties, and she still worked so hard for Esther and her family. Esther decided to take her on a weekend trip to San Antonio. She told Kevin about her plan and asked him to take care of the kids for the weekend. He did not seem happy but did not oppose the plan. The night before, Kevin stayed in the garage for a little while. When he came back out, he told Esther to take his Mercedes-Benz instead of the big van she usually drove.

The Mercedes-Benz was a big deal to Kevin. He bought this brand-new convertible to replace his red race car right after David was born. Kevin looked very satisfied every time he cruised around in the Mercedes-Benz convertible with the top down. After Joseph was born, they replaced the Camry with a big van for the growing family. Esther agreed to Kevin's proposal without a second thought. She thought that maybe Kevin needed to drive the van and take the kids out over the weekend.

Esther and Hua took off on a sunny Saturday morning with smiles on their faces. How much they needed a break! The sky turned dark on the way, though, and it started raining. Esther turned on the window wipers; the wipers moved but did not wipe any water away. The rain soon became very heavy and was pouring down on her car as if from buckets, and Esther could not see the road at all.

Did Kevin know about the faulty wipers? Esther wondered. As an experienced driver, she knew she could quickly get into an accident.

Hua sensed her anxiety and asked, "What happened?"

Esther was able to calm down and pull the car to the shoulder of an overpass. There was not even a railing there. Discombobulated by this incident, she took out her cell phone and tried to call Kevin. The phone would not turn on.

"What happened?" Hua asked a second time.

Esther's mind raced at a hundred miles a second, trying to make sense of what had just happened. It could not all be coincidence.

The rain became even heavier, connecting the sky and ground like a gigantic waterfall. The wind also picked up and swept raindrops back and forth violently like the hair of a gray-haired witch. Esther and Hua watched the waterfall from inside the little convertible Mercedes-Benz, terrified.

Did Kevin do something to the car and the phone?

This thought was even more terrifying to Esther than the gushing rain outside the car.

How could he do something like this? It could have killed me and my mom! And likely, nobody would even know the real reason why we died!

Esther hoped that she was wrong. She hoped that it was all a coincidence. But it was very strange that he wanted her to drive his car. He had never done this before.

There was a popular saying in Texas: If you do not like the weather, just wait for ten minutes and it will surely change. The rain stopped soon. Esther drove the car to an auto body shop to see what went wrong. The rubber strips on the windshield wipers were missing!

The strips would not walk off by themselves! Kevin probably took them off!

Esther's heart sank. She knew Kevin did not like to take care of the kids for the whole weekend. But the idea that he would do something like this to put her and her mother in such danger was beyond her comprehension. It was chilling.

What kind of a person is he?

He used to be like a shining and precious coin to her. However, when she flipped the coin now, she saw a totally different side—one that was rusted and abrasive. Even worse, she feared it might have been a counterfeit all along!

Esther and Hua continued their trip and had a good time in San Antonio. They had many conversations and the two grew even closer to each other.

Esther could not wait to ask Kevin what he did to her car and her phone, but at the same time, she was afraid to even bring it up. She thought she already knew the answer but feared it was true.

My own husband might secretly be plotting to kill me and my mother, and nobody would ever discover the truth!

The likely truth haunted her; she did not want to look at it. She finally asked Kevin what happened. Kevin took her phone, turned it around, opened the back cover and pushed the sim card back into its space.

"That's it," he said like she was an idiot.

Esther just stared at him. Shock and disbelief rocked her to her core.

"Why did you do this? Did you want me to die?"

"I would not have a good life anyway," Kevin replied.

Esther could not comprehend what he had just said.

So, because you cannot have a good life, you would rather I die? What about the kids? she wondered, horrified.

She was speechless while these thoughts ran through her head. Kevin walked calmly away from her. They never talked about the incident again. Esther was never able to shake her fear and shock, though. She did not want to think about it, but her trust in Kevin had eroded away and was replaced by utter fear.

What else is he capable of?

Just like her home, which went through a few earthshaking battles and lost its foundation, her love for Kevin was about to crash down into ruin. She did not know who to talk to about this incident. Finally, she opened to Leah.

"How can you say this about Kevin? How can it be possible for him to do something like this?" Leah was furious. She did not believe Esther.

"This is what happened," Esther said, though she did not want to believe it either.

After all that happened with Kevin and his parents, Esther was nearly willing to take all the blame as long as her marriage could survive. Yet, her sense of dignity kept telling her that it was not all her fault and that she did not deserve this mistreatment.

Something was terribly wrong in her life, and she did not know what it was. There were arguments in her head all the time. She was still constantly fighting against her parents-in-law, her husband and even herself in the virtual battlefield of her own mind. She saw herself making wrong decisions and picking the wrong choices in everyday life. From the bottom of her heart, she cried out, *What happened?*

CHAPTER 20

Small Voice

Her dad, Qing, was finally granted a visiting visa and came to the United States to join her mom, Hua, and help the young family. With her parents taking care of Joseph and all the household chores, Esther finally had joy and peace back in her life.

On the first night Qing came, he greeted Kevin. Kevin simply ignored him. As a matter of fact, Kevin ignored him the whole time he stayed with the family. Kevin came in and out of the house like it was a free hotel. He ate every meal that her parents prepared and enjoyed all the care that they provided but would not say a word to them. He faithfully fulfilled his vow of retaliation against Esther. Esther was surprised by his unappreciative and disrespectful attitude. She did not like it at all, and she even felt ashamed of it. However, she chose to ignore it and kept the peace. She was still hopeful he would change after all the efforts she and her parents made for the family.

One Saturday in September, Esther took her parents and the kids out shopping and for lunch like always. David fell asleep on the way to Walmart. Esther took Joseph and Qing to the store and left Hua in the van with David. When they returned to the vehicle, David was awake and crying madly. Esther could not quite figure out why. Maybe he felt left out and was jealous over his little brother? Maybe he just missed his mother? Esther was not able to calm him down, so she proceeded to drive to a Lebanese buffet restaurant for lunch.

The buffet was the most wonderful meal in the world for a busy family with young children. The customer walked in, and the food was right there available to eat. Everybody could find his or her favorites out of all the choices. More importantly, her parents could have a break from cooking all the time—something Esther felt they needed.

Surprisingly, David would not stop crying. Usually, he was a very easygoing kid. Esther carried him out of the restaurant and stood outside with him in her arms. David was still crying hysterically. It was a hot and humid late summer day in Houston, Texas. With a forty-pound, crying toddler in her arms, Esther's face turned as red as a ripe tomato, and sweat dripped down her cheeks. After a little while, Qing brought Joseph outside; he, too, was crying loudly. Joseph may have wondered why David was crying and felt like something must be wrong. Or maybe he just wanted to be with his mom and brother.

Esther picked up Joseph with the other arm. Now she had two crying toddlers totaling more than seventy pounds in her arms. The Lebanese restaurant was very popular; all kinds of people came in and out. There were Caucasians, Asians, Middle Easterners, Mexicans and more. They looked at the mom and sons with the same smile, one that showed their understanding and sympathy.

They must have all gone through the same thing though we look different, Esther thought to herself.

She did not know whether she should feel happy that her two precious boys found comfort in her arms or feel sad that she had to carry them alone. But this time she had peace of mind, knowing her parents were on her side. They were eating their lunch as quickly as possible so that they could give her a break from the kids.

Studying for the EMBA program became more enjoyable to Esther with her parents here supporting her wholeheartedly and helping her. It was not stressful for her anymore to go to the program knowing her kids were in good hands. Esther spent two whole days every other weekend at the beautiful campus. She had forty-odd classmates, and they had a great time together. Esther made some new friends along the way. She had three carpool buddies: Tom, Peter and Linda.

Tom was a handsome British gentleman in his thirties who worked as an accountant. He worked around the world and married a beautiful Brazilian woman. Tom did not have a four-year bachelor's degree, so this executive MBA program was a great opportunity for his career advancement. Peter was an electrical engineer with a young family of three kids. He was from Chile, and his English had a noticeable accent. He always reminded the teachers when break times and the lunch hour came around. He planned to open his own business after the program. Linda was a middle-aged Caucasian woman who married a Venezuelan and worked for a big oil company as a geologist. Besides two full-time jobs, the couple also ran a hotel business at a remote island resort in the husband's hometown.

Every other weekend, they carpooled to and from the campus. They were already tired in the morning when they met after a week of work, kids and family. They usually greeted each other with "I am tired!" which later became "I'm tired of being tired." Somehow, they were able to pull through the two years, though.

With this group of classmates from very diverse backgrounds, Esther was reminded again that behind every different Western face there was an immigrant story similar to hers, whether of this generation or a few generations back. Furthermore, behind every seemingly successful life there were plenty of struggles and heartache from work and family and, in general, life.

In many ways, these two days every other weekend with the EMBA program were a needed treat for Esther. The campus was beautiful and peaceful. Standard red-and-white brick buildings stood around like fair ladies, calm and elegant. Around them were well-shaped oak trees, nicely trimmed bushes, huge patches of green grass, and fountains. Esther and her classmates were also fed well throughout the lectures and group studies. They ate all three meals together and even enjoyed beer and wine with dinner. Soda, juice and snacks were provided throughout the entire day. Sometimes in the afternoon they enjoyed freshly popped popcorn or freshly baked cookies. Esther usually took some snacks home, which were always a huge hit with the two toddlers.

Esther became more and more comfortable with her classmates. She led a few major group projects during the final semester. Her team was comprised of one middle-aged Caucasian man, Greg, who was a vice president in a major insurance company; an Indian man, Raja, who was a middle manager for an IT company; and an African American, Ted, who worked for NASA. One major project they worked on was to develop a business plan. Esther picked Kevin's business, hoping it would help repair the rift between them and mend their relationship. The group developed a comprehensive market plan for his business. Kevin never came to any of their group meetings. However, he quietly took all the suggestions and never showed any appreciation.

For a long time, Esther was the sole giver in every aspect of her home. It was her children and her strong sense of responsibility that pushed her and kept her moving forward. Finally, with her parents returned to her side, she was replenished emotionally, mentally and physically. Like a tree that went through a few seasons of drought and now replenished with rainwater, she was flourishing again.

It was a typical Sunday off from the EMBA program; Esther took her parents and kids out to Asian town. The Asian town of Houston was booming; shops and restaurants tailored for young generations sprung up like bamboo shoots after a spring rain.

They had a nice lunch in a newly opened Vietnamese restaurant that was famous for its delicious noodle soup. Its owner, Sam, was a close friend of Leah's. Since cash was still the only payment method in the noodle shop and Esther was short of cash, she decided to go to a nearby ATM machine afterwards to get cash. She dropped off her family first at a Chinese grocery store so that her parents could start shopping while taking care of the kids. She then headed to the standalone ATM machine, which was outside of a bank and next to a very busy street. While walking back to her van after getting cash from the ATM, she noticed a small blue car parked right next to her van. All the windows of the car were tinted very dark.

"I would not be able to see them even if they were looking right at me," she muttered to herself.

Esther got into her vehicle and drove off; she went back to the restaurant and paid for the lunch. She then took her van to a gas station at a major intersection to fill up the gas tank. Just as Esther stepped out of her van, a small voice told her:

"Lock the door!"

Three words—loud and clear. It was not a plea but a command. It was not from anybody; nobody was around her. It was from inside herself! However, it was not from her conscious mind because she immediately started to argue with the voice.

Why do I need to lock the door? What could happen?

Esther was still holding the door open when she was arguing with herself in her mind. She could almost push the lock button with her index finger; it would take no time. But Esther decided not to.

What could happen?

Esther stepped out and closed the door without locking it. Her big van was in between a gas pump and the entrance to the convenience store of the gas station. While standing behind the van on the left side where the pump was, Esther noticed the vehicle shaking a bit. She was puzzled. Then it shook slightly again. Esther walked along the back side of the van to check the right side. A small blue car emerged from the right side and passed her before she made the turn. Esther noticed the passenger side door of her van was not all the way shut. Esther opened it and closed it, assuming her dad did not shut it properly. After filling up the tank, Esther went back to her seat and reached for her purse to put her credit card back in. Her hand touched nothing! Esther looked at the passenger seat and could not believe her eyes.

The purse is gone!

How could this have happened?

Esther was in shock, and she did not know what to think. She drove her van away to the grocery store where her family was. She parked her vehicle and tried to calm herself down. She had no time to waste; she had to cancel all her credit cards immediately! Luckily, her cell phone was left out of her purse and was still in the van. Personal cell phones had become popular by then; she had a very simple flip phone. Esther called and cancelled all her credit cards.

Finally, all the dots connected, and Esther had a clear picture of how her purse was stolen. She went back to the convenience store and told them what happened. They showed her a security video. Just as she already assumed, a blue car pulled in between the store and her car. A man emerged from the car's passenger side and got into her van and grabbed her purse. The videotape was of very bad quality. Although the action was recorded, neither the license plate of the car nor the thieves could be clearly identified. There was nothing the store or even the police could do. With so many more severe crimes out there, no police officer would spend one second on such minor theft.

It was all gone: her purse, wallet, address book, credit cards, driver's license... They were nothing fancy or expensive, but they were hers. It made her angry as she imagined that the thieves just kept the one hundred dollars cash and tossed all the other things that meant little to them but so much to her. In the end, the financial loss was minimal. The mental loss, however, was great. Esther felt a deep sense of violation.

After all the dust settled, she realized the blue car at the gas station was the same car that parked next to hers near the ATM machine.

They must have thought I withdrew tons of cash! They followed me all the way from the bank to the restaurant and then to the gas station!

If she had listened to the voice and locked the door, the thieves' evil plan would not have been successful. In some way, she enabled their plan by rejecting the voice.

In the end, Esther had no one to blame but herself. Her question was answered but in a terrible way.

Anything can happen, she knew now. *Really bad things can happen.*

How close thieves were! They were all around! She realized she must be protected when things went well and that it should not be taken for granted.

The voice wanted to protect her this time, but she rejected it! It had to be a good spirit watching out for her that foresaw the danger. The spirit had to be inside her all the time, but she had never heard its voice before. Was it the first time when the spirit talked to her? Or more likely, was she too busy to hear it before?

Now Esther knew how bad it could be to reject the voice!

Esther told Kevin about the incident at the dinner table. She did not hope to get any empathy; yet somehow she felt obligated to tell him about the incident. Kevin responded with another incident he experienced. When he was in a Fidelity store one day, a man came back in from the parking lot and reported that his car windows were smashed and his computer bag stolen.

Kevin talked about the incident in a mocking tone and made a comment about the man.

"He looked so stupid."

Esther realized that she must look stupid to him, too. She felt as if a bucket of ice-cold water was poured on her head. Her heart was saturated with sadness, as it had been many times when it came to Kevin and their marriage.

She had a sudden realization—the incident was an allegory for her life. Since her parents-in-law came to live with her, she had to constantly defend herself in the real world and in her own mind. Her dignity was crushed by the constant accusations from her parents-in-law and her husband that she was not good enough, which had been tacitly—and sometimes not so tacitly—conveyed to her every day. These accusations seemed to be their justification for their mistreatment of her.

Should I pretend that the way they treated me is normal? Is this what I deserve?

Even after they left, arguments continued in her head. Their condemning voices were still talking, and she had to fight back. Kevin's stone face and distant attitude constantly reminded her of their condemnation. Esther found herself defending herself in an ongoing internal battle, which made her angry all the time. Deep inside, she could not help but keep asking the same questions.

What have I done wrong? Did I not just give birth to your second son? What have I received in return?

She often lost sight of what she was arguing against in real life. It was clear this time that she argued against kindness and protection. She suspected something was wrong with her. The fact that she rejected kindness and protection astonished her more than the monetary loss or Kevin's coldness.

Why did I reject protection? Why did I argue with kindness?

It was so easy to obey the voice. Yet, for some reason, she did not. She knew a similar incident could happen again if she did not change. This time the loss was her purse; next time, it would be something more valuable.

Intuitively, she knew that another moment of utter desperation as described in the idiom of "四面楚歌," just like Joseph's one-month-old portrait session, would come up again and that she would not survive it if she were not prepared.

Her parents left right before she graduated from the executive MBA program. They had to go home because their apartment building in China was soon to be torn down for another new real estate development. Esther bought a European vacation package for her parents. Her parents spent almost a month in Europe and had a great time before they returned to China. She felt so much better that she could repay her parents a little bit for all they did for her.

Her parents seemed so flawed to her through her youth; now they became her saviors and fortress. It was only possible through their help that Esther and Joseph were restored to their health. Now Joseph was a joyful and energetic toddler. It was only possible through their dedication that she could finish the EMBA program while still working full-time. Her parents felt accomplished and rejoiced, knowing that her life was back on track. As for the two little boys, they were showered with love from their grandparents, and they could not be happier.

At her graduation ceremony, Kevin did not show up with their two boys until long after the ceremony had ended and almost everybody had left. Esther saw her classmates surrounded by their families and friends who gave them many gifts and flowers. Esther had none of that. She borrowed flowers from a classmate to take some pictures. When Kevin finally showed up with their children, Joseph was running a fever; he was like a withered flower. Kevin said he could not find medicine for Joseph.

Esther told Zia many of her struggles in marriage. Zia and her family were churchgoers. One day, Zia taught Esther to pray to God through Jesus for help.

"Just tell God what you want wherever you are, even when you are driving. At the end, say, 'in Jesus's name.' God will help you."

Esther followed her instruction and prayed one time behind the wheel when the arguments in her head became unbearable. She did not see a dramatic benefit after her prayer, but it took her mind off all the internal arguments for a little while. It seemed a better thing to do than arguing with herself and the past!

CHAPTER 21

Big Light

Zia invited Esther to her church many times. Esther always refused because she used to think she alone was strong enough to handle life. But now, with two young boys relying on her and all the troubles in her life, she was not so sure anymore. A few months after Esther graduated from the EMBA program, she finally went to the church with her two boys on a Friday night.

The church building was very ordinary. It looked more like an office building; there were no fancy stained-glass windows or statues. It did not even have a cross anywhere around the building. But the congregants were extremely warm and welcoming. Many of them were Chinese, and some of them were Indians and Caucasians.

What was unusual with the church was that it provided meals every Friday night before Bible study and every Sunday after morning worship. Most of the food was brought in by church families. It was really a treat for Esther! After working full-time and taking care of the kids for a week, a free meal was a gift from heaven. Better yet, Esther had several hours alone for herself from her kids. The boys had their own Bible study classes. It was a luxury that she had not enjoyed for a long time since her parents went back to China.

The whole congregation gathered after dinner to sing gospel songs and share personal experiences before Bible study classes. A man who was laid off from Coca-Cola shared his gratitude for all the support and encouragement from God and the church family. Toward the end of the session, a leader asked if anyone was a newcomer. Esther did not really want any attention; she would rather hide underground in a hole. But everybody turned to her and was smiling at her. Zia was also pushing her. Esther finally stood up and introduced herself. She was welcomed with a big round of applause.

Going to church on Friday nights quickly became a routine for Esther and her boys. David fell in love with church and made many friends. Joseph, on the other hand, was a restless two-year-old and often played with toys throughout the class. For Esther, church became a place of rest. She sadly realized another huge cost of immigration: she simply never had a break! Her work and her kids kept her busy all day long, and she did not have her family around to help. Now, at least at church, she enjoyed a bit of respite for a few hours once a week.

Esther was usually the first one in line for dinner on Friday nights yet the last one to finish her food. Often, she would start with feeding Joseph while David was still sleeping in the van. David had just turned four and moved to the upper class in a Montessori school. He did not have an afternoon nap at school anymore, so he always fell asleep by the time they arrived at church. Esther would check on David from time to time since she knew David would feel scared if he woke up and found himself alone in the van.

But it happened anyway one day. A man came into the dinner hall and shouted, "Whose son is left alone in the car?"

Esther rushed outside and found David crying hysterically, his face red and sweaty. Esther opened the door and put her arms around this frightened soul, feeling guilty all over about it. David calmed down very quickly; soon he was merrily eating and enjoying his class.

Esther started reading the Bible. The Book of Proverbs captured her heart, and the words shone light through the heavy and dark clouds on her mind.

"Do not rebuke mockers or they will hate you; rebuke the wise and they will love you," said Proverbs 9:8.

Maybe Liu was a mocker. It was probably the reason he was so sure of himself and even rejected the doctor's instruction for David. Maybe it was not all her fault that she could not respect him. Esther thought about it, feeling a little relieved and yet sad.

Is Liu really a mocker? Then what about Kevin? Have I married a mocker and joined a family of mockers?

Proverbs 22:10 said, "Drive out the mocker, and out goes strife; quarrels and insults are ended."

His parents must be mockers.

All the quarrels came when they came, and all the quarrels left when they left. But in the end, those battles scorched the earth behind them. Frankly, Esther had never met anybody like Kevin's parents who had college degrees but lacked basic respect for other human beings, including their own children. They seemed to believe they had the right to control the lives of their children. Chinese tradition required her to respect them unconditionally, yet her conscience would not allow her to. Now she realized it was not her problem.

How can you respect a mocker even if he is old and your relative?

"The tongue has the power of life and death, and those who love it will eat its fruit," said Proverbs 18:21.

Feng did use her tongue like a sharp knife, and she did mean to damage and kill. Along with Liu and Kevin, they bruised Esther all over with their malicious words. They certainly killed the joy of her marriage and her home. On the other hand, Esther often bit her tongue and held her feelings inside for fear that her words may hurt others. Many times, she ended up hurting herself because she did not speak up.

Proverbs 25:19 said, "Like a broken tooth or a lame foot is reliance on the unfaithful in a time of trouble."

Esther reflected on all that happened after Joseph was born.

Maybe the reason for all the chaos and suffering was that Kevin was unfaithful?

She had once thought of Kevin as a perfect husband; he did not perform so perfectly for the last few years only because of the bad influence from his parents. She was so sure that he would return to the old version of a perfect husband after his parents went back to China. But now she started to doubt her belief.

Was he immature or immoral or both? The same question that she asked many years ago came back to her heart.

Was he only capable of receiving but not giving? She had some more doubts about Kevin.

From graduate school to an engineering job to her Green Card, Esther handled it all by herself. Since the day Esther started dating Kevin, Esther only picked up more work for herself to care for him and then his family. Kevin did not need to contribute much, not even after David was born because Hua took care of every matter. However, during her second pregnancy and after the birth of Joseph when she could not handle it all, Kevin failed terribly as a husband and did not give her the support she desperately needed.

After two childbirths, two years of study at an EMBA program, and all the struggles of family life, Esther just wanted to slow down and sink into the reality of her life and make sense of it. The family had grown, and now Esther was a working mother of two young boys.

Esther did not know who Kevin was or where his heart was at this point. He still did not bring in any money for the family. Esther had no idea how his business was progressing. His stone face softened a bit after her parents left, but he was mostly absent from her and the kids. Esther often felt like she was a single mother.

She also liked the Book of John in the Bible. This verse caught her eye: "Then you will know the truth, and the truth will set you free" (John 8:32).

What is the truth? Esther wondered.

She emerged from the false doctrines of her youth back in China. She assumed that she had the truth by living in this free country. However, now she was not sure about this assumption anymore. Her life, especially her marriage, seemed more like an illusion.

The saving grace for her life was always her two boys. David was a perfect student in a Montessori school. Not only was he a very quick learner, but he was also a social magnet. He was a good helper to his teachers and always held the door for everyone. A classmate of David admired him so much that he asked his parents if they could bear a child just like David.

One day when she picked David up from school, he took a carefully wrapped cookie from his pocket and said, "I saved this for Joseph."

All her struggles and hardship dissipated in the face of such a sweet love between her precious sons. She noticed how she treated David was often reflected in how David treated Joseph. Her mood and attitude were contagious. She knew she was setting an example for her two boys, and she was determined to set a good example for them.

Joseph, on the other hand, was quite a different story. He was a restless and energetic toddler. He could be dangerously impulsive and sometimes ran across a parking lot for no apparent reason. He also was a little slow in his language development.

One Saturday morning, a visit to a local Chinese school turned into a frantic search for Joseph. Esther took the kids there to enroll them in weekend Chinese classes. She hoped her two boys would learn her mother tongue and stay connected with their roots. The semester had not started yet; all the classrooms were closed and empty. It was an enclosed, donut-shaped building with classrooms on both sides of long hallways. The registry was set up at the entrance of the building on the first floor. While Esther talked to a teacher at the registry, her back was turned toward her kids. After a couple minutes, Esther realized that Joseph was gone.

Esther rushed through the building and searched every classroom, shouting Joseph's name. David was right behind her, repeating his brother's name. The hallways looked so long, and the building echoed with their anxious shouts. Esther was so scared that something could happen to Joseph that she started crying. David reached for her hand and started to cry, too. A few teachers joined in their search. It was the longest twenty minutes she ever experienced. When they finally found Joseph, he was playing in a huge gym on the corner of the second floor and was blissfully happy.

Esther did not know that her parents-in-law had come back to the United States and were living with Leah. She ran into them while shopping with her kids in a grocery store. Out of respect, she greeted her parents-in-law and asked the kids to greet them. Her parents-in-law barely responded; they were cold like strangers. Leah looked worried as if she was afraid that the greeting may start an argument.

Esther was always grateful to Leah because Leah stood up for her and helped her during the darkest moments of her life. Their communication was, however, reduced to almost nothing at this point.

No wonder she is so distant. Her parents are living with her!

Leah married the man whom her parents and Kevin found on an internet dating site. What attracted her parents the most to this man was his Ph.D. degree from Stanford. He lived in Los Angeles and loved his job.

Leah's parents wanted the man to move down to Houston and live with them. After he refused, the relationship became strained. Phone conversations gradually became arguments and shouting matches. The man finally had enough and wanted to divorce, although Leah was already pregnant at the time. Leah had an abortion after the divorce.

"I am already in my thirties, but I have neither a child nor a man in my life," Leah cried to Feng.

"You deserve it!" Feng scolded.

Leah secretly went back to her former boyfriend, Sam. Sam was a Vietnamese and came to the United States with his parents in the mid-1970s on a boat fleeing from the Communist Party. He was short and sturdy and looked a little rough. He did not have a college degree and worked many odd jobs before opening a popular restaurant. He could speak some Chinese. Leah met him when she worked part-time as a waitress while attending graduate school. He was a manager of the restaurant at the time. Sam liked Leah, and he always helped Leah and her parents whenever they needed help. He would often bring a couple dishes to them; he would take Liu out to go fishing when he was off from work. Her parents had no problem taking in all the help from him, though they looked down upon him as if he was in a lower social class.

Leah conceived with Sam very soon, but she hid her pregnancy from her parents because she knew they would not approve of this relationship. When she could not hide her growing stomach, she moved out of her apartment and went to live with Sam. She lied to her parents that she was laid off and had to move to Arizona for a new job. Her parents stayed in the apartment for a few more months before going back to China.

Before Leah moved out, her parents persuaded her to buy a new house with them. They planned to live with her after they came back the next time and reside in the United States permanently for the rest of their lives. Kevin was involved throughout the whole process of purchase and construction of a new house. With both Leah and his parents absent, Kevin monitored the construction of the house and updated both parties constantly with millions of choices and decisions he had to make.

Esther was oblivious to all that was happening. She stayed super busy working full-time and taking care of two energetic boys. All she noticed was that Kevin gradually warmed up toward her after years of a "cold war." He became more involved with the kids and would plan family activities for the weekends. Esther did not know what made him change.

Maybe he was moved by my dedication, she thought.

It was probably more likely that the chaos of Leah's life and her strained relationship with their parents gave him a clear perspective of Esther's situation last time.

Esther was invited to a company event and could stay in a waterfront hotel for Saturday night for free. Kevin agreed to go with her. It was the first time after all these years that they would do something for just the two of them. Kevin called his parents and asked them to take care of the kids for the night. They agreed to the arrangement on the phone. However, Leah called Esther afterwards.

"Why do you think you deserve to celebrate Mother's Day while my mom does not?" Leah shouted at her.

Esther was again caught off guard.

"What does this have to do with Mother's Day? It is a company event!" Esther explained.

The event happened to fall on Mother's Day weekend. Esther and Kevin were planning to take his parents out for a nice brunch the next day after they came back from the event.

"How do you dare to treat my parents like your servants?" Leah was quite hysterical.

What happened to her? Is she crazy?

Esther could not understand Leah's rage, so she hung up the phone. Leah called again, and Esther gave the phone to Kevin.

"What are you talking about? Are you insane?" Kevin rebuked her and ended the conversation.

Esther was shocked by Leah's change of attitude towards her. It seemed like whoever stayed with her parents-in-law would ultimately turn against her. Leah once was an ally and now she acted like an enemy. Her unfounded accusation had so much hatred, and the level of hatred was so deep that it was scary.

Kevin wanted to attend an expo in Florida for his business soon after. Liu wanted to go with him; however, it was on the condition that Kevin would drive there. His logic was that Kevin would not incur any extra expense for him this way. If Kevin flew there, another airline ticket for him was apparently an extra cost. He wanted to have total control on how things went so that he could feel easy because he was not a burden in his own eyes.

Kevin did not really want to drive all the way to Florida, but he did not want to disappoint Liu, either. He knew Liu wanted to go to the event; if he chose to fly there, it would be like rejecting Liu's will.

It was a destructive kind of passive-aggressive co-dependency that was not healthy for anyone, and it did not get any better from the first time his parents visited.

Esther had pity on Kevin, knowing that it would be really exhausting for him to drive ten-plus hours each way between Houston and Orlando. Besides, it would be two extra days spent on the trip. Kevin could not be in his shop for those two days, and Esther would be all by herself taking care of the two kids for those two days.

The whole idea did not make any sense to Esther. She checked a few airlines and found surprisingly cheap round-trip tickets for less than a hundred dollars. She was overjoyed with her find and called Kevin immediately, hoping the price would change Liu's decision. Kevin was hopeful, too. However, Liu rejected the suggestion and stuck with his idea.

Kevin ended up driving all the way there and taking Liu with him. After the trip when Kevin returned home, he claimed that it was a really good idea to drive there.

"There were so many brochures and samples! They were too heavy for me to take onto the plane; I would have had to pay lots of money for them," Kevin said as if he hit the lottery.

Esther knew Kevin was making up an excuse for Liu's selfish decision. The excuse must have been Liu's idea, and Liu must have looked very hard to find it.

The same night, Kevin came to Esther's bedroom and kissed her.

"Do you know you have not kissed me for more than two years?" Esther asked.

"Really? This long?" Kevin pretended.

"If you ever treat me like this again, I will leave you!" Esther warned him.

Kevin gradually opened to Esther again, except for the areas of his business and his finances. She knew he probably made pretty good money, although he still did not bring a penny home. She did not want to pressure him; she waited patiently, hoping one day that he would share all his secret financial information with her.

She was hopeful her marriage would be restored.

CHAPTER 22
China Visit

After the EMBA program, Esther put more effort into her work and looked for ways to use her newly acquired business knowledge and skills. She also joined a few career and social clubs and became more involved in the community. She was ready to live a more successful life.

Soon after, Esther found that a few junior engineers were promoted to senior positions, but she was left behind. The promotions were not publicly announced. Those engineers did not have graduate degrees and worked for fewer years than she had. Esther should have been promoted with them, if not earlier! Nobody even discussed the possibility of a potential promotion with her. Esther felt blindsided, and she was furious.

How could this happen? she wondered. *Is it because they were Caucasian? Or they were male? Maybe they looked more dedicated because they traveled to a job site more often?*

Kevin encouraged her to talk to her bosses and threaten them with a charge of discrimination. Esther had a good relationship with her managers; thus, she did not want to go so far as to file a charge. She did not like confrontation either, especially with her bosses. However, she wanted to question their criteria for promotion. She was so afraid she could not express herself clearly that she wrote down her arguments. She read from the script when talking to them. Her supervisor and manager showed their understanding of her frustration. However, Mike was so mad after Esther read a few lines from her script that he almost kicked her out of his office. He finally calmed down and agreed to give her more opportunities to qualify for the next round of promotion.

Such an opportunity was soon handed to her; she was assigned to an independent survey on an offshore drilling rig in the North Sea. The goal was to find internal corrosion of the columns and come up with a repair plan. Esther received a three-day offshore survival training in Louisiana to prepare for the trip. The most difficult training for her was to escape from a helicopter that crashed into the water and to climb up a rope ladder to a rescue helicopter. She never knew a rope ladder was so soft, and she had to rely on her own physical strength for survival!

The offshore trip was both exciting and productive. She flew from Aberdeen, Scotland, and rode a helicopter for an hour to the drilling rig. The rig was like a little island by itself surrounded by endless sea. Living on an offshore rig was a brand-new experience for her. Most of the crews on the rig were male, but they were all courteous to her. She was accompanied by a rig safety engineer and a few workers for her work. She had to climb up and down inside every column of a semi-submersible while fully equipped with heavy steel toe boots, a helmet and safety glasses. The insides of the columns were dark and humid, and they had to make sure there was enough oxygen inside every time they climbed inside one. She successfully finished all the tasks after three days. Besides the work, she enjoyed watching beautiful sunsets on an open sea.

Despite these opportunities, Esther found that her future with Pride Oil seemed quite limited. Management did not seem interested in using her EMBA skills at all. In their perspective, she was an engineer and nothing more, just like Mike told her before she even started the program. She knew she had to look elsewhere. She was confident that she would find a great opportunity and that her career would take off sometime soon.

She planned a vacation back to her hometown in China with her kids before she started looking for a new job. It would be the very first time for her kids to go to China. Kevin did not want to go with them, and his excuse this time was that his business was still in its early phase and needed his presence and monitoring. His refusal did not even bother Esther much at all, unlike her first trip back to China. Now she was numb to disappointments.

It was a few years into the new millennium, and China had already joined the World Trade Organization. China's economy took off in the 1990s after the Tiananmen Square event, and it grew at a stunning annual rate of around ten percent. Esther could hardly recognize her hometown. The area around the college dorm where her family used to live was once rice field after rice field. Now it was a concrete forest filled with high-rise apartment buildings and shopping centers. There used to be mostly buses on the street when she grew up and very few sedans, which were reserved for high-ranking officials. Now the streets were so much wider and packed with personal vehicles. The whole city expanded into the surrounding countryside and was so much bigger! Esther could easily get lost in her hometown. More of her friends had their own apartments and personal vehicles.

It was such a pleasant reunion with her family. A couple of years had passed since her parents returned to China. Qing and Hua and the entire family were overjoyed to see Esther and the kids. They enjoyed family outings to West Lake and nearby parks. Qing loved to carry Joseph on his shoulders, and little Joseph could not be happier. David was a little too heavy to ride on his grandpa's shoulders, but he loved to wrestle with Uncle Jian whenever the two met. Hua would take the kids to feed pigeons in the parks. With two curious grandsons by her side and white pigeons flapping wings around them, Hua had the happiest smile.

Joshua, Ling's son, was already a teenager. Jian's daughter, Hannah, was very cute and lovely. Joshua and Hannah would come over all the time to play with their two younger American cousins.

Blood is indeed thicker than water. Esther was amazed at how quickly her two sons connected with their relatives.

HangZhou was not only beautiful but also smelled sweet in early fall. The air was filled with the light yet sweet fragrance of Osmanthus fragrans. This flower was beloved by the people of HangZhou and was the city flower. Osmanthus fragrans were planted everywhere in HangZhou, giving its residents a pleasant surprise every October. Individual flowers were very small and modest, and they came in a form of clusters and lasted for only a couple weeks. Yet, their fragrance was so sweet that they compelled people to slow down and take a deep breath.

Esther finally got to climb up the boulders on Baoshi Mountain once again. West Lake was still so beautiful and peaceful; the mountains in the distance were still so blue and enormous. The water wrinkled beautifully like a silk dress when the breeze passed through like gentle fingers. The city on its east side was so much more modernized and filled with many skyscrapers and huge billboards.

She sat on the boulders and looked at the lake for hours, as if she wanted to bring back all the seasons she missed. She saw the alternating smoky green of willow trees and warm pink of peach flowers greeting many happy visitors on the Bai Causeway in the springs. She saw red water lily flowers in full bloom standing out from the rich, green leaves like beautiful ballerinas in the inner lake in the summers. She saw tree leaves turning red, yellow and golden all around the West Lake in the late fall. She saw heavy white snow reflecting golden sunlight on the Broken Bridge in the winters.

At the Middle of Autumn festival, the family took a big dragon boat to the islet "Three pools mirroring the moon" (三潭印月). This festival was held on every August 15th of the lunar calendar; the moon on this exact night was believed to be brightest for the whole year. This festival was meant for family reunions. Many poems and stories were written throughout thousands of years of history for this festival expressing love and longing for family and hometown. A special desert, "Moon Cake," was dedicated for this festival and was a huge business around this time of the year. This festival fell on different dates of the Western calendar each year and happened to be in early October this time.

The islet was the largest among the three in the lake and was most famous for three stone pagodas close to the shore. It was a perfect night; the moon was bright and full and beautiful. A lit candle was put into each of the pagodas. The candlelight shone through five round holes in each pagoda and reflected on the water, resembling the reflection of the moon. Under the beautiful moonlight, with gentle ripples shimmering on the water, there seemed to be innumerable moons dancing in the lake. The enchanted scene captured everybody's heart; even two little boys were quiet and immersed in this incredible beauty.

They also enjoyed delicious food from many restaurants. There were very few restaurants in the city when Esther grew up. Her family never went out to eat when she was young. Now restaurants were all over the city, with different types of food from all over China.

One memorable meal was at a five-star hotel where May worked as a general manager. May was quite settled in China and was promoted to the position not long ago. The hotel was right next to West Lake by the Su Causeway. Around the hotel lay a huge field of well-trimmed grass. A row of willow trees on the bank waved their branches along the wind like welcoming hosts. It was a very fancy ten-course meal. It started with cold dishes; duck tongue was among them, which was very popular. The main dishes included fresh grouper, Dongpo meat and a slow-cooked duck soup with bamboo shoots. It ended with seasonal fruits, including lychee.

Esther's favorite was Dongpo meat. The dish was named after the same poet that the Su Causeway was. Su was his last name and Dongpo was his first name. He was not only a famous poet who loved Hang-Zhou, but also a beloved official for the city during the Song Dynasty. The meat took a long time to cook. It was arranged like a traditional temple and looked bright and tender and mouth-watering. When Esther put a piece of meat in her mouth, it simply melted.

What could be better in life? Esther thought.

It was a different story with David and Joseph. When they were asked what they would like to order, they could not wait to ask for fried rice and fried dumplings. They showed so much enthusiasm for their favorite food, which made everybody laugh.

American kids! Esther also laughed. There were so many more treasures in Chinese culture. She was determined to keep her kids connected with their roots.

They took a family portrait in the oldest studio in town. The last time they took family photos was right before Esther left for the United States. Twelve years flew by, and so many things changed! The family expanded and the third generation grew up. However, they lost Ling whom they missed every day in their hearts. Somehow, unspoken memories of Ling bonded them together and made them all closer.

Qing and Hua sat in the front with big grins on their faces. Esther stood next to Jian behind their parents. She put her hands on Hua's shoulders. Jian's wife was on the other side of Jian. She was a big-hearted lady with an easygoing personality. Hannah stood next to Qing and put her elbow on his shoulder. Joshua was next to Esther, and he put his hands on David, who stood in the front and next to Hua. Joseph, being the youngest, stood in between Qing and Hua. Everybody smiled happily!

Esther also visited with middle school and college friends. Some of them were running architectural design firms and were crazy busy. China was like a gigantic construction site, with many ongoing residential and commercial developments. Some of her friends worked for high-tech companies. Esther heard that a local company called Alibaba was expanding very quickly.

She visited May and her husband, Ming, in their house. May was battling with health issues again, though. Her body was a little swollen because of all the medication she had to take. Her once striking beauty was no longer visible.

No one can escape the spell of time, Esther sadly thought.

Ming's business was doing very well. With his humble attitude and low-key personality, he gained much support from his former bosses and colleagues in the city government. Their only son was about David's age. Their son stayed in a boarding daycare center for the weekdays and only came home for the weekends because both parents were too busy at work.

Every young family was allowed to have only one child, according to a national policy of One Family, One Child. May admitted that they probably did not have time or energy for another child anyway, even if the policy was different. Yet, they did envy that Esther had two children.

It was very rare for young Chinese to own a single-family house in the early 2000s. Their house was in a suburb of HangZhou and had a huge yard and many old trees. The house had many luxuries that Esther did not have in her own house in the United States. What impressed Esther the most was the master bathroom. It was fully equipped and included a fancy toilet with a seat warmer and a bidet. It was obvious that May enjoyed her upper-class status in the society.

Esther also took the kids and went back to her parents' hometown, WenZhou. Her grandma had long since passed away, before David was even born. Esther regretted not having the opportunity to see her grandma again. What a hefty price she paid for her American dream! She missed all the developments in China over the last twelve years. She missed spending time with her parents and her family. She did not get to see her sister Ling one last time. She missed the chance to visit her grandma one more time.

Her life would be very different if she had stayed in her homeland. *Would it be better?*

Still, she did not doubt her decision to move to the United States. Her new country still represented freedom and opportunity. Twelve years after she left China, she had established herself in the United States with a good career and a family with two young sons. She was proud of her accomplishments. The only imperfection was that her husband, Kevin, did not come with them.

Her grandma's previous farm town was now more like a city. Just like what happened in HangZhou, the rice fields were all gone. Instead, there were high-rise apartments and factory buildings. Her cousins captured opportunities of free enterprise when China switched its focus to economic development in the late 1970s after the Cultural Revolution. They ran their own businesses of all kinds for decades, ranging from orchid farming to manufactory of everyday goods like shoes and sunglasses all the way to accessories for personal vehicles. Some of them had already diversified their businesses and delved into other businesses such as real estate. One of her cousins expanded her real estate business throughout China. The next generation grew up helping their parents with family businesses and now started taking leadership roles.

Her aunts and cousins gave them a big welcome. Banquets were given in her name, and both David and Joseph were treated like royalty. The two little boys were once again spoiled.

While their time with family and friends in China was as pleasant as a sweet dream, the trip back home brought Esther back to reality. During the nine-hour flight across the Pacific Ocean, Joseph could not sit still for one minute. The plane cabin was huge, with only one big TV screen on the front. There was no onboard entertainment at all. For nine hours, Joseph ran around the cabin, stopped at every restroom and played with every doorknob. Esther was exhausted from watching over him. David, on the other hand, fell asleep right after he read a book.

At the Los Angeles airport, both kids fell asleep. When they needed to board the next flight, Esther carried sleeping Joseph with her right arm and his head resting on her shoulder. She pulled sleepy David forward with her left hand.

"Why can't you carry me?" David murmured, half-asleep as they headed toward the plane.

She carried a huge backpack and another small purse hung down from the other shoulder. She had probably more burdens than a soldier on the frontlines. Yet, there was no complaint of any size in her heart; she was happy and content with her boys around her.

Kevin picked them up at the Houston airport with a big smile. Apparently, he missed his wife and kids. Esther saw hope for her marriage and family.

She started looking for a new job right away. With her engineering experience and executive MBA credentials, it was not long before she found a great position with a leading energy company, Prudent Oil. She was assigned to a billion-dollar project, which was to develop an off-shore oil field in alliance with China Oil. Her responsibility was to oversee the entire structural engineering portion of the project. She became a critical member of the owner's project management team.

CHAPTER 23

The Abyss

Not long after, Kevin broke some major news to Esther. They were chatting in the kitchen after dinner. Little Joseph was happily riding his tricycle around the kitchen island. Kevin quickly became very angry and raised his voice when he brought up Leah's name. Joseph was shocked by his father's anger and started crying. He looked up to Esther, who gestured to him that it was not about him. Little Joseph calmed down and continued his merry ride.

Leah had finally told her family the truth. She had resided in Houston the entire time and never moved to Arizona. She had moved in with Sam and given birth to a baby girl. They were now married.

"She has been living in Houston the whole time! She is busy getting pregnant and giving birth, while I am building the house for her!" Kevin shouted. "I took pictures and texted her about the progress every day! She fooled me! And my parents!"

Crazy lies, Esther thought to herself. But at the same time, she felt deeply sad that Leah had to go this far to have a child of her own. Without a doubt, her parents would not give their permission for her marriage to Sam. Without a doubt, they would have told her to have another abortion. Esther was very sympathetic towards Leah. As a woman, Esther understood Leah's urgent desire to have a child and start a family in her mid-thirties.

After all, is it not her right to have her own family and her own child?

Now Esther had more understanding of why Leah yelled at her for no reason last time. Leah was already pregnant; however, she had to hide her pregnancy from her parents who were living with her under the same roof. She must have had many conflicting thoughts and was mentally unstable. Esther shared her thoughts with Kevin.

Kevin softened a bit, yet he protested, "Doesn't she care whom she has her baby with?"

Esther packed many bags of baby clothes and toys for Leah's daughter, and Kevin took them to Leah. His parents were very angry when they heard about the generous gifts.

"Why are you so nice to her? She is a bitch! She does not deserve any sympathy!" Feng yelled on the phone.

"We do not accept this child! She is the daughter of a dog!" Liu declared in his usual cold voice.

Feng made three dolls to represent Leah, Sam and their daughter. Feng put their pictures on the dolls. Because she did not have a picture of the newborn, Feng used a picture of Leah's dog instead. She stuck needles into the dolls and repeated curses of death onto them every day. Feng was not ashamed of her actions, and she told her children exactly what she did.

Esther was beyond shocked and felt a chill travel up her spine when she heard about their attitudes. She could not comprehend her parents-in-law and the depth of their hatred towards Leah and her family.

Is Leah's marriage so shameful that she is better off to die? Do they have the right to decide whether and how she lives? Is saving face more important than their own granddaughter?

Are they evil? Esther could not help thinking this way.

Kevin once again grew more and more distant from her and the kids as if he was sucked into another world. He would not talk to Esther for days and weeks. Esther often wondered what was going on in his mind.

Yes, a new business is not easy, but I haven't asked for one penny from you, Esther thought. *Yes, you need to take care of your parents. But you have responsibilities to your wife and your kids, too! Why do you leave all the responsibilities to me? I am taking care of two kids and working full-time and paying all the bills!*

Esther was tired of reasoning with him; she knew it would go nowhere. She barely had the energy to initiate a serious conversation after a long day's work, especially when the other party never showed any interest. His attitude was loud and clear.

What can you do now that you are bound to two kids?

He retreated into his own world, one to which Esther was not invited. And Esther started losing interest in being part of it this time around.

In her spare time, Esther spent many hours upgrading the house and adding new furniture. One of the changes she made was to replace the carpet with wood for the floors, which would help alleviate David's allergy symptoms. She did everything by herself for this upgrade, from selecting the vendor and choosing the color and style of the floor, to making the appointments and coordinating the actual installation. The night before the installation, Esther was not sure about the color she chose. She tossed around in bed for the whole night but did not talk to Kevin about it. After all, the man did not seem to care about anything she was doing or thinking. Esther felt very lonely while Kevin was sleeping right next to her in the same bed.

The next day, the crew came and installed the floor. They first moved furniture around. Esther made sure that they placed Kevin's desk in such a way that he could start working as soon as he arrived home. It was exactly what Kevin did; he ignored all the stuff going on, went to his desk directly, and started on his work without a word. His action saddened her.

Is this man my husband?

She could not help but wonder how their marriage ended up in such a spot. It became clear to her, though, that something was very wrong.

Soon after Kevin told Esther that his parents wanted to come back to the United States again. Apparently, his parents would live in her house since they were not on good terms with Leah. The news frightened her. Intuitively, she knew her marriage could not survive another round of attack.

"Do you want to see frowning faces when you come home from work? You know what will happen if we all live together again." Esther carefully raised her objection to Kevin. She practically had to tiptoe around him these days.

"I do not," Kevin answered without any emotion; he looked tired.

"We will have to divorce!" Esther added.

Kevin did not say anything.

"How about we buy another house for your parents in the same neighborhood? They could live close by, and we can stay peaceful," Esther suggested.

Kevin did not answer. Esther would not mind that Kevin spent all his money on his parents if they could just leave her family alone. However, one thing that his parents wanted so much was to not appear to be a financial burden. An extra airline ticket to Florida put their logic on full display. Kevin was so ready to buy an extra airline ticket for Liu, but Liu did not want to be responsible for the extra cost.

The extra cost of a house was so obvious and much bigger than an airline ticket! There would be no way for them to accept a house. Esther knew they would not accept this suggestion. She felt desperate when facing their way of thinking. There may be more to their way of thinking, though.

Maybe they must live with their children under the same roof because they are miserable all by themselves. Furthermore, they probably find enjoyment in controlling their children's lives. In other words, screwing up their children's lives!

Esther figured out that this may be the real reason behind their actions.

Are they acting this way unconsciously or deliberately? She was not sure.

Nevertheless, Esther decided to take matters into her own hands. She started looking into government-aided apartments for the elderly in Chinatown. Those apartments were the best options available for Chinese elderly not only because they were virtually free but also because of their convenient location. Shops and restaurants were within walking distance, and Chinese was spoken on every corner.

If they can stay here in a seniors' apartment, they cannot be angry about me for not being able to live in our house.

Esther believed she had found the best solution, and Kevin seemed supportive of the idea. Esther found a new apartment building that was being built and would be ready by the time his parents arrived. Better yet, she had a personal connection with the developer who was a well-known businessman in the community. Esther met him in a minority leadership meeting. She contacted the man and arranged a meeting for her family to meet with him. The kind man explained that selection of residents for the new apartment would be very much like a lottery system since the demand was so much higher than the supply. He hinted that he would do his best to help.

One late afternoon, Esther received a phone call from a general manager of the new apartment building.

"Applications for new apartments can be submitted tomorrow morning when the office opens. But word is out, and people are lining up outside of my office right now," she said. "You better come and get in line as soon as possible; otherwise, it would be too late."

Esther sent Kevin there right away, and Kevin waited in line throughout the whole night. The next morning when the office opened, there were already more people in line than available slots. Kevin was among the lucky ones and was assigned an apartment unit. Those who came in the morning found out they were already too late to even apply, and many fierce arguments broke out. Esther had a sense of hope that she might be able to save her marriage now that her parents-in-law would not have to live in her house.

Way before the apartment was ready to move into, Kevin started talking about letting his parents come to the States. Esther did not know why they were in such a hurry but knew that she could not raise an objection to delay their trip. One morning, Esther received a phone call from Kevin who urged her to buy tickets for his parents. She did not want to, and she knew Kevin was fully aware of her thoughts on the matter. However, it was very difficult for Esther to say no to Kevin. She still wanted so badly to please him.

Esther knew Kevin was not treating her fairly, let alone lovingly. As a matter of fact, he was so cold to her most of the time that it was almost like a grace that he cared to call her and ask for her help. She hung onto the little warmth of his voice and hoped it would somehow do a miracle to their relationship.

A wife desires to please her husband by nature. But this nature could be abused and cause much harm. The harm is usually towards the wife. Yet, it has a profound damage on her children and her entire family that may not be known until years later. It takes wisdom and courage for a wife to make sure that this nature will do good instead of harm. It is best, though, that she does not have to put herself in such difficulty when she must guard this nature.

Esther did not have this wisdom yet.

Maybe it will not be too bad since they will be moving out a few months later when the apartment is ready, she persuaded herself.

Esther called a travel agent whom she knew well for airline tickets. The prices were very favorable, and she bought tickets the same day.

She did not feel at ease about the purchase, and an inner voice told her to stop at every step. Yet, she pushed the voice away again and again.

Kevin called his parents right away and told them about the tickets. He added at the end of the conversation, "Esther welcomes you, and she is the one who bought the tickets for you."

Her heart sank. She knew it was a terrible idea to allow his parents to live in her house. She did not stop the bad idea; she helped it to become a reality. She hated herself that she could never say no to Kevin.

His parents arrived at midnight. It was late afternoon of the next day when Esther first saw them. While she was preparing dinner in the kitchen, Kevin took his parents out of the house. Esther had no idea where they were going. Feng did not cast a single look in Esther's direction, pointing her nose toward the sky.

Liu came to Esther like he was an old acquaintance. He said in a cheerful voice, like a little child's, "Oh, you are cooking broccoli."

Esther simply nodded. She was not surprised by his strange greeting. Kevin came back to the house a minute later. He pretended that he needed to drink some water.

"I am taking my parents to my sister's house," he told Esther.

It dawned on her—his parents wanted to teach Leah a lesson! She had no idea what they were going to do, but she sensed it might be something serious. She felt a chill crawling up her spine. She pleaded with Kevin, "You need to talk to your parents and calm them down."

He clearly wanted to say something but held back. He looked uneasy and even a little nervous, like a dormant volcano about to erupt. He had to be urged by his parents to go back quickly to the car. They probably ordered him not to tell Esther anything, like they always did. He left without a word.

Esther worried so much for Leah and desperately wanted to warn her. She looked all over through her address book for Leah's phone number but could not find it. It was several years since Leah's senseless accusation, and the two women never talked to each other afterwards. Even after Esther sent all the baby gifts to Leah, Leah did not contact her or say a word of appreciation.

Esther went through her address book again and tried to find someone who might know Leah. She placed a few phone calls but could not get ahold of anybody; it was dinnertime and everybody was busy. There seemed to be a big void between her and Leah, which swallowed up her voice of warning. Finally, she gave up and switched her focus to her kids.

Kevin came back home alone later. Esther had already sent the kids to bed and was finishing up in the kitchen. He looked a bit shaken.

"Where are your parents?" Esther was puzzled.

"They stayed with my sister," he answered expressionlessly.

Maybe things are not so bad, Esther felt a little relieved. *After all, they are all family.*

Right after midnight, Esther was awakened by a heavy banging on the front door. She got up and went to the living room. She was almost blinded by all the blinking lights from police cars outside her house. Several police officers were talking to Kevin at the front door.

"He is pretending he doesn't know anything!" one officer said to another loudly with a laugh of disbelief. Kevin was still murmuring.

"Do not take your parents to your sister's house again," they warned in a serious tone and left. Apparently, his parents were sent back to the house by the police and were in their room upstairs.

Esther was astonished. She could not comprehend what was going on.

"What happened?" she asked Kevin.

But he did not say anything.

Esther received a call from Leah a couple of days later, and they met for lunch. Leah told her what happened that night. Leah and her family were having dinner at their house when they heard loud noises outside. They had just moved into their brand-new house not long ago. It was the same house that her parents wanted her to buy and planned to live in with her for the rest of their lives. It was the same house that was built under Kevin's supervision from beginning to end. Many moving boxes were not yet open and were still stacked in the garage. Their cars were parked at the front of the garage and right outside the kitchen.

"Thief!" Sam responded to the loud noises and rushed out of the back door.

It was Kevin and his parents who surrounded Sam's truck and were damaging it. Liu was banging on the front hood with a big rock. Feng busted the driver's side window with a hammer. Kevin used a knife and scratched the entire driver's side.

Upon seeing Sam, Kevin grabbed him and pointed a gun against his head before he pushed Sam back into the house. His parents followed. Terrified, Leah grabbed her baby and ran out of the house through the front door. She screamed for help on the street. Her parents ran out after her. Sam also ran out, followed by Kevin. In the middle of the street, her parents turned around and grabbed Sam. They kicked and beat him. Kevin joined his parents and kicked Sam harshly in his crotch. Sam did not fight back. Several neighbors came out and tried to stop the beating. The three finally stopped and retreated to the house. Leah, with her baby in tow, took Sam to a nearby hospital to get checked out and wrap up his wounds.

In the hospital, Leah and Sam came to their senses and realized that they needed some protection. She called 911 and asked for a police officer to accompany them back to their house. It was almost midnight when they returned, only to find her parents in their house. Liu and Feng already went to bed in the master bedroom. They refused to leave when the officer asked them to.

"This is my house," Feng screamed.

"Can you prove that this is your house?" the American police officer asked, confused.

Feng grabbed a pot. "Look! This is my pot. I brought it from China."

The police officer looked at the pot; it was an American brand. He laughed and shook his head in disbelief.

"You have two choices: either go back to your son's house or go to jail."

"I want to go to jail," Liu answered.

"I do not want to go back to my son's house because I hate his wife!" Feng protested. "I am going to die soon. My doctor said that I only have three months to live!"

It was neither the first time nor the last time when Feng declared she would die soon. They were sent back to Esther's house by a police car. The next day Leah and Sam filed a restraining order against Kevin and her parents.

"I don't know what to do." Leah repeated the same phrase again and again. She looked confused and dismayed.

Esther's mind went blank. She did not know what to think. Things turned out to be so much worse than she could have ever imagined. She felt dizzy.

What would happen to me if they could treat their own daughter and sister this way?

How could my husband be so crazy and violent?

Who am I living with?

Her heart kept falling into a bottomless abyss.

CHAPTER 24

Total Darkness

Esther went home and did not breathe a word about her conversation with Leah to Kevin or his parents. She went on with her routine—going to work and taking care of the kids—and pretended she knew nothing. She was afraid that they would instantly label her as their enemy if they knew she knew about the incident and was on Leah's side.

Esther often felt like she was a background plant in the house. This overlooked plant took care of the kids and the house and paid all the bills. Her parents-in-law did not talk to her, and her husband rarely acknowledged her. Every night Kevin went to his parents' bedroom and talked to them behind a closed door right after dinner. He would stay in their room for hours until after the kids went to bed. She did not complain, though. She did not want any of their attention because it would only lead them to attack her.

What she did not know was that her parents-in-law had considered her as an enemy from the very beginning. This time around they left her alone because they had bigger enemies: their own daughter and her family.

Kevin finally decided to tell Esther what happened that night. His version of the story was that Leah and Sam attacked his parents.

"Why would your sister and your brother-in-law attack your parents?" she asked, pretending that she was hearing about the incident for the first time. She looked him in the eyes. He would not look back at her. He did not answer her question.

Kevin and his parents hired an American defense lawyer for the civil lawsuit Leah brought against them. Esther knew about this lawyer. He was well-known for his nasty demeanor and nonstop flirtation with every Chinese woman whom he could talk to.

"Why did you hire this guy? He has a bad reputation," Esther asked, feeling ashamed by her husband's association with him.

"You are right; he can be nasty. It is exactly why we need him." Kevin was proud of his choice.

Esther was speechless.

Not long afterward, Esther found many pictures on her camera showing wounds on Liu's arms and legs. There were many wounds of different depths and lengths. The wounds were clearly self-inflicted by knife to manufacture evidence against Leah and Sam. From what Leah told her, there was no time for Sam or Leah to injure Liu at all, let alone so many times. Esther was stunned and disgusted by the sight of these wounds.

Why did he hate his own daughter and his own flesh and blood this much? Esther could not comprehend it. *Furthermore, did he try to fool the United States justice system by manufacturing false evidence?*

What she heard about the Cultural Revolution became a reality in her own home. During the Cultural Revolution, friends and families turned against each other and manufactured false evidence for political persecution. History often repeated itself because of deep-rooted values and tradition. Although Esther left China and built her life on the other side of the planet, Chinese tradition had followed her. Now the worst part of this tradition manifested in her home in the land of America.

Esther was beyond furious. She now realized that she was living with evil spirits. She showed the pictures to Kevin and shouted, "What are these pictures? Is this the Cultural Revolution all over again?"

Kevin did not reply. The pictures were deleted from her camera soon after.

One late afternoon while preparing a meal in the kitchen, Esther happened to turn around and saw Liu walking into the room behind her. He was staring at the back door, and he was not looking her way. A strong desire to kill was written all over his face; she felt a chill running down her spine. She had a terrible feeling that something was about to go very wrong, and she was learning to trust such feelings.

Weeks and months went by. The trio still had their endless meeting behind the closed bedroom door every night. Kevin took his parents back to his sister's house a few times, but apparently no agreements were reached. The lawsuit continued. Esther tried to pull Kevin out of this insanity.

"You know your sister just wants to have her own child," Esther said to Kevin in a soft tone. She tried hard not to stir up his anger.

"Does that mean she can just sleep with anything?" His voice was filled with anger and disdain.

What did your words even mean? Esther wondered.

"You have known Sam for a long time. He is also a human being." Esther was careful to give her reasoning.

"Do you mean that my parents are not human beings?" Kevin was angrier.

Why cannot everybody be human beings? Is not this a fact? Esther was puzzled by his reasoning. But his attitude prevented any further conversation.

Esther had a few more serious conversations with Kevin and asked him to reconcile with his sister. Every time they talked, Kevin softened up and seemed convinced. A few hours later, though, he returned to Esther and totally changed his mind. His mouth opened, and his parents' words came out. He accused Esther of being manipulative and full of scheming tactics. Esther felt hopeless because her husband was being pulled further away to a place of no return, and she could do nothing.

Leah contacted Esther a few more times and updated her on the latest events. Esther took her out a few times for lunch. Esther had a lot of sympathy for Leah; they both were persecuted by this family at the most vulnerable time—childbirth—in their lives. It mystified her how there could be so much misery during childbirth, which was supposed to be the most joyful time for a family.

Esther felt that she and Leah forged an unlikely alliance due to the same rejection by their family. At least somebody understood her pain. However, one conversation broke the alliance. Leah told Esther that Kevin showed up at her house a few more times, even though her restraining order against him was still in effect. Sam had purchased a gun and decided to act if Kevin attacked him again.

"There won't be a second time. I won't let him attack me and my family anymore!" Sam declared.

Leah told Esther that they would retaliate if Kevin did anything to their child.

Why involve my children? Esther was astonished to hear the threat.

Sensing Esther's anger, Leah explained that she cared deeply about David and Joseph. But her child was more important to her. She inferred that if something happened to her child, Kevin would have to feel the same pain as she did.

But this means my children! What about my pain? Why do my children have to suffer?

Esther stared at Leah in absolute horror, as if she was staring into the eye of a hurricane. Her world was already swept halfway into this big storm, and now her kids would be the next ones to be swallowed up?

After all that I have done for you, this is how you treat me? Esther could not help but think this way as she stared, dumbfounded, at Leah.

Esther knew Leah was reluctant to voice such a threat; nevertheless, it was a real threat! It was a crazy, horrific threat—a threat to her children! She knew that Leah was trying to warn Kevin off from further harmful actions. What she could not accept was that Leah was using her two innocent children as tools in Leah's own family war!

Esther was never more fearful in her life. This family war was like a hurricane that kept intensifying and expanding, ready to destroy anything in its reach. Esther had this terrifying feeling that somebody had to die before it was over.

Again and again, the picture of a desolate house with its roof blown away came to her mind. Kevin, who was supposed to be the roof for the house, was long gone. Esther was the last wall standing, trying her best to shield her kids from the flying debris all around them. Esther was fearful that her house was engulfed in the hurricane and could be shattered into pieces in the blink of an eye.

Esther tried again to convince Kevin to settle the case.

"Leave Leah and her family alone! What if they retaliate by hurting our kids?" Esther begged. She did not mention that it was a real threat from Leah; instead, she pretended it was just a mother's worry.

"How dare they!" Kevin raised his voice like he was the king of the world. His confidence soon gave way to a sense of doubt.

Esther did not know whether this conversation helped to slow them down. They still talked behind that closed door every night. One day, Esther happened to go to Feng's bedroom and saw a letter written by Feng. The letter was written to a judge of the civil case. Feng listed all the sacrifices she made for Leah and condemned Leah for her betrayal.

"My daughter, who I raised up with sweat and blood, betrayed me!" Feng dripped a few drops of blood on the paper to emphasize her point.

Esther was more terrified at the sight of the blood. She felt like a total darkness had fallen on her house and her life. The darkness grew denser every day and could swallow her up. She needed light desperately.

She could have had some light if she had been baptized the month prior. Her church had a baptism meeting, and she thought she was ready. However, during her readiness talk with a church leader, she confessed that she did not have one hundred percent faith in Jesus. Her faith was probably around seventy percent. She was told to wait and think it over.

Why do I always have to be so honest? Esther questioned herself. If she could just give the answer that the leader wanted, she would have been baptized by now, and surely, she would have light in her heart that could break through the darkness!

But honesty was her nature, especially when it came to faith, which was such a serious matter. She could not cheat herself; furthermore, she did not dare to cheat God who knew her heart. Honesty was in the blood of her family. Her dad Qing confessed the scribble on a piece of paper was his writing during the Cultural Revolution. The confession cost him years of wrongful persecution, yet he never had a doubt about his confession.

"Somebody else would suffer if I did not confess," he gave his reasoning in a casual conversation. Having a clean conscience meant more to him.

Esther had more respect for her father nowadays. She used to think Qing was a little weak; now she realized he had great strength for being honest throughout his life regardless of all the wrongs and struggles he had to endure. She saw firsthand how deceptiveness increased and intensified in Kevin's family and was about to destroy the whole family.

Esther could not blame herself for being honest. But the light she experienced after she started reading the Bible became dim in the face of the overwhelming darkness around her.

I need light!

CHAPTER 25

Deadly Hurricane

Esther's mental picture of a roofless house manifested in a busy hurricane season. Hurricane Katrina not only blew away many roofs but also breached the levy and flooded the city of New Orleans. The whole city was devastated. Houston opened its arms to the displaced residents of New Orleans and welcomed them with Texas-sized hospitality.

Just a month later, Hurricane Rita became a threat to Houston. Days before its expected arrival, news about Rita from all media platforms intensified and bombarded every resident. All the forecasts predicted that it could be worse than Katrina and more damaging. Memories of Katrina and its aftermath were still so vivid, people in Houston started to panic. Every family pondered the idea of evacuation. The day before its landing, roads and streets were already flooded with cars fleeing the city. It took Esther three hours to get home from work instead of the usual thirty minutes.

Esther discussed the matter with Kevin for a few days, and he suggested that Esther take their kids and drive to Dallas by herself. May's sister was still living in Dallas and had already invited them to go to her house. Kevin had to stay behind with all his inventory, some of which was stored outside in the open. It was too late to move them indoors. It was also too late to get insurance for the inventory; Kevin called a few insurance companies at the last minute and was outright rejected.

Esther started packing for the trip in the late afternoon while worrying about the drive to Dallas under such terrifying circumstances. She did not know how long the drive would take since so many people seemed to get on the same roads. She did not know whether they would be caught by the hurricane on the way there. One thing she did know was that two little boys wanted to eat and poo no matter where they were.

The boys will need a little potty.

Esther lost her confidence at taking this trip on her own at the sight of the little potty. In the meantime, Kevin came back to her and told her a different plan that he came up with his parents. Esther was hopeful that the new plan would give her much needed help. Their plan was that Esther would take Feng with her on the trip, and Liu would stay behind and help Kevin take care of the store and the inventory. Esther almost threw up when she heard the plan.

In addition to the two little children, they also wanted her to take care of Feng. This time around, she would not believe the lie that Feng could help her take care of the boys. Furthermore, Feng could have a medical emergency on the trip because of her terrible health condition. If something happened to Feng, Esther for sure was doomed for the rest of her life.

Esther was reminded of Feng's childhood story in which Feng was put in the front of a pack of adult merchants in the dark forest where many wolves wandered about. She now totally understood the fear of the little girl. She grew angry at this selfish proposal but managed to push her mounting fury down.

"Who is going to help me?" she stared at Kevin in disbelief.

Kevin sensed the absurdity of the entire proposal and ended the conversation. Immediately afterwards, Esther unexpectedly received an international phone call from China. It was her brother, Jian.

"Don't leave home! It is safer to stay home where you can find help. It is too dangerous for you to be on the road alone with the kids!" Jian was very firm.

Esther remembered she had told her dad on the phone about the evacuation plan the day before. Her family in China also knew about the hurricane and was closely watching its development. Esther was able to stay in touch with her family through phone calls in the middle 2000s because the cost of an international call to China had dropped significantly. However, an international call to the United States from China was still expensive and inconvenient. It was the first time Jian had called her since she came to the United States, and it was so timely. To Esther, her brother's advice was a message from God. She decided to stay home instead of evacuating.

In the face of great danger, it was her family from the other side of the earth who gave her much needed help. Although they were so far away physically, their love was right here with her.

True love supports you no matter where you are.

The city government released their statement later on the TV and encouraged residents of Houston to evacuate. More than one million people from all over the city scrambled to exit, piling onto the roads and highways. The side of every highway exiting the city quickly became a parking lot while the other side was totally empty.

For days, cars were stuck on highways in the unforgiving September Texas heat. A drive to any nearby major city that would usually take several hours turned into a several-day nightmare. What made it even worse was that cell phones did not work anymore. The systems were overloaded and crashed because everybody tried to connect to friends and family. Those on the road were on their own without any help. It was a time of terror and desperation.

Many people abandoned their cars on the roads. Some ran out of gas because they could not get their cars to a gas station in time. Some ran out of food, so they walked long ways to look for food and drink. Some people died on the road due to heat and exhaustion.

Later a bus loaded with nursing home patients caught on fire and exploded right outside of Dallas. It was a horrific scene: a bus burning in the middle of miles and miles of personal vehicles. Twenty-four people on the bus died in the fire.

Esther could not imagine what would have happened if she had taken the trip to Dallas with her kids and Feng. She did not believe that they could have safely made it. Feng could possibly have passed out or even died during the three-day road trip. Even if they made it, the terror of being stuck on the highway with the worries of running out of gas and food, without any means of communication to family and friends, and with a burning bus in sight, would probably have haunted them for the rest of their lives!

The next morning, when everyone was fleeing the city, Esther and the family prepared the house for the hurricane. Before Kevin left for his work, he asked Esther to go to the store with him.

"What about the kids?" Esther was confused.

She was surprised by his immature and selfish request. Nevertheless, she felt a little bit of comfort because her husband needed her in the face of danger. He was distant and cold for a long time. Kevin withdrew his proposal, but he seemed frightened and uneasy when he left for the store.

Hurricane Rita weakened before its landing and took a surprising turn to the northeast after it landed. Houston was barely affected. The damage caused by the unplanned evacuation was far greater than damage from the hurricane itself. Esther felt lucky that she and her kids did not have to go through all the suffering. She came to a painful realization, though, that Kevin was not reliable either in family conflicts or in natural disasters.

Esther continued to live carefully in her house, trying not to attract any attention. But one thing made her so angry that she could not hold back. Feng's big red comb was in her shower.

"Why did your parents take a shower in our bathroom? They have their own bathroom right next to their room," Esther asked Kevin.

"My mom said it would save you some money in housecleaning if we all used the same bathroom." Kevin acted innocent as if his parents were doing her a big favor. Esther hired a cleaning lady to clean the house once a month. She did not mind paying a little more to clean the upstairs where his parents lived. One time, however, his parents refused to let the cleaning lady enter their rooms to clean.

Esther was disgusted by their excuse. Nevertheless, she did not continue the argument because she knew she could not win against their pretention. The next day, she found her beauty razor broken and lying on the ground in the shower.

From her experience, the razor would not break from falling to the ground because it was sturdily built. Even if her parents-in-law dropped it by accident and it broke, they should have picked it up and put it together. After all, it was her shower to start with! Esther knew that his parents wanted to start a fight against her despite her efforts to avoid it.

"What is this? Why did your parents break my razor?" Esther asked Kevin. This time she was ready for a fight.

"What is the big deal? It simply dropped!" Kevin became angrier than her.

He picked up the razor, put it back together and then threw it to the ground violently. It did not break. He picked it up and threw it again. It still did not break. He did it a third time. It remained in one piece.

Esther looked at him calmly. Finally, Kevin left the room in a rage.

Esther decided to leave her shower to her parents-in-law and take showers in the kids' shower instead.

"Why are you using this shower?" Kevin asked with a sense of guilt when he found out about the change.

"I don't mind," Esther responded in a cheerful tone.

She counted down the days that she had to suffer while her parents-in-laws lived in her house. The seniors' apartment in Chinatown was going to be ready for them to move into in six months. After they moved there, her life would be restored. It was her only hope.

CHAPTER 26

The Unthinkable

Esther enjoyed her work on the mega-billion-dollar offshore oil field development project, which was both exciting and challenging. The project designed, built and installed multiple offshore facilities, including production platforms and a FPSO. Esther joined the project when design of the offshore facilities was well underway in the United States and construction just began in China.

Esther was now the lead structural engineer for the project. It was quite smooth to work with her fellow team members. Most of them were gray-haired oil field veterans and saw the ups and downs of the oil industry over the course of many decades. Again, she was the only female engineer as well as the youngest on the engineering team. She was also well accepted by her Chinese counterparts in this alliance because of her Chinese background.

It was very difficult to work with the contractors, though. In addition to their obvious defensive nature, her youthful appearance did not earn her immediate respect. Every time she challenged an engineer—who was usually much older—she faced strong objection. She never gave up; she leveraged support from top managers on both sides as well as from her fellow team members and had her requests implemented.

One time she discovered a huge design flaw. A drilling package was designed by a small contractor while the offshore platform where that drilling package would be placed and supported was designed by the main EPC contractor. The small contractor forgot to inform the main contractor of a significant weight increase of the drilling package; thus, the support on the platform was neither adequately nor properly designed. It would have been disastrous if the mistake had not been caught in time. She pointed out the flaw without embarrassing the contractor. Moving forward, she set up regular coordination meetings between the two contractors so that this type of mistake would not happen again.

Another time Esther found an overlooked design practice that could have caused huge field problems. Many pipe support beams were designed as cantilevered beams that were supported only on one end and free on the other end. Although the design satisfied all the requirements, Esther believed the beams would deflect and not support the pipes, based on her field experience. Consequently, the pipes would be overstressed and fail, which could cause major production problems. Esther requested that the design be changed and all these beams be supported on both ends.

The EPC contractor did not agree with Esther. The contractor's main concern was that this simple design change would require additional material and man-hours in the field. Changes to the supports that were already in place would be especially costly and painful. This time, some of her own colleagues sided with the contractor and did not support her.

Esther called for a formal meeting and brought together management teams of both sides. They made a compromise and decided beams of three feet or longer would be changed and be supported on both ends. Her credibility was further validated toward the end of the project. Those short beams of less than three feet that were left unchanged deflected and twisted and failed to provide proper support just as she predicted. The contractor had to go back and made changes to every single beam on the field, which cost them much more money. Little by little, Esther gradually gained respect from the contractors.

Since all the platforms were being built in China, the management team planned to send her to the construction site to check out the progress. This time she was going back to China as a lead engineer of a major international project! Better yet, she was going to take a few days off afterwards and visit her family. However, the trip was delayed twice for different reasons and was put off for two months. She finally made it the third time in November.

It was a pleasant trip. Esther felt spoiled; she got to fly business class and stay in five-star hotels in China. The area around the construction site was so new and modern; so much had been built over the past few years in this once-small fishing village. She met the entire construction team. The progress of construction went well under the iron control of a construction manager. He was a seventy-year-old British man with about fifty years of experience in the offshore industry. He ran the site almost like a dictator and had strict rules for everyone. Although workers' complaints were widespread, their performance at the site was outstanding.

On her second day after arriving at the construction site, she received an unexpected international phone call from Kevin. Something must be very wrong.

"What happened?" Esther was quite nervous.

"An incident happened," Kevin said in a shaking voice.

"What was it?" Esther's heart was seized with fear. She was fearful for her children.

"My mom died." Kevin started to cry.

"What happened?" Esther was astonished. She felt a slight relief that her children were fine, but she could not comprehend how Feng died so suddenly. Feng was always in bad health but nowhere near death when Esther left for this trip.

"It was an accident," Kevin sobbed. "Can you come home earlier?"

"Sure! I will! Let me talk to my boss," Esther responded with a sense of responsibility like a soldier ready to go to war.

"Take care of yourself! Do not do too much! I will come home and help you!" she added.

Esther decided to leave the construction site and go home the same night. Her manager was fully supportive and assigned a chauffeur to drive her back to Beijing where she could catch an international flight. What made it more complicated was that she had already planned to visit her parents at the end of the business trip. Her parents had waited for her for over two months since her trip was rescheduled twice. Esther did not want to disappoint her parents; however, she knew her husband needed her more at this point. She called her parents and told them about the situation. As she expected, they totally understood and agreed with her decision. They told her to comfort Kevin and sent their condolences for the loss of his mother.

On a two-hour ride back to Beijing, Esther was on the phone nonstop and managed to change all her flights. The earliest available flight back to the United States was the next morning. She called Kevin a few more times before her flights. Kevin turned cold again; his vulnerability in his first phone call was held back. He said that he would explain the situation when she got back home. Esther also called Leah to find out more information instead. What she heard was like a jar of ice-cold water pouring down on her, leaving her freezing from the inside out.

It happened right at the clubhouse of her neighborhood. In front of the beautiful gardens was a small parking lot where Liu practiced parking a car. Esther knew her parents-in-law planned to live in the United States permanently, and Liu wanted to drive around Houston. Kevin often took Liu out and taught him to drive on the weekends. They did not tell Esther their plans or ask for her opinions. She could only guess their intention by watching their actions. She knew from experience that she could not trust their words.

Feng stood behind the car on the sidewalk while Liu practiced backing the car into the parking space. Liu stepped on the gas so hard that the car jumped up the curb and crashed into a brick light stand. The car did not strike Feng directly; rather, it startled her so much that she fell backward and hit her head on the cement ground. She lay in a pool of blood and died right there in front of the red-shingled clubhouse.

Leah received a call from Kevin and rushed to the hospital. Feng was long gone. Before Leah had a minute to grasp the fact and mourn the sudden loss of her mother, Liu and Kevin attacked her verbally.

"It was you who ruined your mother's life!" Liu pointed at Leah with his finger and spat at her face.

Kevin joined his dad in the attack. "You made Mom miserable!"

The unthinkable incident terrified Esther, and she started to shake. Feng's death was so tragic; yet, it was the attitude of Liu and Kevin that startled her even more.

"Why did your dad say this? Was it not he who caused your mother's death? Why does he turn around and accuse you?" Esther asked Leah, puzzled and angry.

"My dad said it was his fault that my mom died, but my fault was much bigger since I did not make her happy when she was alive." Leah sounded a little numb, apparently overwhelmed by sorrow and pain.

"Why did he do this to you? Doesn't he feel guilty?" Esther could not believe what she heard. She wanted to put her arms around Leah.

"He said he already knelt before Kevin and asked for forgiveness," Leah said, as all her strength was drained.

While Feng still lay there in a pool of blood in front of the red-shingled clubhouse, many police cars and ambulances arrived at the scene. Kevin also rushed there. The first thing Liu did was kneel before Kevin.

Is Kevin the only person who was impacted by this incident? What about Leah? And the grandkids? Esther could not understand Liu's reasoning.

Esther now realized that Liu may be the origin of all the miseries. She used to think it was Feng.

"My dad and my brother spent the whole night shouting at me and condemning me! It was like the Cultural Revolution all over again—they are the Red Guards, and I am the enemy of Chairman Mao!" Leah was like a deflated balloon. She probably would have rather been thrown into a corner and left unnoticed.

Liu tried very hard to hide the accident from others. He would monitor Kevin's conversations with others and ask Kevin about the person whom he talked to after every phone call.

This explains why Kevin did not want to tell me the details, Esther thought.

Liu still wanted to apply for his driver's license, even after the incident. Kevin and Leah reluctantly took him to a local DPS office. Upon arrival, Liu jumped out of the car and rushed toward the office with great enthusiasm. He was like a little child running for his prize. Kevin lagged behind and started sobbing. Liu sensed that his joy was inappropriate and finally stopped pursuing the driver's license.

According to Leah, Kevin was totally crushed. He cried almost the whole time for the last couple of days.

Esther had mixed feelings on the trip back to Houston. She thought that all the chaos may subside with Feng's death; however, now she was doubtful of this hope. She was also scared. Things always turned out to be worse than she could have ever imagined.

What else could go wrong?

At the same time, Esther felt fortunate that she was so far away from this unthinkable incident. If she had stayed home, she would have also been attacked by Liu and Kevin. Even worse, they may have somehow accused her of Feng's death.

She realized that the timing of her trip could not have been a coincidence. She was sure that God protected her. He timed her trip perfectly; her China trip was delayed twice, and she was able to make the trip the third time when this incident happened. She was amazed by the way God protected her. He removed her entirely from the whole incident and put her as far away as possible on the other side of the globe.

She was so grateful for God!

CHAPTER 27

Broken Dream

Kevin again was silent and cold when Esther arrived home. He would not talk to her. She busied herself as usual taking care of all the housework and the kids, hoping that it would cheer Kevin up. She bought flowers and visited Feng at the funeral home; she even knelt before the coffin to show her respect.

A few days later at home, Kevin told Esther not to tell anybody that Feng passed away.

"Just tell them that my mom went to live with Leah."

Esther was confused at his request. She thought about it and decided it must be Liu's idea. She did not feel like she could follow such senseless and disrespectful instruction.

She carefully raised her opposition. "Do you think it is fair to your mother?"

"Why can't you make me a little bit happy?" Kevin shouted at her angrily. Their conversation ended.

On the day of the burial, Esther sent Joseph to school and took David with her to the funeral home. She figured that Joseph would be a little too restless for this serious occasion. There were only five people at the burial site: Kevin, Liu, Leah, Esther, and David. Esther bought red roses and handed one to each person. They put the roses on the coffin, and Esther put an additional one on for Joseph.

When the coffin was lowered and covered, Esther held David's hand and then whispered to David to hold Kevin's hand. When David touched Kevin's hand, Kevin lifted his eyes and looked at David and then at Esther. Esther looked back at him to show her support. Kevin looked numb and emotionless, yet he had a tiny bit of appreciation in his eyes. Holding hands with Kevin through David in front of Feng's grave, Esther felt a little bit of connection with her husband.

Many months went by after Feng's burial. Kevin remained as cold and silent as a dead volcano. Most of the time, it was still like two families living under the same roof. Kevin and Liu were one family, and Esther and the kids were another family.

Kevin and Liu now seemed closer than ever. Kevin would drive Liu around and take him out for a meal whenever he had a break. Whenever they went out, Liu would carry Kevin's bag and follow Kevin closely like a servant while Kevin walked ahead like a king. Furthermore, it was as if, to Kevin, Liu now represented Feng. Kevin loved Feng and hated Liu when he grew up. He owed all his achievements to Feng. However, Kevin seemed to redirect all his affection to Liu now that Feng had passed away. The fact that Liu directly caused Feng's death did not seem to matter.

Maybe Kevin wanted to take good care of Liu since Liu was his only remaining parent? But how could he change his feelings so dramatically? Esther was very puzzled. She also was angry that Kevin continued to ignore her and their kids as they remained at the bottom of his priority list.

Thanksgiving soon arrived, and the whole family planned to go to a holiday gathering at Esther's church. This was the first time the whole family would go out together in the same vehicle since Feng passed away. Liu went to the van before Esther; he then returned to the house and pretended to check on the back door so that he got to the van the second time one step behind Esther. Esther realized that he wanted to take the front passenger seat but not to appear that way.

The fight for the front passenger seat was initiated by Feng when the two mothers came to the United States at the same time for the wedding. The fight continued every time his parents came to stay with them; Feng always took the front passenger seat when they went out together. Esther always thought this fight over a seat was ridiculous. She ignored the fight and withdrew herself entirely from it. She would always quietly take the backseat and sit with the kids in the second row. Liu would sit in the third row. She stopped going out with them altogether after a while because she did not want to be around them at all.

Right before Feng's death, Liu started to take the front passenger seat in their outings while Feng sat in a backseat. It signaled a major power shift. Esther knew the significance of this change. She was quite puzzled, but she was too busy to give it one more thought.

This time, when Liu and Esther arrived at the vehicle at the same time, Liu pretended to give the front seat to Esther and said, "You take this seat!"

Knowing his true intentions, Esther also pretended and said, "It is better for me to sit in the back so I can take care of the kids."

Liu took the front seat, looking justified and content. The drive turned out to be chaotic as Kevin was not familiar with the route and Esther gave out driving directions from the backseat.

At church, Zia approached Esther and asked, "Where is your mother-in-law?"

Esther looked around to check on her family. Kevin was sitting with Liu in a corner by themselves, busy eating without talking to each other at all. Her two kids sat close to her at the next table with their friends. One kid said something funny, and all the kids burst into boisterous laughter.

There is no way I can lie about this fact! Not even for my kids' sake! She was determined that she would not participate in their lies this time and forever after.

"She passed away," Esther made it brief. "It was an accident."

Zia went over to Kevin and Liu and gave her condolences. Kevin looked very angry on the way back home. Esther pretended nothing happened.

The senior living apartment was finally finished; the news of its completion was in the headlines of every local Chinese newspaper. Those who were allocated a unit were like lottery winners and were the envy of many seniors around the town. However, Kevin and Liu did not seem to be happy about the move—or maybe they just pretended they were not happy. They acted like Esther kicked Liu out of their house.

Now with Liu living in the senior-living apartment, it was the four of them in the house again. However, Kevin still did not talk to Esther at all. He stopped eating dinner at home, either. The only time she saw him was late at night. By that time Esther had picked up the kids from daycare after work, cooked the meal and fed the kids, and done a million other things already. She was usually reading to the boys on the sofa when he walked into the house. It was the same sectional sofa they owned for a while, and a floor lamp stood behind the turn. The light glowed warmly down on the three of them. It was a rare moment when she could relax with the boys for a little while before they went to bed.

When Kevin walked in, he would not even look at them. Instead, he headed right to his study room. All that Esther could see was his back. She could literally see Feng's face on his back laughing at her.

"Ha Ha Ha! You will never have him!"

David would usually jump down from her lap and run after Kevin. He would end up sitting on Kevin's briefcase and playing chess with Kevin in the study room. Kevin continued working on his computer while playing chess with David halfheartedly. Joseph also would jump down and go play with his toys. This gave Esther a little break before rounding them up for bed.

On Esther's birthday, Esther suggested going out for dinner. Kevin was only interested if Liu could join them, so she reluctantly agreed. The restaurant was very close to Kevin's store. It was a rainy afternoon, and the traffic was extremely busy during rush hour. After a long day of work, Esther picked up both boys from their school and then picked up Liu from his senior apartment before driving across town to the restaurant. She was totally exhausted by the time she arrived. It probably took Kevin less than five minutes to drive there, and he simply showed up by himself. They ate dinner in silence. There was neither conversation nor laughter among them. Kevin was attentive to Liu as if it was Liu's birthday. He totally ignored her and the kids.

What's the point of all my efforts? Esther swallowed more sadness.

Esther had no idea what Kevin was thinking or doing. He was a closed door to her, which she lost interest in trying to open. The only time Kevin talked to Esther was to drop a few bombs of insults or guilt.

"I should have divorced you way earlier. Then I could have given my mom a few good years of her life," Kevin told her a few times. He used these words like a sharp knife and stabbed her right in her heart and twisted it around a few times.

Esther did not talk back most of the time because she did not want to start an argument with him; after all, he just lost his mom. She chose to ignore his condemnation because if she took it in for even a second, it would cause a fierce argument in her head that drove her crazy one more time. One time, however, Esther could not keep silent.

"Let us divorce! I do not want to end up like your mom," Esther said quietly.

Her despair grew in her heart that she could never be able to make Kevin happy. He would not be happy unless his parents were happy; at least, it seemed this way. She knew she could never make his parents happy because they seemed to have determined from the very beginning that they would not be happy with her. Now Feng had died, and the fact that she was not happy with Esther could never be changed.

Esther guessed the only way she could make Kevin and his parents happy was to become like them. They would be happy if she could participate in all their lies and violent acts. They would be happier if she volunteered to be a scapegoat for all the misfortune and unhappiness.

Misery loves company.

Esther knew that she was not their kind of person. Her parents brought her up to be honest and kind. She may be at a loss in terms of what she wanted for her life, but she was very sure about what she did not want. She did not want to become a person like Feng. She knew if she went down this wrong path of becoming like Feng, she would have a terrible ending just like her.

It was clear that Kevin was becoming more and more like Liu. He hated Liu when he grew up, yet he became a younger version of him—maybe even a more dangerous one! It was like the same evil spirit that Liu carried around got hold of Kevin and swallowed him up. Or it may be more like that the same evil spirit that stayed dormant inside Kevin was aroused by Liu and kept growing until it took him over. Esther hopelessly witnessed his change right in front of her eyes. Sometimes she wanted to grab hold of him and shake him violently so that the evil spirit would fall off and the once sweet and innocent version of Kevin could come back. She hoped so much that version was still deep down inside Kevin, but she could be wrong. She doubted sometimes that version was ever there in the first place.

If Esther became like Feng, her marriage with Kevin would become just like the one between Feng and Liu, which Kevin absolutely hated in his youth. Unconsciously, Kevin tried to repeat his parents' marriage and thus the misery.

Her biggest fear, though, was that her two precious boys would grow up to become like Kevin and thus Liu. Her life would be doomed if her sons became like Liu!

A child to his parents is like a fruit to its tree. Parents feed the child with their thoughts and values like a tree feeds the fruit with nutrients.

Family dynamics often repeat from generation to generation. The same tragedies occur throughout generations, which is called a generational curse. It takes deep awareness and great courage to recognize such a curse and break away from it.

Esther opened up to Zia about her marital troubles, and Zia suggested Christian counseling. When Esther sat down with Dick, a kind-looking gentleman in his sixties, she started crying before she even opened her mouth. She cried throughout the whole sixty-minute session. Dick suggested that she write down the events and send the paper to him before their next meeting. Esther did just that, with her tears all over the paper.

When she showed up the second time at Dick's office, Dick looked at her and said, "Wow!"

He could not believe the kind of oppression and abuse Esther endured. The next thing he told Esther was, "I think you should file for divorce!"

"How can you say this? I am here to figure out how to save my marriage!" Esther was astonished.

"Marriage takes two people," Dick replied softly. "It cannot be just you who wants to make it work!"

"But God hates divorce!" Esther was desperate.

"Pick up your Bible and turn to Mark 10. Please read verses 4 and 5… Moses allowed the Israelites to divorce because their hearts were hardened. Your husband's heart is hardened," Dick replied calmly.

Esther never thought about this option. Throughout her life she always achieved her goals; she did not mind how difficult the goals were or how hard she had to work for them. She came to the United States all by herself with a scholarship for a graduate study. She found all her engineering jobs by herself. She helped her parents get visas after five rejections. She completed an intensive executive MBA program while raising two kids and holding a full-time job.

Now, saving her marriage was her goal. She wanted her husband back so badly! She wanted desperately to make her marriage work. What she wanted the most in her life was to provide a dream home for her precious sons. Her home was her American dream.

But Dick may be right. She worked so hard on this goal, but it did not seem to work. As a matter of fact, the harder she tried, the further Kevin stayed away from her. Like holding on to the sand in her palm, the tighter she squeezed, the faster it slipped away. It seemed that much of the sadness and pain she experienced was self-inflicted by her desperate efforts.

Furthermore, she was probably fighting for something that was long gone. Her marriage was like the sand gone from her palm. It was like a beautiful mist that was there in the early morning but dissipated when the sun came out.

Maybe he already left this marriage? Does the marriage still exist after all?

There was one last thing Esther had not tried yet in her efforts to save her marriage. She often wondered whether she should drop by Kevin's store after hours and see what was really going on.

Is there another woman?

She never did, though. She did not have time. After one full and busy day at work, she picked up the two kids, cooked for them, cared for them, and got them ready for the next day. She did not have a friend whom she could just drop off two little kids with for several hours. Everybody was busy and had a full plate, including Zia who had just had a third child. Things would be so different if her parents and her family were close by! It was a hefty price she had to pay, living by herself on the opposite side of the globe away from the rest of her family.

Esther was also afraid of being humiliated by Kevin in public. His cold and rude attitude towards her spoke loudly of his rejection of her. She was ashamed of the humiliation at home, and it would be unbearable if she encountered the same humiliation at his workplace.

Do I care that there may be another woman in his life? she asked herself.

No! She became surer, with the help from Dick.

CHAPTER 28

The Refuge

Her work gave Esther the sense of dignity she longed for. She was not a rookie anymore and showed more confidence in voicing her ideas and opinions. She gained respect from all the contractors and her coworkers for her knowledge and intelligence. She made another business trip back to China. Throughout the twenty-hour plane ride, every joint in her body ached. She had never felt so much physical pain in her life. She knew it was a manifestation of the agony in her heart.

An off-duty flight attendant who managed to get a free flight happened to sit right next to her. The Caucasian lady shared her whole life story with Esther. After a couple of failed marriages, she married an African American man and was happier than ever. Esther also shared her struggles in her marriage.

"Love should not hurt this much," she said to Esther plainly.

Maybe Kevin did not love me anymore?

Esther wished this period of difficulty would fade away just like it did the last time. She hoped Kevin still loved her. She could be wrong.

Did he ever love me?

The kind of affection he showered her with when she was young and pretty was probably not love. All he needed to do was gladly accept all her love and reap all the benefits from it. She was a very independent woman, and she seldom needed his help and support. But every time she did, he failed. And it only got worse! One time was when she needed his company on her first trip back to China while six months pregnant; another time was when she needed his care after she gave birth to their second child, Joseph; then it was when she needed his protection during Hurricane Rita. As a matter of fact, he had not provided basic support as a husband in every aspect of their marriage for a long time.

The more she poured out her life to him, the less worthy he seemed to view her of his love. Worse yet, he tried very hard to convince her that it was her own problems that caused her to be unworthy of his love. He seemed justified in his terrible attitude towards her and his absence as a husband and a father.

When she considered love in terms of support, the answer became clear.

Esther was astonished by this painful realization. She could not even smile when she went to the Great Wall with her coworkers. It was almost twenty years since her first visit. Back then she had just graduated from high school and was as happy as a bird. Now she was more like a soaking wet hen. This hen had two little chicks under her wings and struggled to keep standing, let alone walking. She needed a place to hide from the wind and rain in her life.

Esther was baptized at Easter; her refuge was under God's wings. She did not even tell Kevin about it, since he would not have been interested anyway. Also baptized were nine other church members, including Lily. Lily was a few years older than Esther, and the two became very close. Lily had a very difficult husband and could relate to Esther's struggles. Esther's two young kids joined her after the baptism, and they posed for a picture. When she held her two sons on her lap, she felt peaceful for the first time.

A few coworkers were overjoyed when they heard this news. Karl, who was a part-time pastor and longed to go back to full-time ministry, bought a Bible for Esther the next day. The other was Dennis, a gentleman from Hong Kong, who assured her that she was on the right path. Gradually, she discovered many Christians at her workplace. There was even a Bible study group that gathered once a week during lunch hour. A new world opened for Esther, one where she saw light and joy.

But her concern and fear mounted at home. Every day, Kevin carried a handgun in his briefcase—the same gun he used to threaten Sam before. He never explained clearly why he had the gun with him. Esther guessed that he needed it for protection since he had many cash transactions in his business and his store was not in a safe neighborhood. His seemingly harmless interest in gun ownership had started to grow a few years prior when he and his dad attended a few gun shows. Kevin then signed up for a shooting class, earned his license and bought a gun.

The presence of a gun posed quite a threat to Esther after she knew Kevin pulled the gun on Sam. Fear took root in Esther's heart; every young child's tragic death due to a gun that she read or heard about in the news now stood out as a flashing warning sign to her. Every morning before she left for work, she would check his briefcase. It was always wide open with the gun sticking out prominently. The computer was right next to the open suitcase. She knew that her two little boys could wake up early and play some computer games on the computer before Kevin took them to daycare. She did not dare to talk to her kids about the gun because they were still too young to understand. She did not dare to mention her concerns to Kevin, either. It might give him a new way to threaten her. She would simply push the gun down deep into the bag every time.

Maybe he was already threatening me with the gun! Esther wondered whether that could be the case.

Days and months went by. Kevin remained like a dead volcano to her. He did not bring any money home. He did not talk to her at all. With Dick's help, the endless arguments and condemnation in Esther's head slowly calmed down. She saw her reality that her once seemingly perfect life, as distant as a past life, would not come back anymore. Maybe divorce was the best solution.

Maybe it is better not to try to hold it all together?

One night, Esther woke up from a nightmare. In the dream, Liu walked into their bedroom where Esther and Kevin were sleeping on two separate single beds. Liu put his bed in between them. Kevin seemed reluctant, but he neither said anything nor stopped Liu from doing it. Esther opened her mouth but could not utter a single word. She felt so horrified that she woke up. At that moment, she knew her marriage was over.

What about the kids?

She worked so hard to give them the best life. Now they would have to grow up in a single-parent household. The very thought broke her heart.

One Sunday afternoon, Kevin took the kids out as usual to shop and have dinner with Liu. It was the only time of the week he would hang out with the kids. He took the kids to his store at night afterwards. In front of his store was a huge yard with all kinds of marble and granite slabs. The slabs were stored standing up in wooden frames and were very tall. The yard was enclosed by a fence and a gate. Kevin parked the car outside of the gate and went into the yard, leaving both kids in the car. As time passed, it became pitch dark. David and Joseph grew increasingly fearful and started crying. They decided to look for their dad, so they got out of the car and walked into the yard holding hands. They found their dad squatting in front of a slab and checking on something.

When Kevin saw them, he laughed at them and asked, "Why are you crying? You are like girls."

David told Esther about the incident when she gave him a goodnight kiss. She was astonished at Kevin's senselessness and felt sorry for her two boys. She could feel their fear; the fear she had was spreading to her kids. She comforted David and told him that she would talk to Kevin about it.

She would tolerate mistreatment of herself if she had to. But when it came to her children's well-being, she would tolerate nothing and nobody, not even Kevin. She was afraid that Kevin's mind was so distorted that he was becoming dangerous to his own children. Her staying in this marriage was not good for the kids if their safety was threatened. The frightening thought of divorce now seemed a better solution even for her kids.

By now Kevin would not talk to her in any way. He did not talk to her at home. He did not pick up her phone calls. Esther wrote an email to Kevin about the incident. The next day, Kevin told Esther that he filed for divorce and already had a lawyer. He stood across the living room from Esther, and he had the business card of his lawyer in his hand.

"You can hire him as your lawyer as well," he suggested as if it was a favor.

She did not want to take the card. But she walked across the room to take it from his hand. He did not give her anything except rejection for a very long time. He even looked a little sympathetic when she took the card.

She must have looked like an idiot to him. She figured it was better this way.

Esther called her parents. They were all worried when they heard her voice. After a moment of silence, Esther informed them of her decision.

"I think I will get a divorce."

"Sure, it is okay." It was like her parents were waiting for her to bring up the subject. They sounded relieved. "Do not drive yourself to insanity in order to stay in the marriage."

"We have been worrying about you!" Hua admitted.

"If it is his idea to divorce, take it and leave right away. He may change his mind later." Qing was very clear and firm. He never liked Kevin. Her parents' attitude surprised her. Their support gave her much-needed assurance.

She also talked to Leah about the matter.

"The old Chinese wisdom suggests to rather burn down ten temples than tear down a marriage. But I tell you otherwise. Leave him and run for your life!" Leah said. She never talked to Kevin after Feng's funeral.

The option of divorce used to be scary and unthinkable, but now it became a better choice for herself and her kids. It seemed like the people around her already knew this fact! They were just waiting for her to come to this realization.

How will the divorce process go? What will happen? Questions mounted in her heart.

The only daily activity Kevin helped with in taking care of their children was taking the kids to school every morning. If they divorced, he would then stop doing this one thing. It would be all on Esther.

How do I manage to add one more thing to my already overwhelming daily schedule? It was scary to even just think about what she needed to do every day. She was more frightened to look into the future.

How am I going to raise two boys all by myself?

When she was pondering on this question one early morning, a small and steady voice told her,

"You can raise them on your own!"

"Can I?" Esther asked in her heart. This time, she did not argue with the voice. She took this assurance to heart that she could somehow accomplish this impossible mission.

She was hoping Kevin would move out. He told her that he was looking for an apartment. He called her one time and told her about two apartments that he was considering.

"Which one do you think is better?" he asked.

She knew that something was fishy. He had not asked for her thoughts in such a long time. She did not know his true intentions, and she did not care anymore. Maybe he was waiting for her to break down and beg him to stay.

"Choose whatever you want!" She was disgusted and hung up the phone.

He seemed to change his mind not long after that and stopped talking about the apartments. One night, he woke her up after midnight and demanded that she close the garage door.

"Why do you want me to close the garage all the time?" he shouted. He usually went to sleep after her, and it was his routine to close all the garage doors. The garage doors could be controlled by a remote inside the house, and it would only take him a push of a button to close them. Apparently, the argument was not about the doors; he just wanted to initiate a fight. Esther did not want it! She got up from her bed and closed the garage doors with the remote control. She did not say a word. Kevin left the bedroom in a rage and slammed the door behind him.

Was his proposal of divorce just a threat or was it a real plan? Was he now trying to drive me out of the house? Esther was not sure about his true intention, but she did not care anymore to find out.

Instead, she wanted to figure out what she wanted to do. She was sure that she did not want to live with him anymore. She became more and more scared of him. She checked a few women's shelters for possible temporary arrangements for her and her two kids. Sometimes she doubted her own fear, though. But a conversation on a Family Violence Hotline validated her fear.

"You are right. You are not imagining. Your fear reflects your situation," the agent told Esther.

Esther planned on moving out secretly and avoiding any direct conflict with Kevin. She wanted to escape from him. Yet, she had no idea where to go. She moved some clothes and important documents to Zia's house. She rented a PO box for her mail. She then planned a vacation with her kids in Seattle, knowing for sure that they were not returning home afterwards.

The last time she drove back home before flying out to Seattle, her heart was seized with fear. It was in the early afternoon, and she drove back from work to pack for the vacation. She was afraid Kevin was home and would find out about her plan. She did not know how he would react.

Her house, once as beautiful as heaven, now was more like a hell. She prayed to God for protection during the whole drive. When she made the last turn before arriving at her house, her fear disappeared. A few city workers with orange vests were working on her house's sewage line. They even blocked off a little area at the front of the house with orange tape. She remembered sending in a request for the repair a few days ago.

Their presence was like a sign of peace. She knew then that God answered her prayer. Kevin was not home; she gathered everything she needed. She left a note for Kevin that said she and their kids would be on a vacation.

The three of them stayed at Jean's house and had a great time in Seattle. Jean, her former graduate school roommate, was a very good host. At the time, she was completing her residency program for psychiatry. She and her husband were financially well-off because he started working for Microsoft right after college and accumulated a significant amount of wealth from the company stocks. They had to send their six-month-old son with her parents back to China, though, because both were very busy with their work.

Esther and the kids visited Mount Rainier. It was Esther's second time there. The first time, she came to visit Kevin right after their wedding when Kevin worked for Microsoft. The views were the same, yet her situation was very different.

A once beautiful marriage was gone.

She was deeply sad. On the other hand, her two kids were quite excited to see snow for the first time. They happily played in the snow and hit each other with snowballs.

The day before they headed back to Houston, Kevin called. He asked about the mail transfer request he received.

"Yes, we are moving out," Esther told him in a quiet voice, "but I do not know where we will live yet. I just rented a mailbox."

Kevin sounded a little bit surprised yet did not object to the idea. He did not ask them to come home.

"What is up, Mom?" David asked Esther after she hung up the phone. He was in the same room and apparently overheard the conversation.

"We are not going back to our house," Esther told David calmly. Yet, grief overwhelmed her like waves of the ocean pounding the seashore.

David burst into tears. He did not ask why they weren't going back, as if he already knew. Esther embraced him and started crying with him. Their heads pressed together; they cried for a long time. The unspoken sadness saturated them, yet they found comfort in each other's arms.

Esther and her two kids checked into a hotel after they came back to Houston. She told the kids that it was an extension of their vacation. School soon started. Esther took a picture of the kids on their first day of school. David was starting first grade and Joseph was starting kindergarten in the same private school. The boys wore their school uniforms and looked so sweet with their cheerful smiles. As usual, David put bunny ears above Joseph's head. The elevator door in the background, however, revealed their abnormal situation.

I will make sure my sons have good lives, Esther vowed in her heart.

Esther and her boys left the hotel and moved into an apartment after a month. Esther tried very hard to maintain a sense of normalcy for her children, and the kids seemed to get along all right. All their typical activities resumed, and life seemed to go back to normal. In a chess tournament soon after, David took first place and brought home a trophy almost as big as him.

There were occasional moments, though, when the kids could not hide their confusion and sadness. One night when Kevin called, David broke down and cried, "I miss Dad!"

Esther felt terrible. Kevin blamed Esther for hiding the kids from him, yet he never asked them to come back home, and he continued with the divorce filing.

At a YMCA swimming meet, a parent approached Esther and asked what was going on with her family. She told Esther that Joseph was asking other kids whether their dads lived with them.

"My dad doesn't live with us," he told his friends.

Esther did not know how to address the issue with the kids. She did not even know herself how the issue would turn out. One night after a Cub Scout meeting, Jack called and asked what happened. Jack and his wife, Heather, were Caucasians and used to be her neighbors. Their son, Peter, was a very good friend of David's since kindergarten.

"David told Peter that you were living in an apartment."

Before Esther could answer, Heather picked up another line.

"What is going on?" she asked. "Are you okay?"

The couple were well-educated and worked for a major oil company. Jack grew up on a farm in the Midwest and became the first college graduate in his family. He worked his way up to a mid-level manager position in an engineering department. Heather came from an elite family from up North and graduated from Harvard Law School. She was working as a corporate lawyer. Heather was an assertive woman, so she sometimes appeared bossy. However, her caring voice warmed Esther's heart at this moment.

"We moved out of the house." Esther could hardly control herself.

Instead of making any comments, Heather volunteered to provide her life story. "I divorced before. Jack is my second husband."

Her words shocked Esther. They were like a perfect couple. Their marriage seemed so like a fairy tale that it was always the envy of all the people around them. Behind their seemingly perfect marriage there must have been their fair share of struggles. Her words brought light and warmth into the darkness of Esther's life. Esther had a deep appreciation for her kindness.

"Heather is my first and only wife," Jack clarified.

He was a typical engineer and always wanted to be precise. Esther almost burst into laughter. Her defenses crumbled down, and she started to cry.

"I will just leave you two alone." Jack left the conversation.

Esther and Heather talked on the phone for a long time. Heather told her all about her first failed marriage. She told Esther that she picked herself up afterward and moved down to Houston from the Northeast, where she met Jack and started a new life. Heather would never reveal such a personal story if it was not for Esther's current situation.

Esther felt a renewed sense of hope.

CHAPTER 29

Shark Tank

A few months passed by, and Kevin was moving full speed down the path of the divorce. Esther found out that his lawyer was known for helping his clients to hide their assets and screw up their ex-spouses. Kevin's choice of lawyer exposed his real intention. Esther had to look for a lawyer to represent her. In a rush she picked a female Caucasian attorney who seemed eager to win her business. The lawyer helped prepare a very long investigation request and then served the request to Kevin and his lawyer.

They had an initial mediation session and reached a few agreements. One of them was to freeze personal bank accounts except for necessary living expenses. Another one was for Esther to return to the house to collect her personal items. During the whole mediation session, Kevin looked at her with contempt as if to say, "You really think you can fight me?"

It simply disgusted Esther.

When Esther went back to the house to gather her belongings, the house looked like a coffin to her. Its pale-yellow walls had lost their glow and looked more like the weeping face of a phantom. The inside looked dark, empty and lifeless. An assistant of Kevin's lawyer was already there to watch over her and make sure she only took what was agreed upon. Esther collected albums, books and clothes and put them in her van. Waves of sadness again saturated her, and she started sobbing. The assistant looked sympathetic and helped Esther take some items to the van.

The house used to be her home, the place where her family lived and grew. The house used to be her pride, which showcased her ambition and achievements. The house used to be her dream, where her heart and soul were attached. Now her home was broken, her pride turned into shame, and her dream shattered.

It was the only house her two boys ever knew, where they were conceived and grew up. However, it was not their house anymore now. Also gone was the worry-free childhood of her sons.

Esther noticed that the main entrance to the study room was blocked off by the desk, as if Kevin was barring her from this room. She wanted to pick up a few more little items from the study room, so she went in through a side door.

The assistant stormed in and yelled, "Get out. You are not allowed to come in here!"

"Why?" Esther was very sure that there was no such restriction in the agreement. She was also astonished by the assistant's dramatic reaction.

The assistant pushed Esther out of the study room and blocked the entrance.

"This is my house!" Esther protested; she was enraged.

But the assistant would not move. Apparently, she had an order to protect the study, though Esther did not know the reason. Esther called her lawyer, who advised Esther not to get into an argument. Esther left the house shaking with anger and humiliation. She never wanted to go back to the house anymore!

Around Thanksgiving, Kevin called the kids and asked to talk to Esther. Esther reluctantly picked up the phone. Kevin apologized for the whole thing and begged her for another chance. Strangely, he did not mention dropping the divorce. Esther did not accept his apology. Kevin showed up outside their apartment door a couple of nights later. He knocked at the door.

"Who told Dad our address?" Esther looked at her two kids in anger. She had told them many times not to tell their dad where they lived.

"Dad insisted that I tell him." David looked at Esther in fear, shaking. Esther knew it was very hard for a seven-year-old to resist his father. She did not rebuke him. She told Kevin to leave, then proceeded with her usual nightly routine. Kevin told her later that he waited outside in his car until the lights went off.

Esther wondered whether there was any chance they could get back together. Even if they could, she wondered whether they could manage to have a better and lasting relationship. She trusted that Dick could help her figure out the chance, so she arranged a few appointments for Kevin to go see Dick. Kevin went to see him once and stopped.

"Kevin did not see any problem with the way he treated you," Dick told Esther.

On the first Sunday of the new year, Kevin came to church to drop off the kids, and he brought some gifts for Esther. One of the gifts was a huge tin of candy with, however, a few broken chocolate pieces in it. The other was a bag of raw shrimp, which was a present from Liu. Esther did not quite understand why Kevin would present these items as New Year's gifts to her. She refused to take them. The idea of accepting anything from Liu was disgusting to her. Kevin looked outraged when he left.

Kevin stopped any attempt at reconciliation afterward. Soon, it became clear that Kevin broke all the agreements that were set up in the first mediation. Millions of dollars in his accounts were sent to China and disappeared. Everybody was shocked at his lawlessness.

Did he truly want to win me back for the last few months? Or did he just need time to move money out without being exposed right away? Esther wondered. The latter was more likely the case; Esther was again shocked by the deceptiveness of his character.

The mediation fell apart. The whole divorce process took a devastating and exhausting two years. It was not only ugly but also brutal. Kevin was clearly happy to use every chance he could find to screw Esther a little bit more. He changed his lawyer and hired an even more ferocious one. At the end, he filed for bankruptcy. He surprised Esther again and again as to how low he could go as a human being.

Moreover, she had to constantly fight with her own lawyers. She wound up changing her lawyer in the middle of the divorce because the first one was obviously not competent. Often, she wondered whether her lawyers, to whom she paid an hourly rate of $300, were working for her. In a court appearance, her lawyer sat right next to Kevin's lawyer and had a long talk. They seemed to have known each other for a long time and were quite close. Her lawyer did not bother to lift his eyes to find where Esther was.

Another time when she was visiting her lawyer in his office, she wanted to make a copy of a document, but the lawyer did not consider it necessary. When Esther insisted, he would not allow her to use the copy machine in his office. He told her to go out and use a public copy machine.

"Why can't I use your office copy machine?" Esther was confused. She was the client and paid him a great deal of money.

"You don't take the word 'no' very well." He looked aloof.

It was a freezing and dark winter day. On the way to a public copy shop, she wondered why she tolerated such abuse. It was too late to change lawyers again. She felt sorry for herself, and she was determined that she would never have this shark tank experience ever again.

In addition to the divorce proceedings, her life was packed with work and the kids. On the work front, she was promoted one more time. Her suggestion to start a well cleanup project earlier to boost initial production was adopted. She became a project manager of the well cleanup project and led the effort across many disciplines, including engineering, procurement and construction in the United States and in China.

She took a few business trips back to China. She was able to arrange her trips in such a way that she could take the kids with her during their school breaks. She would drop the kids off with her parents and go off on her business trips. The kids had a great experience while being spoiled by their grandparents and relatives. They even briefly attended the same elementary school Esther went to thirty years earlier. Teacher Yang, her favorite Chinese teacher of her fifth grade, was now recognized as a top-ranked Chinese teacher in the nation. He was also promoted to be the principal of the school and held the position for many years.

Esther managed for her kids to attend every extracurricular program available, from sports to chess to Chinese classes. Going to church every Friday night and Sunday morning gave them much-needed stability. Free dinner on Fridays and free lunch on Sundays were like manna from heaven. They were replenished physically, emotionally and spiritually every time they went to church. They were like a boat securely anchored in a big storm.

David excelled at school and at everything he did. He loved to go to church. His Sunday school teacher, Wendy, adored him.

"He is so attentive and loves Bible stories!" Wendy told Esther.

Wendy and her husband, Greg, came from Taiwan and were on the leadership team of the church. Both were highly educated and worked in the medical field. Both of their kids went to Ivy League schools. Wendy would check on Esther from time to time and pray with her. She was very wise and humble. Her suggestions were always very clear and helpful.

Joseph, on the other hand, remained a restless yet sweet little boy. He still mentioned from time to time that the old garage held two cars, his mom's and his dad's. This mental picture probably expressed his sorrow and his wishes. Her little boy's secret wishes saddened Esther, as she knew he would be disappointed.

At the end of the divorce, they had to settle a few issues in court. One of them was child support. Kevin testified that he only made $10,000 the year before. He offered to pay $500 per month for both kids and rejected Esther's request for him to pay for half of the kids' private school. Her lawyer pointed out that Kevin made a lot more money than he claimed because his salesperson made an average of $60K a year. It was obvious to everybody in the court that Kevin was lying. By now Esther was not surprised by Kevin's lies. However, his contempt for the law and absolute neglect of his children were still shocking to her.

The judge asked Kevin, "Are you testing our IQ?"

The judge ruled that Kevin would pay the maximum amount of monthly child support of $1500; however, he would not need to pay for the private school. When Esther walked out of the courtroom, she was sure that she would never take another look at Kevin ever again in her life! Kevin watched her leave, and he looked a little sorrowful.

Finally, Esther could go ahead and plan for the kind of life she wanted for her kids and herself. It was still a scary thought that from now on she would be raising her kids alone.

In her last session with Dick, he told her, "You can decorate your house the way you want and create the kind of memories you want for your life!"

His advice gave her some much-needed revelation—that she now had the freedom to live her life truthfully. That was exactly what she was going to do!

And my boys will grow up to be great men!

CHAPTER 30

The Assurance

Esther still hoped to keep her kids in their school. The private school was known for its excellent early education curriculum and very competitive chess clubs. Both her kids were doing very well at school, and they loved playing chess. However, the cost for both kids was so high that she could not afford it all by herself. Her kids wrote letters and begged their dad to help them stay at the school. Kevin simply ignored their pleas.

There was one thing Esther did not like about the school, though. The principal insisted that Joseph take medicine for ADHD even after a doctor verified that he did not have the issue. Esther had no intention of drugging her son just to please the school! It was so prevalent in the United States for people to use drugs to solve any issue as if they could do magic. It may be the easiest thing to do, but it certainly was not the best way and could be dangerous, especially with young children. Esther decided to move the kids to a public school.

Esther took the kids with her to a peaceful neighborhood that had a great public school system. They found a nice and modest two-story house. Its exterior brick wall of old dark red and brown colors had a touch of charm and elegance. Inside, the house was well planned out and felt warm and comfortable. A curved stairway with wooden handrails led to a second floor with four bedrooms and a playroom. As her two precious boys sat on the stairs and smiled at her camera, arms around each other's shoulders, she knew this would be their new home.

The move was scheduled for a Friday afternoon. A moving company would come and move the major pieces of furniture by truck. Esther was going to take all the small items in her van and then drive to her new house before the truck arrived there. She thought it would take a few hours to get it done and that she could finish everything by herself.

Soon she was amazed by the number of small items she had accumulated over the two years. She made trips up and down between her apartment on the third floor and her vehicle in the parking lot. The flight of stairs seemed harder to climb each time. She did not realize the inconvenience of living on the third floor until this last moment.

How did I manage to live on the third floor for the past two years?

Her body was totally exhausted and went on a strike before she could finish with the last two moving boxes. She sat on the floor of the apartment and could not move at all. This was the first time Esther had ever reached her physical limit. It was too late to call someone to come and help, especially just to carry out the last two boxes. And the moving truck had already left and was headed to her new house!

At this very moment, somebody rang the doorbell. It was a repairman. Esther had called for service a few days before to get the apartment ready to move out. The man showed up just in time! Esther knew that he was the help from God. The repairman took the two boxes down the stairs for her. She was able to drive her vehicle and arrive at her new house in time before the moving truck arrived.

Esther and her kids quickly settled down in their new house. She bought all her furniture in one trip at one store that filled up the whole house. She threw away all the wrapping paper and plastic. This house was for her and her two kids to live in and enjoy!

Like all full-time working single moms, Esther juggled many balls simultaneously. Every day was a nonstop hustle. There were so many decisions to make every day, from meals to school and from her work to the kids' activities. There was no room for errors in planning. She did not have any complaint, though. She was so happy that she was not burdened by the divorce process anymore. It was like dropping a heavy dead weight from her shoulders and from her heart.

Esther even managed to throw a big birthday party for David right after the new school year started. David had all his good friends at the party, some from the old private school and some from the new public school. Many neighbors, old and new, also came. More than fifty people attended the party in all. A professional magician was invited to the party. He performed many tricks and made everybody laugh. At one point, both of her kids were performing with the magician while all their friends stared attentively. The smiles and the laughter warmed her heart, and she knew she could make it.

But it also became clear that she needed some help for her life, at least with the dinner. There were always events right after she came home from work. Every night some extracurricular activity was going on, whether it was a soccer practice, or a Boy Scout meeting, or a book night. The weekends were even busier. On Saturdays, the boys played chess in the morning, attended Chinese classes in the afternoon, and played a few ping-pong games at the end of the day. Esther would do grocery shopping, chat with friends, pay bills and a million other things while the kids were in classes. Many times, she just could not find time to prepare dinner.

One Saturday afternoon she talked to Heather. Heather still could not get over the fact that the kids left the private school.

"Are you getting any help with your housework?" Heather asked at the end of their conversation. Heather had already quit her job and was a stay-at-home mom now. She had a nanny to help with the kids. She could not believe that Esther was handling all these tasks by herself. Her question prompted Esther to give the matter some serious thought.

Esther and her kids finally came home after all the classes that night and ate takeout Chinese food. The kids relaxed and played some games while Esther washed clothes and dishes. They prayed right before the kids went to sleep. Esther prayed that God would send some help to her. David prayed that he could go back to the private school. Joseph prayed that Santa would send him a Nintendo Wii.

There were still a ton of chores for her to do; the chore list was endless. She often felt like her back was about to break by the time she brushed her teeth. But there was also a sense of exhilaration from all she accomplished during the day. This night, though, after the kids went to sleep, Esther called her parents and asked them to come and help her.

"I bought a house and there are enough rooms for you. Do you want to come?"

Her parents seemed preoccupied with their new apartment and taking care of her nephew, Joshua.

"We are so busy. Joshua is already a sophomore in high school, and he needs care and attention. Also, we need to buy a new TV and a new sofa. The old TV is not working very well," they said.

Esther could not believe her parents overlooked the obvious struggles she was going through as a single working mom. She could not control herself and started crying.

"You do not think I need any help, do you?" Esther lamented. The other end of the line went silent.

"We will come. One of us will come," Qing finally murmured.

Esther could not wait to leave her parents as far as she could when she was growing up. Now she desperately needed them to come to her side. She was so confident when she stepped onto this new land for the first time. Now she could not make it on her own and had to beg her parents for help!

Right before Qing's arrival, Esther strained her back. It was late Friday afternoon. After the kids went to Kevin's house to spend the weekend with him, Esther cleaned her vehicle right before going to church. There were always millions of things to do, and she was so used to squeezing in just one more thing to her packed schedule. When she stretched her arm and reached for an empty water bottle under a seat, her back muscle froze and her back locked up.

She managed to walk back into the house and lie down on her bed. Lying down was extremely painful, and turning onto her side was almost impossible. Her body probably knew better than her conscious mind again: she was overworked and needed rest!

"Why did you not come to church tonight?" Lily checked on her from church. After she found out what happened, Lily came directly to her house after church and helped her go to sleep.

Her house was packed with visitors from church over the weekend. They brought in so much food that would last a week. Many shared their own stories of physical illness and recovery. They gave her a lot of advice on where to get treatment for back pain and how to get well.

Esther was overwhelmed by the outpouring of love and support. She was also surprised by her own ignorance because she did not even know some of the visitors who went to the same church for years. Her physical weakness opened another side of life that she had not paid any attention to before.

By the time the kids came back at the end of the weekend, Esther was a little better. They were nevertheless shocked to see their super mom in such a weak state. She wanted to get up and prepare dinner for them.

"Mom, I can do it. I will warm up the food!" David was like the man of the house.

"Mom, let me give you a massage!" Joseph's sweetness melted her heart.

She knew she could make it. She saw hope from her two precious boys. She heard love from her parents' voices. Her dad was already on his way to the United States to save her. She tasted support from all the meals that her church friends brought in. She would continue to find wellsprings of strength in many likely and unlikely places.

* * *

Fourteen years later, the world had barely come out of the Covid pandemic. It was a sunny spring morning. Esther was home alone, working on her business. David had graduated from college the year before and now was working in Boston as a consultant in the medical field. He applied to medical schools the year before and went through many interviews. Joseph was studying art in a top art school in New York.

The phone rang, and it was Daivd.

"Mom…" David paused and then shouted, "I got into Harvard medical school!"

"Really?" Esther could not believe it. She knew David was outstanding, but Harvard?

"I could not believe it, either! It was like a dream!" David started laughing. "I got into both programs, Pathways and HST. I need to pick one!"

Tears welled up in her eyes.

"Why are you crying, Mom?" David asked.

"I am so happy for you, David! I am so proud of you!" Esther could hardly control herself.

After she hung up the phone, Esther burst into tears and cried loudly. She never cried so loud all those years. The whole house echoed with her cries. She knelt before the cross and kept crying.

All the years of sweat and tears! All the years of struggles and pain! All the years of sorrow and shame! In the face of this incredible blessing, they were all worth it.

Finally, she was sure of her choice.

"Thank You, Lord! Thank You for giving David this opportunity! Thank You for bringing our family this far! Thank You, Lord!"

A few days later, morning sunlight came in through the windows of the living room and shined on a dark red cross on the wall. Across the room, a bright red folder was lying on top of a shiny black baby grand piano. On the red folder were the words, "Harvard Medical School."

www.ingramcontent.com/pod-product-compliance
Lightning Source LLC
Chambersburg PA
CBHW060347310726
48976CB00003B/748